PRETTY
relentless

Lacey Black

Pretty Relentless

Pine Village Series, book 4

USA Today Bestselling Author

Lacey Black

Lacey Black

Pretty Relentless

Pine Village Series, book 4

CHAPTER
one

Ava

Nine and three.

That's exactly where my hands are positioned on the steering wheel as I drive home. It's dark, but not late. I left Gabe and Blair's wedding reception at eight, giving myself plenty of time to get home before the roads potentially get bad from the weather. Not that they will, but you never know. Weather in northwestern Wisconsin can change at the drop of a hat, so I'm always prepared for whatever life throws my way.

Except, I'm not prepared for my car to sputter and die, literally in the middle of the deserted roadway. I do everything I can to steer my Kia Seltos off the road, but I'm only able to get the front end to the shoulder before the vehicle stops moving completely. My rear end is still very much in the roadway, which makes me panic a little. Fortunately, Eldridge Road isn't incredibly busy, thanks to being on the opposite side of town from Bluff Preserves National Park, so hopefully I won't cause an accident with my haphazardly disabled vehicle.

Flipping on my emergency hazards, I retrieve my cell phone from the clutch purse sitting on the passenger seat. My hands are a little shaky as I tap in my code and pull up the messaging app. I could call instead of text the tow truck driver, but he's sitting at the wedding reception I just left, and with the music, I'm not sure he'll be able to hear the ringing.

> **Me:** Hi, Marcus, this is Ava Rutledge. My car just broke down on Eldridge Road. It's not completely off the roadway either. I know you're at the reception, so is there someone I can call for help?

The bubbles appear almost instantly.

> **Marcus:** On my way.

> **Me:** I hate to pull you away from the celebration.

> **Marcus:** It's fine. I wasn't staying much longer anyway. I'll head to the shop and grab the tow truck.

I fire off a quick thank you to Marcus, feeling awful he's having to leave Gabe and Blair's wedding reception to come bail me out of trouble, but I suppose that's what happens when you're the only repair shop and tow service in our area. Since my rear end isn't completely off the road, I don't want to leave it until morning. It could cause an accident for a passing vehicle, despite having the emergency hazards on.

I wrap my arms around myself, hating the fact I'm not wearing a winter coat. It just didn't go with the dress I wore to the wedding, but I'm desperately regretting that decision now. This sweater is warm but does not provide nearly enough comfort in a disabled car in the dead of winter. I make a mental note to stock up on emergency supplies for my trunk very soon.

A pair of headlights fill my rearview mirror and stop directly behind my car. My heart starts to beat hard as I reach over and press the lock button. Twice. I clutch my phone in my hand, ready to dial 911 when the person who stopped behind me opens their driver's door. I can't tell who it is or what kind of vehicle, thanks to the blinding lights in my mirrors. My heart pounds even harder as I feel the person approach my door and knock on the window. I lift my phone, ready to call for help.

That's when I catch a glimpse of a familiar face.

"Hey," he hollers, lifting his hand and giving me a friendly, nonconfrontational wave.

"Mr. Pierson?" I holler through the closed window, surprised to find the father of one of my fifth-grade students standing beside my disabled vehicle at this time of night.

He flashes me a warm, disarming smile that makes my heart flip in my chest. "Just Gavin, Miss Rutledge. To you, I'm just Gavin."

My mouth goes completely dry. "Uh…"

"Can I help?" he hollers through the window.

"No, I'm good," I reply, my teeth starting to chatter. "The tow truck is on its way."

"Come on, Miss Rutledge. You must be freezing. Let me take you home," he insists, his hands shoved in the pockets of his jeans as he bends over, trying to shield his face from the cold.

Reaching for the handle, I unlock the door and slowly push it open. "Maybe I should wait for Marcus," I say, mostly to myself than to him.

"If you want, fine, but I'd feel more comfortable if you'd wait in my truck." Gavin remains completely still, waiting until I make my decision. "It's toasty warm," he adds, and I'll be honest, that last statement outweighs all the reasons why I should stay in my car.

"Okay," I reply. The chill sweeping into my vehicle has me reaching for my purse and ready to exit.

"Here," Gavin says, offering me his hand while I'm climbing out. It's an incredibly gentlemanly thing to do, and I admit, I totally eat it up. Chivalry is not dead.

I try not to focus on how warm, yet rough his hand is as he leads me to the passenger seat of his truck. A shiver sweeps through my entire body, one he clearly notices. "Please let me take you home, Miss Rutledge. It'll take a little time for Marcus to get here and load up your vehicle. There's nothing you can do until morning."

I hesitate, running through my options and quickly realizing I don't have many. Yes, I could stay here, waiting for Marcus to do his thing, but that would mean he'd have to give me a ride home at some point too. "Okay," I finally reply, knowing this is for the best. "Thank you."

Everything else happens quickly. Gavin helps me into the passenger seat of his truck, the heater hitting me square in the face and feeling like that first drink of ice water on a hot summer day. It's the best sensation, and I find myself placing my hands in front of the vent to help warm them up.

Then, something else hits me. "Oh, my key." I dig into my purse for the fob, unclipping it from my ring of keys.

"I'll set it under the floor mat, so Marcus has it," he tells me, reaching for the small, black device. My fingertips brush his palm as he gently takes the fob from my hand. "Be right back," he adds, shutting the door and blanketing me in the warmth of the truck interior.

He goes to my Kia and places the key fob under the mat. He takes a look around, probably making sure I have everything I need, and shuts the door.

I pull out my cell phone once more and fire off another text to Marcus.

Me: Key fob is under the mat. Someone is giving me a ride home.

He replies back a few seconds later.

Marcus: Sounds good. I'll tow it back to the shop and take a look at it first thing in the morn.

Me: Thank you, Marcus, and again, I'm sorry to pull you away from the reception.

Marcus: All good, Ava.

The driver's door opens, and Gavin slips inside. I look through the windshield just in time to see snow flurries start to fall, making me even more grateful I'm not sitting in my broken-down vehicle right now.

"Thank you, again," I say as soon as the door is closed.

"It's no problem, Miss Rutledge," he replies with a warm, friendly smile.

I catch a whiff of his clean scent, whether it's soap or cologne, it tickles my nose and makes me want to inhale deeply. I don't, of course, because that would be weird, and while I've always been considered an odd duck, leaning in to smell someone would definitely elevate my weirdness level.

"Ava," I blurt out, my brain kinda spinning.

"What?"

"My name. You keep calling me Miss Rutledge. You can call me Ava," I tell him, feeling a blush creep up my neck that has nothing to do with the heat inside the car.

He flashes me another smile, one that makes my nipples tingle and my thighs clench. "Ava," he repeats, as if trying out the word, and I'll be gosh darned if it isn't the sexiest sound I've ever heard.

"Annabelle," I practically holler, wishing I could crawl into a hole. "Sorry, I didn't mean to yell that. What I meant to ask is how she's enjoying her Christmas break. I know it's only been a day, but I'm sure she's enjoying the time away."

He throws his truck into drive and slowly pulls away from the side of the road, leaving my disabled car behind. "She has no complaints yet, but I'm sure once Christmas is over in two days, she'll be itching to return to school and her favorite teacher," he tells me, sending a wink my way.

"She's such a great student. One of the hardest working kids I've ever had in fifth grade," I tell him as we continue to drive along the dark roadway. I've been teaching for fourteen years already, so that's saying something.

"I have no idea where she gets it from. I wasn't that smart when I was in school," he replies with a chuckle. "You're up here in Strawberry Hill, right?" he asks, quickly switching conversation directions.

"Oh, yes. Second road, blue house on the right."

He taps his thumb on the steering wheel while he drives. "Annabelle loves being in your class. You're all she talks about," he informs me.

Thankfully, he's unable to see the blush on my cheeks as he keeps his eyes on the road. "I appreciate you saying that. She really is a wonderful student. She's on track to be our top reader, as well as top speller this year."

He laughs. "Doesn't surprise me. Do you know she asked for books for Christmas this year?"

Hearing that makes my heart sing. I was one of those students. You know, the nerdy ones who got all excited to go to the book fair and actually buy books? I was a regular at the library and always competed in summer reading challenges. I won four years in a row, competing as a child in the adult category.

"A girl after my own heart," I reply with a smile, placing my hand against my chest.

Gavin chuckles as he starts to slow as we approach the subdivision. He turns onto the second road, which winds around to the back of the small grouping of houses. We slowly make our way to the row of houses, mine being the second one on the right. He pulls into my driveway and stops in front of my attached garage.

Reaching to release my seat belt, I say, "Thank you so much for the ride."

"You're welcome."

The click of his seat belt lets me know he's unfastening his too and causes me to look his way. "What are you doing?"

He gives me a breathtaking grin. "Walking the lady to the door."

"That's not necessary," I insist.

"My mama would tan my hide if I didn't walk a lady to her front door at the end of the evening," he replies in the cutest Southern drawl, reaching up and pretending to tip his nonexistent cowboy hat.

I find myself smiling, despite the fact this wasn't a date. "It's not necessary, really. I'm only walking fifteen feet," I say, even though I know it'll fall on deaf ears. He's already opening his door and climbing out.

Gavin meets me at the passenger side and opens my door, extending his hand. My fingers glide against his as I take the offered hand and allow him to help me down. The black wrap dress I'm wearing molds to my skin, hitting just below my knees. With the help of Hallie, I paired it with a pair of mid-calf boots with little kitten heels that make me walk like I'm a newborn foal trying to stand for the first time. Flats are my normal shoes and the only thing I wear in the classroom, so why I let my friend talk me into something with heels is beyond me.

Walking up the sidewalk to my front door, I'm about to release his hand and thank him for the escort when my right foot slips on the freshly fallen snow. There's just enough on the ground to wet the sidewalk, causing it to get a little slippery. Add in the fact I usually wear boots in this type of weather and I'm an accident waiting to happen.

My leg starts to slip out from under me, but I'm kept from falling to the ground thanks to a strong arm wrapping around my waist. "Careful," he murmurs, his warm breath tickling my ear.

"Thank you," I reply, trying to right myself before shuffling the rest of the way to my front door. Of course, with every step I take, all I smell is him. Gavin. His clean, woodsy scent wraps around me like a warm blanket and comforts me.

When we're both firmly stationed on the small concrete stoop, the old overhang shielding us from the falling snow, he lets go of my hand. I slip my key into the lock, releasing both the knob and deadbolt locks. Turning to face him, I'm torn between inviting him in as a show of appreciation for the ride home and slamming the door in his face after blurting out another thanks because I'm awkward as hell.

"If you need a ride anywhere tomorrow, you're more than welcome to call me, Ava."

"Oh," I reply, my heart pounding in my chest. "Thank you for the offer. I'm sure you have better things to do than shuttle me around town."

He gives me a smile that makes his hazel eyes look more green than brown. "Actually, I'm certain you're wrong there. I'd be honored to take you wherever you need to go."

Is he flirting with me?

"I have a vehicle I can borrow, but I appreciate the offer."

"Well, it stands at any point this weekend."

I nod, knowing I don't have his number in my phone but not really sure if I should say that aloud. "Thank you. And thank you for stopping. I'm sure I would have been fine waiting for Marcus but do appreciate the fact I didn't have to sit there in the cold any longer than necessary."

He gives me a full-wattage smile. Even with his scruffy jaw, it makes his entire face light up. For the first time, I notice how incredibly sexy Gavin Pierson is. I feel bad I've never looked at him that way before, but he's always been my student's father. Yes, my student's attractive father, but that's it. Now, I can't help but realize how gorgeous he is.

He reaches out and brushes a strand of my hair off my cheek. "I'm glad I stumbled upon you, Ava."

My throat is thick as I swallow over the lump. "Me too, Mr. Pierson."

Again, he flashes me a grin that could melt the glaciers in Antarctica. "It's Gavin," he says with a wink.

"Gavin. Thank you." I turn toward the door, ready to end the weirdness that always seems to surround me. "Oh, I hope I didn't take you away from anything important tonight." I know he lives in town, over by the Methodist Church, which makes me wonder...

What was he doing out on Eldridge Road?

It's not incredibly late, but it's an odd time to be out and about, especially with the snow coming.

"You didn't," he assures me. "I, uh, like to go for drives. It helps me clear my mind to drive around, listening to music. It's how I think and process whatever's on my mind."

"I'm sorry I disturbed that," I state, feeling bad for messing up his quiet time.

He holds my gaze for several seconds before replying, "I'm not."

I tear my eyes away from his and turn toward my front door. "Thank you, again."

"You're very welcome."

Pushing open the door, I start to take a step inside my house when his voice makes me pause.

"You look beautiful tonight, Ava."

I glance over my shoulder and feel this...*thing*. My heart starts to pound, and my throat goes completely dry. I want to reach out and throw my arms around him, reveling in the feel of his wrapped around me.

And...I want to kiss him.

My student's father.

Which is a hard limit for me as a teacher. Even one in a small town, I have rules in place for a reason. Yet, I find myself wanting to throw those rules straight out the window for the first time in my life. No, not in my life. I did that a few times in college, and they always seemed to come back and bite me in the rear at some point.

That's why rules are so important. They provide structure and balance in my life and remind me to always do my best at keeping on the straight and narrow.

Getting involved with a student's dad would definitely *not* help me achieve that.

"Thank you," I whisper, knowing he can probably see the blush his comment caused.

Shoving his hands in his pockets, he takes a step back, giving me plenty of space to enter my home. Just as I go to close the door, our eyes meet again, and I give him a polite wave goodbye. The corner of his mouth curls up, and as soon as the door is closed and locked behind me, I turn my attention to the peephole. I watch as Gavin smiles, looking down at the ground for a moment before turning and walking toward his truck.

And since I'm still standing here, watching, I see the moment he pauses and turns back to my door, as if he's about to run back up and knock. He doesn't, however. Instead, he climbs inside the cab of his truck and slowly backs out of my driveway.

Long after he's gone, I stand here, watching through that tiny hole. I'm just not sure if I'm grateful he didn't run back up to the door or saddened. I'm firmly standing between the two, wishing we could explore this attraction we both seem to have and knowing it's for the best we can't.

Sighing, I finally push away from the door and head toward my bedroom. It was a beautiful wedding celebration, and despite my vehicle breaking down, it turned out to be a not-so-bad ending too.

Gavin intrigues me, which is why I need to keep my distance.

Nothing good can come from getting involved with a man like him. He could only be classified as a gorgeous complication to my carefully constructed life.

One I don't need.

But that doesn't stop my mind from wondering.

Yeah, but what if...

CHAPTER Two

GAVIN

Damn, she's beautiful.

I've repeated that phrase over and over since I found Ava Rutledge stranded on the side of the road. I tried to keep myself in check, remaining as respectful as humanly possible, but it was difficult with her wearing that black dress and boots. She looked positively breathtaking.

Always does.

I've known Ava for quite some time, but as more of an acquaintance. Someone who grew up in the same town, attended the same school. She is three years older than me, a senior in my freshman year of high school when I caught my first glimpse of her. I was too young for her and way out of her league, but that didn't stop my teenage brain from fantasizing about her.

Of course, I was just a kid with a crush, but I spent that entire school year secretly watching her and wishing she were mine. She had the sexiest freckles on her cheeks and wore wire-rimmed glasses. After she graduated and went off to college, I'd catch sight of her every now and again when she'd come home for break, and while

I dated my share of girls in high school, I was always sweet on Ava Rutledge.

Crushes are brutal like that.

Over the years, we've occasionally been at the same place at the same time, and while I don't consider it a crush anymore—just recognition of a beautiful woman—I have a deep respect for her. She attended college and returned to her hometown to teach at the very school we all walked the halls in as kids and has done well with her life, despite the fiasco of that terrible college photo resurfacing a few years back.

I, on the other hand, have had my fair share of ups and downs. A failed marriage, bitter custody battle that took forever to settle, and a credit score that doesn't seem to go anywhere, thanks to my ex and her ability to trash everything with my name attached to it. But the best thing to come from even the worst day in my life is my daughter, Annabelle. She's simply the best piece of me, and I refuse to let her mother dampen that.

She's the most inquisitive little girl I've ever met, always has been. Even as a young child, she asked the dreaded question...why? She wanted to know how everything worked, and from the moment she was able to read, she read everything with words on it. Okay, not everything, but she always has a book or will go online to research something that fascinates her.

I wasn't kidding when I told Ava I didn't know where she got it from. I was a C student, and sometimes barely even that. I didn't like school, especially reading, and from what I've learned about my ex-wife over the years, she wasn't exactly a stellar student either. She got by, mostly by using her looks when she could.

I have tons of stories, but now isn't the time. No one wants to hear about how Julia used any and all means possible to get a leg up in life.

And I definitely won't get into anything involving her *legs* right now, but I will say they were usually spread.

When I reach Eldridge Road once more, instead of turning left and continuing my drive through the countryside, I opt to turn right. I'm curious as to whether Marcus is there yet to retrieve Ava's car. It's only a few miles up the road, and thanks to the falling snow, there isn't any traffic out right now.

The road is somewhat flat, but there is a big bend coming up. As soon as I drive around it, the lights of Pine Village come into view. They're off in the distance, but there, nonetheless. I can also see the blinking orange lights of Ava's disabled Kia. Decelerating, I slowly approach her vehicle, noting how perfect and fitting it is for her. It's a small, sporty SUV with all-wheel drive. I've seen her scoot around town and on snowy country roads with ease and love how comfortable she looks in it.

Just as I prepare to pull over and make sure no one fucks with her car—despite having yet to pass another vehicle—I see the flashing lights of Marcus's tow truck up ahead. He's on his way, which means there's really no reason for me to hang around. It's not like he needs my help or anything. Marcus has been working on automobiles since he was old enough to walk, cutting his teeth on oil changes and brake lines. His grandpa owned the original shop, and as he grew up, raised by his grandparents, that's where he spent all his time.

He learned from the best and, about five or six years ago, purchased the shop.

I give him plenty of room as I pass, watching in my rearview mirror as he pulls the flatbed truck in front of Ava's disabled vehicle. Knowing there's nothing I can do but head home, I continue forward, reaching the city limits of Pine Village fairly quickly. I move through the streets, recalling how I'd walk them or ride my bike as a kid. I grew up not too far from where I'm at, so I head in the direction of the house my parents still live in after forty years of marriage.

I'm the youngest of three, and the only one to stay in our hometown. I love the small-town vibe, while my older brother and sister thrive more in the city. Both live in St. Paul, Minnesota, just a short thirty-minutes on the opposite side of the Wisconsin/Minnesota border, so they're still close enough to check on our parents and get together for birthdays and holidays.

When I turn onto Grinnell Drive, I spot the familiar light in front of the living room window on, and I can practically see my parents sitting in their respective recliners, watching late-night television. You would think it was the news, but it's not. They're huge Jimmy Fallon fans, watching it faithfully with a bowl of popcorn and a bottle of beer.

My parents are cool like that.

I always thought I'd be just like them when I grew up. As the youngest, I sort of got away with everything by the time I was in high school, but even though I was an ornery shit, I always longed for the relationship my parents seemed to have. Oh, it wasn't perfect. They argued and, at times, told each other where to go, but at the end of the day, they talked it out and vowed to do better.

My marriage to Julia was nothing like that.

Not even close.

I pass my parents' house, wanting to stop but not at this hour. Not that it's late, but I'm sure my mom worked hard to prepare for tomorrow. We'll be gathering at their place for Christmas Eve dinner. Since it falls on a Saturday, it was easy to plan around my siblings' schedules and when I have Annabelle. I get her all day tomorrow, and while the thought of not seeing her on Christmas morning kills me, that's the way the holiday schedule falls.

Julia and I split the time fifty-fifty, and while it was a huge fight and long court process to get to that point, I don't regret it. Having my daughter with me as much as I can was my goal, and thanks to a very expensive lawyer, we were able to get shared custody, despite how difficult Julia made it. The major holidays are rotated, so while Annabelle is with me Christmas Eve and her mom Christmas Day this year, next year will be the opposite. I make the best out of it, making sure my grievances with Julia don't touch our daughter.

As I worm my way through the city streets, taking in the houses decorated with Christmas lights, my mind returns to Ava. I don't think she's dating anyone, which surprises me. She's smart, beautiful, and has a good head on her shoulders. I've never understood why some guy hasn't scooped her up yet. But you never hear of her dating anyone, and believe me, in this town, you'd hear. Everyone makes your business their own.

Eventually, I drive home, pulling into my attached garage and parking. I use these drives to help relax me, but I feel like after finding Ava stranded on the side of the road, I'm anything but. I'm tense, and my mind is consumed by her. As much as I try not to think about my daughter's gorgeous teacher, I can't stop.

This is definitely going to be a long night.

"Ready?" I ask Annabelle as I pick her up on Christmas Eve morning. It's exactly eight o'clock, and my daughter is full of smiles and excitement.

"Yes," she informs me, making sure her coat is zipped and her gloves in place. "I'm so happy it snowed last night. Now it feels like Christmas."

I take her overnight bag, which contains what little bit of stuff she doesn't already have at my house. "We're leaving, Julia," I holler at my ex, who, surprisingly, hasn't graced me with her appearance at the door.

"She's still sleeping," Annabelle states, making sure the door is locked behind her as she closes it.

We walk toward my truck, and when she climbs in the passenger seat and I have her bag placed on the floorboard, I ask, "Did she work last night?" I know full well she didn't. It's not harvest season, and even then, Julia rarely works evenings because of our daughter.

"No, just up late, I guess. I woke her up when I was getting ready and told her I was leaving."

I nod before closing her door and heading for the driver's side.

Julia works at her dad's grain elevator in Hudson, about ten minutes away from Pine Village. She takes care of a lot of the office side of the business, and in fact, that's how we met. I was driving a truck for a farmer, hauling grain to the elevator one harvest, and bam, there she was.

Gorgeous.

We hit it off right away, and the next thing I knew, we were talking about marriage. Like three months after we met. I was twenty; Julia barely twenty-one. Got married, had a kid two years later, and battled until the day we finally acknowledged it was over.

It wasn't all bad, don't get me wrong, but we learned pretty early on that we weren't right for each other. Yet, we still tried for the sake of our daughter. However, in the end, divorce was our only option, especially after I suspected she wasn't faithful. She never confirmed it, but my gut tells me the rumors were accurate, especially since the guy she was supposedly screwing was my former employee—who quit the moment his name was mentioned as being linked to her.

But all that is in my rearview mirror.

I'm happy and healthy, raising my daughter, working as the local contractor, which I love, and doing my thing.

"When are we going to Grandma and Grandpa's?" Annabelle asks.

"Three. We'll do presents and eat dinner. Great-Grandma Pierson is going to come over for a bit too after church. I think Grandma wants to do games."

Annabelle smirks. "I hope it's Scrabble. Remember last year when Fletcher threw the board across the room when I beat him?"

I chuckle, heading toward the diner. Fletcher is my brother's oldest. He's eighteen and competitive as hell, especially in the classroom. So to lose to his younger cousin was a blow to his ego. "I'm guessing the Scrabble board will be put away this year," I tell her, finding a parking spot right on the street in front of the diner. Turning off the truck, I spin my attention her way. "Even though it *accidentally* went flying from the table."

My eleven-year-old daughter giggles the sweetest sound. "Yeah, *'accidentally,'*" she repeats, using her fingers to make air quotes.

"Come on. Let's go have breakfast, and then you can help me get a few last-minute gifts," I state, grabbing my keys and slipping from my truck.

"Can we go to the bookstore?" she asks, her brown eyes full of hope and excitement.

I pause on the sidewalk outside the diner. "It's Christmas Eve."

"I know," she sings. "What better time to celebrate the birth of our Lord and Savior than with a new book?" she asks, fluttering her eyelashes and offering me a big grin.

Laughing, I open the door and follow her inside. "We'll see. We have to get something else for Bethany," I tell her, referring to my sister's youngest daughter.

"I know just the thing! At Thanksgiving, she was talking about the Star Friends books! We can get her some of those. They're really good," she says as Ellie walks over to where we stand.

"Hey, guys. Have a seat wherever," Ellie states with a friendly smile. "Chocolate milk?" she asks Annabelle, who eagerly nods. When Ellie glances my way, she adds, "Coffee and water?"

"You're the best, Ellie," I tell her, following behind Annabelle as she heads for one of the available booths.

Frannie's Diner is a local staple, serving the best home-cooked meals around. Fran still works, but not nearly as much as she used to. Ellie Dexter has been managing this place for years, starting here in high school. When she got pregnant at seventeen, it was Fran who took her in, giving her a job and a place to stay when her parents kicked her out. She married TD, the local police officer and football coach, last summer, and they seem pretty happy.

Annabelle and I just got our coats off and placed on the booth seat beside us when Ellie returns with our drinks. "Are you ready for Christmas, Annabelle?"

"Yes," my daughter proclaims. "I get two whole days of Christmases. Today with my dad and tomorrow with my mom."

"Well, that sounds like a lot of fun. And a lot of gifts," she adds with a chuckle. "Are you having the French toast or the pancakes today?"

"French toast," my daughter replies.

"Whipped cream and strawberries?"

"Of course!"

Smiling, Ellie turns her attention my way. "The usual for you?" she asks, remembering every detail of my usual order without making one note.

"Please," I reply, tearing open two sugar packets and dropping the contents into my coffee.

"Coming right up!" she proclaims, spinning around to put our orders in with the kitchen.

The bell over the door chimes, and as usual, everyone turns to see who's arriving. Since it's so close to Christmas, we don't have a lot of tourists in town right now, which means the newcomers are most likely local. I turn, spotting TD and Ellie's son, Brody, entering the diner.

TD gives me a wave in greeting, but his attention is drawn quickly to his wife. They share a smile, and as if two magnets drawn to each other, they both move and meet in the middle of the diner. "Hello, wife," he mutters right before pressing a chaste kiss to her lips.

"Husband," she murmurs, practically singing that one word. Then, she quickly turns her attention to Brody. "Good morning."

"Morning, Mom," he mumbles, his hair slightly askew and his eyes heavy.

She chuckles. "Booth or table?"

"Counter," TD states, slapping Brody on the back of the shoulder and guiding him toward the far end of the room, where the long counter is situated.

"I'll be up in a few," she chimes in behind them, making a few stops to refill cups of coffee.

"Brody looks a little tired," I say when she reaches our table.

She smiles widely, glancing to where her husband and son sit, talking. "He was up pretty late last night, hanging out with some friends all home from college, and I haven't confirmed it yet, but I think there might have been a little alcohol involved," she says, shaking her head.

I nod. "Nothing we didn't do at that age, right?" I reason, recalling how my friends and I would sneak beer out of our parents' refrigerators and share it at someone's house. The unspoken rule was no one leaves if alcohol was ever involved, something we stuck to even when our dumb, teenage brains wanted to challenge us.

"Well, I wouldn't know," she replies with a chuckle, reminding me of how her life was different than her classmates, thanks to a teenage pregnancy. "But he stayed put at his friend's, and that's all I ask. You either call me or TD or you don't leave."

I nod. "Good rule."

She sighs. "They're technically adults, but it's hard not to still view them as kids. As long as they're smart about it, we have to let them make their own decisions, right or wrong."

"He's got a good head on his shoulders, Ellie."

"I know," she replies proudly.

"Hey, I know it's early, but if Brody's looking for summer work when he gets out of school, I'm always searching. I could definitely keep him busy for the months he's home on break."

She grins widely. "Wow, really? I'll mention it to him, thanks."

"Just have him give me a call or stop by this spring if he's interested. Or if he has a friend who might be." Summer is always crazy busy with construction projects, and having an extra pair of hands comes in very handy, especially since Annabelle is also out of school and I try to spend extra time with her.

"Thanks, Gavin," she replies, hearing the ringing of the bell at the kitchen window. "That's probably your order. I'll be right back."

I turn my attention back to Annabelle and give her a smile. She's the perfect combination of her mom and me, with her mom's round face and brown eyes, but my brown hair and full lips. She catches me watching her and gives me a wide grin. Her front teeth are slightly crooked, an indication she's probably going to need braces someday soon, and her eyes are twinkling with both mischief and anticipation.

"So, about the bookstore..."

CHAPTER *Three*

Last-minute shopping is the worst, especially on Christmas Eve. Throw in the fact I don't have a vehicle and had to borrow one from my dad—which he had to deliver to me, mind you. But he did it with a smile, and even tried to slip me gas money when I dropped him back off at the house so I could finish my Christmas shopping.

I don't have a lot to do.

My dad is done, as is my sister, Analise. I have a gift for my brother-in-law, Chris, but I wanted to add something to it, so I made a quick stop to see Logan at the hardware store for a hand tool recommendation. That leaves my twin nieces, Riley and Molly. I can shop for them all day long, though gone are the days they found cute little matching outfits adorable.

The girls are thirteen now, and, despite being identical twins, are as different as night and day in personality. Molly is as girly girl as they come, always wearing pinks and purples, is a junior high cheerleader, and loves big, fancy hairbows, while her twin, Riley, prefers sports brands, plays soccer, and is learning the guitar.

And I love them to pieces.

I find a parking spot on a side street and climb from my dad's Ford Explorer. Thankfully, he has two vehicles, the Explorer being the one he doesn't drive as much as the truck, so it was easy for him to agree to let me borrow it for a few days.

Making my way to the storefronts, I pass the barbershop and the beauty salon, both closed on Christmas Eve, and go straight to the heavy wooden door of my favorite little shop in downtown Pine Village. Stepping inside, I bask in the warmth, familiarity, and scents of books—both new and old.

Jasmine's Books started as a small used bookstore and has slowly grown into something unique and magnificent over the years. While her used books are a big draw, in a small town like Pine Village, she realized she needed something more. So, she started researching and discovered she could purchase new books through different channels, including directly from the authors themselves. She has a decent selection of signed books—most of them romance. They make the perfect holiday gift, if you ask me.

But Jasmine didn't stop there. You'll also find vendor tables, all selling their homemade crafts, art, home décor, or clothing. Even jellies and honey. It's the best kind of store, offering a variety of products, and I'm not surprised it's busy.

"Good morning, Miss Ava," Jasmine hollers from the front counter.

"Hello, Jasmine. Merry Christmas," I reply, dragging my feet over her welcome mat to clean off any remnants of last night's snowfall.

"Merry Christmas, dear. Let me know if you need anything," she says, returning her attention to the customer she's checking out.

I make my way through the room, taking in the festive holiday decorations, the homemade goodies, and head toward the children's book section. I bypass the used shelves and go to the new offerings, hoping to find what I'm looking for, since there's no way to order it— either through the bookstore or online—and get it in time.

I find a book fitting of my idea for Molly. It's a step-by-step book on crafting all sorts of things from hairbows to jewelry, and it'll be the perfect addition to finish out her gift. Smiling, I start searching for something for Riley. She's not as crafty as her twin, so I opt for a book about women in sports and hope she finds it inspiring and educational. Considering one of the athletes on the cover is Mia Hamm, former soccer superstar, I'm sure she'll enjoy it.

Happy with my selections, I turn to head toward the section housing romance books. I have big plans on decluttering my closets over Christmas break, but I'm certain there will be a little time over the next week and a half to do a little reading too.

"Miss Rutledge!"

I spin around, a smile already spreading across my face the moment I recognize the voice. "Hi, Miss Annabelle," I say, trying to keep my eyes focused on one of my students.

Unfortunately, my eyes betray me, seeking out her father like a castaway searching for ships on the horizon. He's directly behind her, a warm, friendly grin on his own face that makes my heart rate kick up a few extra beats.

"Good morning, Miss Rutledge," he greets, his voice low and gravelly.

Shock waves course through my veins, striking my clit with a force that causes me to gasp.

His hazel eyes fill with worry. "Are you all right?"

I clear my throat, wishing the floor would open up and swallow me whole. "Oh, yes," I reply with an awkward chuckle. Returning my attention to Annabelle, I ask, "Are you ready for Christmas?"

She nods eagerly. "We're going to my grandma and grandpa's this afternoon. My cousins and aunts and uncles will be there."

"That sounds like fun," I tell her, offering an easy, friendly smile.

"Are you going to see your mom and dad?" she asks.

Nodding, I state, "I am, but not until tomorrow. My sister and her family will be there. That's why I stopped in here. I wanted to get my nieces another gift." I hold up the two books I found and let her inspect them. I wasn't joking when I told Gavin his daughter was incredibly smart and inquisitive. She's a book lover through and through, just like me.

"I love to make stuff," Annabelle says as she flips open the book I found for Molly. "Dad, look! You can make all sorts of jewelry and bows."

"Very cool," he says, offering her a grin.

I can't help but notice how amazing he looks this morning. Gavin Pierson has always been a good-looking man, but for some reason, he suddenly appears...hot. He's been in my classroom a few times since the beginning of the school year, but once he left the room, I didn't spend half the night replaying our every contact. Last night—and this morning—his memory kept infiltrating my brain, refusing to let up.

Maybe it's some sort of hero worship syndrome. Being the one to pull over and offer to help. Though, I've never felt any sort of attraction to Marcus, despite being a decent-looking guy. He's always been someone I consider a friend. Nothing more.

Gavin, on the other hand, isn't someone I'd consider a friend. Yes, I've known him most of my life, but only because Pine Village is a small town. He was younger than me, and we didn't hang out in the same circles. Sure, I'd consider him attractive—hot, even—but that's it. Suddenly, after last night, I want to spread him on a cracker and eat him alive.

Hallie might be rubbing off on me.

"I'm here to pick out a book for my cousin, Bethany. I was thinking the Star Friends series. She's eight and talked about her library having them at school. Do you think that's a good choice?" Annabelle asks, pulling my thoughts away from her father.

"I think that's a great choice. *Diary of a Wimpy Kid*, Magic Tree House, and Babysitter's Club are all great for that age too," I offer.

"Oh, yes!" she proclaims, and suddenly, we're both walking toward the children's book section.

"This is very popular right now," I state, pulling one of the newer books off the shelf.

"I've read this one. I love the fairies who share words of wisdom to the main character throughout," she says, that familiar twinkle in her brown eyes. Every time she gets excited about a book in class, her eyes take on this bright light, an exhilaration like no other.

"It's a wonderful story, full of intrigue. I'm glad you enjoyed it."

"Dad, what do you think about getting Bethany this book and the first two in the Star Friends series?"

I glance over to see Gavin smile fondly at his daughter. "Sounds good."

"She's going to be so excited for these," Annabelle announces, moving down the shelf to find the Star Friends books she's after.

"Thank you for making suggestions," Gavin says as he steps forward, taking the space at my side his daughter just vacated.

Shrugging, I reply with an awkward chuckle, "I love books. I could talk about them with anyone."

He holds my gaze with his rich hazel eyes. "Nothing wrong with having passion."

My skin starts to tingle, and my nipples grow hard. Thank goodness I'm wearing a coat and thick sweater. Otherwise, I'm certain he'd see what type of reaction his words have on me. I open my mouth in hope some sort of intelligent reply can be said, when Annabelle interrupts.

"Miss Rutledge! They have that new one in the series!"

I spin in her direction and find her holding up the brand-new Zohra Nabi book we've all been anxiously awaiting. The kids loved the first book I grabbed by that author and knew there was a second book in the works. "I know." Then I add a wink and the hint of a smirk.

Annabelle gasps. "Did you get it already?" she asks, holding the book to her chest.

"It might already be on my desk for when we return from Christmas break."

She squeals in delight, returning the book to the shelf and moving on to browse more.

Gavin leans in close, and his intoxicating scent wraps around me. "I got her The Sisterhood of the Traveling Pants series for Christmas. It seems a little advanced for her, though."

"She's going to love it, and I don't think it's too advanced. She's reading at a junior high level. In fact, some of the books I've recommended are ones I went and borrowed from the sixth-grade literature class," I tell him as we stroll along behind Annabelle as she peruses. "And not just because she's read everything I have in the classroom already."

He chuckles. "She loves your class."

Smiling, I can't help but boast, "She's a wonderful student."

"Miss Rutledge, I have the best idea," Annabelle announces as she returns to where Gavin and I stand. "You can come with us to my grandma and grandpa's house tonight."

I feel like my eyes bug out of my head as her words register. "Oh, thank you so much for offering, Annabelle. I'm actually going to church with my grandma later, but I appreciate the offer."

"You can come after. You're my favorite teacher, and that's practically the same as being my family. She can come too," she reasons, making me smile.

"Aww, well, thank you for inviting us. We'll have to see," I reply, even though it's more so to appease her at this point.

"Why don't you start heading up to the front counter so Jasmine can ring us up?" Gavin suggests.

"Okay," she states before turning her attention to me. "I'm so glad we ran into you, Miss Rutledge, and I hope your Christmas is great." Then, she steps forward and throws her arms around my waist, books and all, and squeezes.

I delicately return the gesture, lightly patting her back. I do my best not to touch my students, but sometimes, at this age, they just want or need hugs. "Enjoy the rest of your Christmas break, Annabelle. We'll see you in class after the first of the year."

She nods, steps back, and heads for the front counter, books in hand.

"She's right, you know."

My attention turns to Gavin. "About what?" I ask in confusion.

"Today. You're more than welcome to come with us to my parents' house, despite the fact it's Christmas Eve. In fact, you're also welcome because of it."

My throat is thick as I try to swallow. "Thank you for the invite, but I'm sure my grandma will have me wrapping all of her gifts after church tonight," I reply with a chuckle.

He nods. "Well, the offer stands. If you decide later you want to drop by for dessert and coffee, please do."

I give him a small smile. "Thank you, Mr. Pierson."

Stepping forward, he invades my personal space. His woodsy scent tickles my senses and causes my breath to hitch in my throat. "Just Gavin, remember?" The corner of his mouth curls up in the most delightful little smirk.

"Gavin." I don't know how I get that single word out. My throat is so dry at his nearness I can't think straight.

He flashes me a smile that makes my thighs clench and heads off toward his daughter. "Merry Christmas, Ava. Maybe we'll see you later."

I nod, unable to form words, and watch him go. I can't help but wonder if he can feel my eyes on his ass, because they are certainly glued there. Even though part of it is obstructed by his coat, I still get a decent view.

Forcing myself to look away, I scan the children's books once more, mostly to give Gavin and Annabelle time to check out and exit the store. Even though it's logical I'd follow them to check out, when I'm near him, suddenly, I feel all out of sorts. My heart races, my palms sweat, and my lady bits stand up and take notice. Even more so than when I met Peter in college, and we began our two-year relationship. Talk about the shy girl who got all tongue-tied around hot guys.

I've never been good around them. Male friends, sure. I don't have any problem talking to TD, Logan, Gabe, Marcus, or any other former classmate. Not because they're not good-looking in their own respect, but when I find myself attracted to someone, my brain just sort of forgets how to be cool.

Not that I was ever really cool to begin with.

Oh, well. I don't have to worry about it now. I need to run home, finish wrapping my presents, and get ready to pick up Grandma. The Christmas Eve service is our little tradition, and now that she doesn't drive thanks to her terrible vision, I get the honor of taking her. That's where my focus needs to be tonight, not on the sexy single dad of one of my students. Especially when I have a very strict "no dating" rule for fathers of kids in my class.

But if—*if*—I was going to break my own rule, it might very well be for a man like Gavin Pierson.

"Thank you for coming. Merry Christmas."

I shake our pastor's hand as we slowly exit the church. "Merry Christmas," I reply, feeling my phone vibrate in my pocket.

"Excellent service, Pastor Charles," my grandma says behind me, shaking his outstretched hand.

"Thank you, Miss Betty. Merry Christmas to you," he replies before moving on to the next member of the congregation.

I extend my elbow, which Grandma takes, as we carefully descend the steps leading to the foyer. My phone vibrates again, and I start to get a little anxious that something could be wrong. Yet, I still refrain from pulling the device out. Grabbing Grandma's coat from the rack, I help her slip it on, retrieving my own while she secures the large buttons down the front.

"Before we go, I'm going to have a word with Zelda," Grandma announces, walking over to where one of her church lady friends stands.

Making sure I'm out of the way, I take the opportunity to check my phone while I wait. I find a bunch of text messages in our friend group and scroll up to find the first one.

> **Ellie:** You guys, Brody just got home and told me his grades. Dean's list for his first semester of college. I'm so stinking proud of him!!

> **Blair:** Yay, Brody!! He's such a smart young man. You have every right to be proud.

> **Hallie:** Yes!! Congratulations, Brody!

> **Blair:** What did TD say?

> **Ellie:** He took me in his arms and held me while I cried. There were times when he was little that I didn't know how I was going to pay for new shoes and clothes and food. I'm just so overcome with gratitude for what everyone did for me and him.

> **Blair:** YOU did this, Ellie. We all just held your hand and helped when we could.

> **Hallie:** Agreed. He is a shining example of his mama.

> **Ellie:** Thank you. Truly. I can't believe I had such an amazing child, despite all the crap life threw at me.

Hallie: That's exactly why he's so wonderful, caring, and smart.

Blair: Agreed. Please tell him congrats from all of us.

Hallie: Yes! We'll buy him a slice of pie next time he's at the diner.

That's the last message sent, and I'm able to jump right in.

Me: Sorry, I was at church with Grandma. Yes! Congrats to Brody. He's a smart young man, just like his mama.

I try to ignore the way my heart trips over itself at the word mama. There's an ache in my chest at the thought of having a baby. I've always wanted one. Well, not just one, but a couple. Unfortunately, that requires someone with sperm to make that happen, and I haven't exactly been swimming in the dating pool lately.

And I know that's how Ellie feels too. They've been trying to have a baby since they got married over the summer, but it hasn't happened yet. I understand her fear completely. The older we get, the more difficult it becomes, with more risks of complications. That's why I hold my classmates so close to my heart. They're the kids I've always wanted but may never have.

Hallie: Everyone have a wonderful Christmas Eve. Hope Santa brings you exactly what you want this year.

"Ava, dear, what do you think?"

I glance up at my grandma, not realizing she had been talking to me. "What?"

"About dessert with Zelda. There'll be pie," Grandma says, a big grin on her face, since she knows I'm a huge fan of peach and cherry pie.

My phone buzzes again in my hand, so I quickly reply, "Oh, that would be fine."

"Great. I'll tell Zelda we'll meet her there," she says, turning and making her way back over to her friend.

I fire off one last congratulations and Merry Christmas message to the group before pocketing the device and meeting my grandma at the door. We walk together to my dad's Explorer, and once I have her securely tucked inside, I move around to the driver's side and start up the SUV.

"It's such a beautiful night, isn't it?" Grandma asks, smiling out the window at the night sky.

"It is. Do you think we'll get more snow?"

"I don't think it's forecast, but that's one of the things about Wisconsin weather. It can be unpredictable," she states with a chuckle. "Just turn up here and head south on Hooper Street."

I follow her directions, driving to where we're meeting Zelda for dessert. Of course, my mind replays Gavin's invitation for dessert and coffee, and I can't help but wonder if they're doing just that—sitting around the table and laughing over cakes and cookies.

"Right here, dear. The one on the left."

I pull into the driveway she indicates, and realization hits me. I know this place.

It's not Zelda's home, but that of her son's.

Gavin's dad.

"What are we doing here?" I ask, gaping at the brightly lit house.

"We're going to have pie with Zelda and her family."

"But..."

"Let's go, slowpoke. I don't want all the good pie to be gone," Grandma says before climbing out of the vehicle.

I'm left feeling overwhelmed by what's happening, but quickly get out of the driver's seat and meet Grandma around at the side of the SUV to escort her inside.

To Gavin's childhood home.

The plot thickens...

CHAPTER *four*

GAVIN

"How's it going?" my brother, Paul, asks, taking the empty seat beside me at the dining room table.

"Pretty good," I reply, sipping water and glancing at the kids all playing games in the living room with their grandparents.

"Business doing well?"

I nod. "Winter is always slower, but I have plenty of indoor jobs to keep us busy for a while."

"That helps. At least you're not framing up a garage right now," he says, taking a drink of his beer.

"No shit," I mutter, grateful to be working inside for a while. We've had those types of jobs before, and they're never fun this time of year. "How's everything with you?"

"Good. Getting ready for tax season, which means I'll be working crazy hours for the next four months, so trying to enjoy a little downtime before all hell breaks loose."

My brother, Paul, and his wife, Tina, own a CPA firm in St. Paul and are pretty successful. They have six accountants under them, some who only work during tax season, while others stay on full time to handle year-round needs for customers and corporations.

"Math," I grumble, throwing in a shiver to make my point. "Why anyone would want to do math every day is beyond me."

Paul chuckles. "Says the man who uses math in measurements all day, every day."

"Not the same," I insist.

"So what else is new? You seeing anyone?" he asks quietly, even though we're the only two in the room.

My brain flashes with an image of Ava, despite the fact we're not dating. "Uhh, no."

"What was that?"

"What was what?"

"The hesitation."

I scoff and cross my arms over my chest.

"There *is* someone. I can tell."

"You can't tell shit," I counter. "There's no one."

Paul chuckles. "That right there. I can tell because you instantly got defensive. Tell me."

I feel the weight of his eyes on me as I try to sit calmly, but as the silence goes on, I start to squirm. I consider my options, but in the end, I know he won't let it slide. He's like a dog with a bone, determined to pull any dirt out of me he can get. When we were little, he used to tickle me until I cracked. Now, he just waits and stares until I have no other option. I'm sure it's a technique he's perfected throughout raising his kids.

Asshole.

"There's someone I...like."

"And?" he encourages, wanting more.

"And, that's it. I would love to ask her out, but I'm pretty sure she will resist."

"Why?"

I glance around, making sure no one is within earshot. "She's Annabelle's teacher."

"Okay, so?"

I shrug. "It's not that simple. She's pretty reserved and doesn't date much. And I'm certain she wouldn't date the father of one of her students."

Paul leans a little closer, placing his elbows on the table. "I don't know, man. You were always a persistent little thing when you were younger. I bet, if you wanted to, you could convince her to give you a shot."

"This isn't like talking Mom into giving us more time to stay up and watch *Batman*, Paul," I reply with a laugh.

He shrugs as the front door opens. "That's probably Grandma. The Christmas Eve service should be over by now," he states, jumping up and going to help her inside. Grandma Zelda may be in her eighties, but she's still incredibly active and very involved in her church.

"I invited a friend to join us for dessert," Grandma announces as she slips her coat off and hangs it on the tree beside the door.

Getting up from my seat, I pull out the chair at the end of the table. "How was the service, Grandma?"

"It was lovely, dear. The Christmas services are always my favorite," she says.

"What can I get you to drink, Grandma?" my sister, Ginger, asks, joining us in the dining room.

"Coffee, please."

"Is it time for dessert?" Mason, my sister's fourteen-year-old son, hollers from the living room, where he is playing Uno.

"Sure is!" Grandma replies, smiling as the kids all seem to come running. A knock sounds at the front door. "Oh, that's probably my church friend, Betty."

I hear the front door open, but my eyes are zeroing in on the peach pie my mom made for tonight as it's brought to the antique buffet table where the desserts are placed. If I don't hurry, it'll be gone, the pan practically licked clean by the Neanderthal I call my brother.

We've always fought over the peach pie.

"Miss Rutledge! You came!" Annabelle hollers, catching my attention.

I look up and find Ava and her grandma standing by the front door, and there's no missing the shock on Ava's gorgeous face. She smiles down at Annabelle, who wraps her arms around her waist and squeezes tightly, much like she did earlier in the day at the bookstore. Then, as if sensing my eyes on her, Ava looks up and meets my gaze. I swear, you can hear the sizzle of electricity as it zings through the air.

A hand comes down on my shoulder and gives a hard squeeze. "Ahhh, the teacher, I assume?"

I swallow hard and glance at my brother, who's wearing a cocky smirk on his smug face. "Shut up."

Quickly changing my route from the dessert table to the front entrance, I meet Ava and Betty as they're taking off their coats. "Merry Christmas, ladies," I say, helping hang their coats.

"Merry Christmas," Betty replies with a warm smile.

"Sorry to intrude, but Zelda invited my grandma over for coffee and pie," Ava says, a look of uncertainty on her pretty face.

"And we're happy to have you," I insist, offering my arm to the older woman. "Miss Betty, would you like some coffee? I believe my mom just made a fresh pot."

Betty steps forward, slipping her hand around my elbow. "I would love some, dear. And Zelda has told me all about the pies," she states, walking with me into the dining room.

Fortunately, since the kids all eat dessert in the kitchen around the smaller table and counter bar, there is plenty of room at the dining room table for our guests. "Well, it looks like she saved you a seat," I say, pulling out the chair closest to my grandma for Betty to have a seat.

"Thank you, sweetheart," Betty says, patting my cheek. "If I weren't so damn old, I'd be giving you my number."

Just as I bark out a laugh, I hear a gasp and a shocked, "Grandma!" behind me.

Betty just shrugs and takes the seat. "Well, my eyesight isn't what it used to be, but I'm not completely blind, Ava." She gives me a friendly smile. "Zelda didn't tell me her grandson grew into such a handsome man. You know, my granddaughter is adorable *and* single."

Again, there's a gasp behind me. "Stop it!" she whisper-yells at her grandma, making everyone in the room chuckle.

Smiling, I glance back, taking in Ava's adorably red face, even though she's trying to hide it behind her hand. Returning my attention to Betty, I flash her a charming grin. "Why, yes, Miss Betty, I am fully aware of your granddaughter's beauty." I give her a wink as my sister delivers mugs of coffee to Grandma and her friend.

While the rest of the adults grab dessert and find seats around the dining room table or in the living room, I give my complete attention to Ava. She's wearing a rich, warm red sweater, and my mind instantly goes back to that night over the summer when she walked into Shiner's Pub in that sexy as fuck red dress. It was unlike anything I'd ever seen her wear before, straight out of my wildest fantasies, really, and rekindled this massive crush I have. All night, I couldn't take my eyes off her as she visited with her friends, celebrating Hallie's birthday. It also fueled the actions I took on myself later that night when I was alone at home.

Now, she's paired her red sweater with black slacks and looks so classic and beautiful. I don't know what it is about Ava Rutledge, but I've never been more attracted to anyone else.

"What can I get you to drink?"

She looks up, her cheeks still stained from embarrassment. "Oh, I'm fine."

"Come on, Ava," I reply lightly. "Let me get you something. Coffee? Ice water? Iced tea? I think there's some soda in the fridge too."

"Umm, all right. I'll have coffee."

Giving her a quick grin, I reply, "I'll be right back. Go ahead and grab yourself some dessert before the hooligans return for seconds." I head into the kitchen to pour two cups of coffee.

The kids are all chatting about the gifts they received tonight and the ones they're hoping to get tomorrow. I chuckle as I hear the oldest talk about wanting a new car, which I know he's not receiving for Christmas, and smile as the youngest gushes about the books she unwrapped earlier. When I have two cups of coffee filled, I return to the dining room.

Ava is sitting at the seat beside her grandma, listening to the two older women chat. "Here ya go," I reply, placing the steaming mugs down on the table. I notice Ava still doesn't have any dessert, but her grandma does.

"Thank you," she replies, wrapping her fingers around the mug, as if to use it to warm them up.

"You're welcome. No dessert for you?" I ask.

"No, I'm all right," she insists, but there's no missing the way her eyes dart toward the array of sweet treats nearby.

"Come on, Miss Rutledge. My mom's peach pie is to die for and is my favorite," I insist, reaching for her chair and ready to help pull it out. "You need to try it."

She slowly stands, and it takes every ounce of control I possess not to place my hand on her back and guide her toward the desserts. I long to touch her, but refrain, mostly because I don't want her to feel like I'm getting handsy. I've never been a big touchy-feely guy, but recently, when I'm around Ava, all I want to do is get my hands on her.

When we approach the buffet table, my eyes seek out the one dessert that's the biggest reason I come to family functions: the pie. Okay, that's not entirely true but it's definitely a huge part of it. Sweet peaches, buttery, flaky crust, and a dusting of sugar that makes my mouth water.

"There's only one piece of pie left," Ava says.

"That's okay, you take it."

She shakes her head, reaching for a brownie with powdered sugar on top. "I couldn't. It's your favorite," she reasons, also taking a chocolate chip cookie.

"Nope, I insist. Mom's peach pie is practically its own food group. She won the church group pie bake-off seven years in a row. If you don't take it, you'd be missing out on one of the greatest gifts in life, and I could never eat it with you sitting beside me, knowing you're peach pie-less and I'm not. It would ruin peach pie for me for the rest of my life."

Am I laying it on thick?

Yes.

Does she appear to be falling for my bullshit?

Also, yes.

A slow smile spreads across her lips. "Wow, how can I say no to that?" She chuckles. "But the only way I'm eating this pie is if you split it with me. I can't eat a whole slice of pie, plus what I already put on my plate, so really, you'd be doing *me* a favor by sharing it with me."

"Deal," I reply.

Just as I go to reach for the pie server, a hand swoops in to grab it first. I turn narrowed eyes toward my brother, who's smirking gleefully and victoriously. I reach out and slap his hand. "Drop the pie server or you'll be eating your Christmas meal tomorrow through a straw."

My asshole brother barks out a laugh and shakes his head. He glances around me and smiles at Ava. "I promise, my baby brother isn't always a caveman. He's only acting like that because he thinks flexing his muscles will impress you."

I groan, and before I can retort with something sarcastic and witty, Ava steps up to the plate and knocks it out of the park. "I get it. I've heard amazing things about this pie, and if you take the last slice, you're second one, I might add, leaving us with nothing, then you might deserve a knuckle sandwich, as my grandpa used to say."

Paul gapes in horror at Ava, while I burst out laughing. When he finally catches his composure, he hands off the pie server. "You two are perfect for each other," he mutters not-so-quietly, reaches for a brownie and shoves it in his mouth, and turns and walks away.

"Oh my God, I can't believe I said that," Ava mutters, covering her mouth with her left hand. "I'm so sorry."

Giving her my attention, I can tell she's clearly embarrassed and a little flustered. "Don't be sorry. The look on his face is worth it. And believe me, he's not upset or offended. He's heard way worse from me over the years and has given it back just as good."

"I was rude," she murmurs softly, shaking her head.

Scooping up the final piece of pie, I set it on her plate. "You were sassy. I liked it, Ava," I state, throwing in a wink before returning the server to the empty dish. "What do you say? Shall we go sit and enjoy our dessert?"

Her cheeks are flushed and her eyes a little sparkly as she nibbles on her bottom lip and nods. "Yes."

Ava returns to the seat beside her grandma, and I take the empty one to her left. No one seems to be paying us much attention as she takes her plastic knife and fork and cuts the slice of pie in half. I can't help but smile as she takes her time, doing her best to ensure the dessert is cut equally.

Pointing to her plate, she says, "Pick your half."

Deciding I love seeing her smile, I lower my face, getting close to the two slices. "Well, the one on the left appears to have a little more peach filling, while the right half has more of the sugary, flaky crust. Hmmm," I contemplate, studying both pieces until I hear her chuckle.

When I look up, my heart does this weird flip in my chest, which makes it almost impossible to draw in a full breath of air. She's so fucking beautiful it almost hurts to look at her. "I didn't realize choosing a slice of pie was such a hard decision."

"The hardest," I insist.

"Well, in my classroom, I'd be telling you, you get what you get, and you don't throw a fit," she teases.

I bark out a laugh, drawing the attention of a few at the table, but I refuse to acknowledge them. My eyes are locked on the beauty beside me. "Are you telling me I'm acting like a fifth grader?" I ask, unable to hide my own grin.

"Well, technically no," she says, holding up the plate so I can take my pie. "Students actually hear that particular line in kindergarten, so..."

Another fit of laughter from me has all eyes on us once more. "All right, so I'm the equivalent of a kindergartener. Got it," I retort, winking as I stab the closest piece and set it on my plate.

She sighs. "That's the one I wanted," she mutters.

"Well, then I guess you should have picked before me."

We eat our dessert, casually talking and engaging with those around the table. It's comfortable and easy, like most of my family gatherings. Only this time, there's the added bonus of having Ava here too.

"Where are you working at, Gavin?" Ava's grandma, Betty, asks.

"Well, I just wrapped up a kitchen remodel for the Gustafsons over on Parkway. I'm taking the next week off, since I'll have Annabelle for part of holiday break. We're going to Minneapolis for a few days to an indoor waterpark."

"Oh, that sounds like fun," Betty replies before she starts talking to my sister about work.

"Annabelle mentioned the trip in class. She's looking forward to it," Ava tells me between bites of her pie.

"I always try to pick somewhere within driving distance to go for a few days over winter break. I know her mom takes her on a big trip during the summer, so this is an opportunity for us to go together and she doesn't have to miss school. Plus, it's easier for me to take the time off from work between Christmas and New Year's. My employee, Max, is appreciative of the time off too and spends it with his own kids."

She nods, pushing her plate away and setting a hand on her stomach. "That was amazing, but I'm stuffed."

After finishing off my own final bite of dessert, I ask, "What did you think?"

"Of the pie?"

"Yes."

"It was delicious. Best peach pie I've ever had."

"See? I was right," I quip, leaning toward her so no one can overhear our conversation.

"You were right."

"Which means you should go out with me."

That seems to catch her off guard. Her beautiful brown eyes widen and the light dusting of freckles on her cheeks only seem to grow brighter as she blushes. "I, uh...I can't."

"Can't?" I ask, and even though I fully expected this answer, it still stings a bit.

"Yes, I have a rule."

"A rule? Do tell," I encourage, getting even closer.

"I don't date parents of my students."

I give her a nod in understanding. "Makes sense, but I think you should reconsider."

Her mouth ticks as she tries not to smile. "Oh, you do, do you?"

"I do, and I'll prove it to you."

Her eyes flash with something that looks like excitement. "Tonight?"

"No, not tonight, but soon. Gradually, over time. I'll wear you down." Leaning even closer so I catch the hitch in her breath and the scent of her perfume. "I'm relentless like that," I add, throwing in a wink.

She clears her throat and glances to her right, probably checking to see if anyone is paying us any attention. "I may not change my mind."

Giving her a wide, panty-melting grin, I inform her, "Rules were made to be broken, Miss Rutledge."

I'm not afraid of a little cat and mouse chase, and something tells me this woman will be one-hundred-percent worth it when caught.

CHAPTER
five

Ava

I reach for my mug of hot cocoa and stretch my legs out on the couch. Usually, I'd spend my Friday nights reading, but I opted to watch the newest real-life crime drama on my streaming service. I don't usually do anything scary or suspenseful on account of I live alone and I'm a bit of a chicken, but I remember hearing about this particular case a couple years ago on the news, and it gripped my heart. Two children went missing, and the parents were responsible. The parents have since had their day in court and were both found guilty, leaving a small community in Tennessee reeling from what happened to these young children at the hands of their parents.

My gray-and-white tabby cat, Tabitha, is snuggled on the blanket at my feet, sleeping. She's the most temperamental cat, usually preferring to hide beneath my bed or spread out behind the couch near my heat register, so when she chooses to make her appearance known by lying with me, I'm not going to balk.

I've always been a cat person. I have nothing against other types of pets, but when I was a little girl, my dad and I rescued a stray that showed up at the farm, and I've been a cat lover ever since.

Socks, named after his white feet on an otherwise black-and-gray body, was my best friend and went everywhere with me. Of course, after Socks arrived, a couple more followed, ensuring our farm always had a litter or two of kittens running around. The barn was always full of feline activity.

Tabitha was one of the barn cats I rescued about three years back. Her mother took off almost immediately after birth, leaving a small litter of two in need of tons of care. Between my dad and I, we bottle fed those babies every day, but sadly, only one survived. I felt a kinship to that surviving kitten, having lost my own mother just two short years before.

Tabitha has been with me ever since.

I carefully reach down and run my hand across her soft back, showering her with pets and attention, while keeping my legs and feet completely still so she doesn't get mad and move. She cracks open one eye and looks my way, annoyance flinting across her face. She adjusts herself, giving me her back, which is both not surprising and annoying. I mean, it's not like I wasn't the one who mothered her to life after her own mom abandoned her, but whatever.

The wind has picked up in the last hour or so, rattling my windows on the north side of the house, which just so happens to be where my couch is positioned. Snow is falling outside, adding to the already covered roadways and yards. I shoveled my front and back steps earlier, but now that it's coming down again and will be for the better part of the night, I'll have a big mess to clean up in the morning.

Just as the documentary begins to reconstruct the tragic scene that resulted in the death of the kids, I hear a loud groan outside, like wood creaking and bending. It reminds me of the scene in *Titanic* when the ship was flexing and getting ready to snap in half.

Holding my breath, I turn toward the window. The shade is still up because I enjoy watching the snow fall, and that gives me the perfect line of sight to see my front porch cave in. The rumble of the material breaking and falling has me letting out a scream. The force of the roof caving in causes my wall to shake and my window to break.

The cat is long gone, probably hiding under my bed at this point. My heart is pounding so loud, I can no longer hear the wind howl outside, but I can now feel it, thanks to the big cracks in my front window that look as if the weight of the roof pressing against it and the gale force winds might do it in completely.

I scramble from the couch and go in search of my cell phone. My hands are shaking as I reach for the device. It takes two attempts at putting in my passcode, adding to my frustration, but finally, I get the digits in properly and tap the first number in my call favorites. It's not too late, so hopefully Dad isn't already in bed, sleeping.

"Hello?"

"Dad, I think my front porch roof caved in," I tell him, as I blink hard to keep the tears at bay. "My window is broken, and I...I don't know what to do."

"I'm on my way, Ava Grace. Give me a little extra time to get there," he says. I can hear him rustling around the house.

My heart drops into my stomach. "The roads," I start, glancing out the kitchen window and watching the snow fall.

"I'll be fine, honey. The truck has four-wheel drive, and I've heard the plow is already out to try to stay ahead of it."

I nod. "All right, but please be careful," I say, sniffling. I'm not sure where this wave of emotions has come from, but it hits me like a ton of bricks.

"Always. Be there shortly, Ava Grace. Stay away from that broken window." His voice is gentle and kind, just like always.

"Will do. Love you," I whisper. The moment he replies, I hang up, cradling my phone to my chest.

I can't believe this is happening. I've spent so much time over the last couple of years making small, affordable updates to my house and property. The front porch, while appearing dated with its lean-to style, slanted roof, seemed sturdy. Apparently, the weight of snow and the constant freezing and thawing of ice has taken its toll on the structure, causing it to collapse.

Redoing the front entrance to my home is on my to-do list. My plan was to rebuild the porch, adding a peak in the middle and extending it out to cover more of the front of the house. Now, those incredibly costly repairs are going to need to be examined sooner, rather than later. I'll have to replace the window for sure, and maybe more. I've been saving since my last home renovation project in the kitchen, but if this issue requires a new roof, I definitely won't have enough for that.

Don't get ahead of yourself, Ava.

I take a deep, calming breath and let it out slowly. There's no reason to worry about things I don't know yet, nor can control.

Slipping out of the kitchen, I head for my bedroom to put on a few layers of warmer clothes and check on Tabitha. I grab the first pair of thick flannel pants I can find and pair them with a random mismatched fleece sweatshirt. When I've added a little more warmth, I drop to my knees and peer under my bed. Balled up against the wall is my cat, glaring at me as if I somehow caused the roof to fall and my window to break on purpose, my cat sighs before closing her eyes and ignoring me completely.

So judgy.

Retrieving a thick pair of wool socks, I take them to my living room and slip them on my feet before heading to the mudroom off the back of the house to put on my snow boots, stocking hat, and winter coat. When I'm finally bundled up, I go through the back door and enter my attached garage, since I'm certain the front entrance is going to be completely blocked by the caved-in porch.

I grab the shovel positioned by the door and prepare to make my way to the front of the house. The snow continues to fall as I head outside, my face getting pelted with wet snowflakes and cold wind, but I push through the discomfort, determined to shovel a path to the front.

Halfway up my driveway, a full-size truck rumbles around the corner and slowly pulls in. Relieved Dad made it to me safely, I give up on my quest to shovel snow and walk his way. He's just exiting the big Ford when I reach his side.

Dad glances to my front porch and whistles. "That's a doozy, Ava Grace."

I turn to see the damage for myself, my throat suddenly dry and tears starting to burn my eyes. "That's not good." The posts that once held up my porch roof are broken, and the roof itself is hanging from where it was connected to my roof and hanging against the side of the house.

"No, but it could be worse. Let me see if I can get up there and check on the brace structure. It's held up, which is why the porch is like that, but we need to assess the damage."

"Tonight? I don't think you need to be climbing ladders in this weather," I tell him.

He looks up, hands on his hips, as he considers our options. "You're right, but I need to at least see what the damage is. Then we'll board up your window so it doesn't blow in or break more. With the roof blocking it, I don't think it will, but the wind is supposed to keep up all night, and I don't want to risk it. We'll board it from the inside."

I swallow hard, wishing there were another way to fix the damage, but I know there isn't. Not at this point of the evening, with limited visibility and resources and the weather not playing nice. "Yeah, okay. I think I still have some sheets of plywood in the garage," I state.

We go to the garage and retrieve the ladder and plywood. It's not a full sheet, but it'll work for tonight and should cover most of, if not all, the window. I help Dad by holding the ladder as he climbs up to assess the damage. "Good news is there doesn't appear to be damage to the trusses or braces. I think the old poles were rotting and snapped under the weight of the snow."

I sigh, trying to shield my eyes from the wind as I hold the ladder. "Okay. Why don't you get down now before you fall."

He chuckles, carefully climbing down the ladder. The moment his feet are firmly planted on the ground, he shakes the gathered snow from his head and refolds the ladder. "All right, let's get inside so we can help protect the window. You can call the contractor tomorrow for an estimate."

His words finally register, causing me to stop in my tracks. "Contractor?"

He glances back, pausing in the middle of the driveway. "Yeah, contractor."

Images of Gavin filter through my head, like a parade of the town's hottest guy. "Umm, I guess I just assumed I could hire you."

He chuckles again, continuing on his trek to my garage. As soon as we're inside, he informs me, "I can do small cosmetic repairs, but I'd prefer you have a professional look at this one, Ava Grace. Besides, Gavin's good."

I nod, my throat suddenly dry at the thought of having Gavin here...in my house. "You're right. I'll give him a call Monday morning."

"Tomorrow, sunshine." His words are adamant and full of concern. "With a potential roof issue, you don't want to wait."

"But...it's Saturday tomorrow, and he might have his daughter," I counter.

"I understand that, but I'm sure Gavin has contingencies in place where his kid is concerned. *My* concern is my kid," he informs me with a gentle smile. "And *my kid* needs to make sure her roof isn't going to cave in on her."

I sigh, knowing he's right. Plus, it's supposed to keep snowing this weekend, which means the build-up on my roof will continue. The last thing I'd want is more damage and a potential water leak. "Yeah, okay. I'll call in the morning."

"Thank you," he says with a smile. "I'll text you his cell phone number."

"Thanks for coming into town to help me," I say, as he hangs the ladder back up on the hooks.

"Of course, sunshine. You can call me anytime." He gives me a big hug before going for the piece of plywood he pulled from the back wall. I retrieve my hammer and some nails, hating the fact we're about to put holes in my walls or trim, but understanding it's necessary. Wisconsin winters can be brutal at times, and the last thing I want is for the weather outside to come inside.

We manage to get the wood in the house, and after taking off our heavy winter attire and pulling my couch out from in front of the window, I hold the board in place while my dad secures it to my trim. "Since the window will need replacing, I think it'll be easier to also change the trim than to try to reuse it and fill the holes. I'm sure Gavin can do that, but if not, that's an easy project for us."

Dad and I have worked together on most of the upgrades to my house. I did hire my brother-in-law to do the plumbing and heating stuff, but otherwise, Dad and I have tackled the rest. I adore spending time with him, especially working side by side. It reminds me of when I was younger and working on the farm. While my sister did her share of chores, she preferred to be inside with Mom, whereas I made sure I was outside, running alongside my dad.

"That should hold until Gavin can come and take a look," Dad announces once the board is secured in place. "You know you can come spend the night at my house if you'd prefer."

I flash him a smile. "Thanks, but I'm okay here."

He nods before putting on his coat and boots and collecting the hammer and nails. "Offer's always open. You need me, call."

"I will. Thanks, Dad," I say, giving him one more hug.

"All right, I'm gonna head home. I'll lock up the garage when I'm done in there," he announces, walking toward the back door.

"Love you," I say, giving him a kiss on his scruffy cheek, which tickles my lips.

"Love you too, Ava Grace. Let me know what Gavin says."

"I will," I confirm, waving as he exits my house, locking the back door behind him as he goes.

Just as I flip off the kitchen light, I hear a shovel scraping the ground. A quick glance out the kitchen window confirms what I already know. My dad is finishing my shoveling. It doesn't surprise me, since he's spent the last five years going above and beyond for my sister and me. Ever since Mom passed away, he keeps himself incredibly busy. I've always thought it was easier for him that way, as opposed to sitting at home in the big house they used to share, surrounded by the quiet and memories.

I listen as he finishes up his snow removal and returns the shovel to the garage. I peek out the kitchen window and watch as he exits, making sure the door is secured before he leaves. I run over to my phone and type out a quick message, hitting send before he pulls out of the driveway.

Me: Thank you. Love you.

Dad: Not a problem, Ava Grace. Love you too.

Smiling, I take my phone to my bedroom and slip it onto the bedside charger. He's called me by my first and middle name for as long as I can remember, much like he calls my sister Analise Nicole, and with each grandchild born—my sister's twins—he promptly continued the same tradition by calling them Molly Mae, middle named after my mom, and Riley Grace, after me. I sometimes wonder if he'll do the same to my children, if and when that day comes.

I've always loved kids. It's why I became a teacher. Well, that and a passion for school. I was the kid who completed the summer reading list, usually within the first three to four weeks of summer break, as well as submitted any additional "practice" work they sent home. Math problems, small writing assignments about what I was doing during break, and even fun history or science projects. I was a teacher's dream, and maybe that's why I found myself steering toward the same profession I looked up to as a kid.

I can't help but wonder what Annabelle will become when she's older. She reminds me so much of myself, always wanting to learn something new.

Making my way to the bathroom in the hallway, I prep the shower and start to remove the extra layers of clothing I put on to go outside. My mind jumps to tomorrow, when I'll call Gavin. Will he personally come over to check out my porch roof and window, or will he send his right-hand man over? I've met Max a few times around town, but don't know much about him. Is it weird that I prefer Gavin to inspect the damage himself? Not just because he's easy on the eyes, but simply because I do trust him as a professional.

All I can do is think about him, picturing him in my space. Even after I've finished my shower and have gotten myself ready for bed.

I'm still thinking about him.

Something tells me this is going to be a long, sleepless night.

CHAPTER
six

GAVIN

My cell phone rings precisely at eight o'clock on Saturday morning, which is the moment I'm pulling into my ex-wife's driveway to drop off Annabelle. The number isn't familiar, but that doesn't mean anything in my line of work. A big part of my business comes from word of mouth, and my cell number is passed around like candy. I don't mind though. Business is business, and being readily accessible via cell phone is a huge piece of that puzzle.

"Hello?" I answer, putting my truck in park as the Bluetooth picks up the call.

"Hi, is this Gavin Pierson?"

A smile breaks out across my lips instantly, and I'd be a damn liar if I didn't say my cock recognized the voice too, jumping in my pants at the mere sound of her voice.

However, before I can reply, Annabelle does, clearly realizing who's on the other end of the line too. "Miss Rutledge?"

There's a brief hesitation before she says, "Yes, it's me. How are you, Annabelle?"

"I'm good. Dad's dropping me off at my mom's," my daughter informs her teacher.

"Oh, I'm sorry to interrupt."

"It's okay," I quickly add. "Is everything all right?"

"Yes. I mean, well, sort of. I had an issue with my porch last night, and it buckled. I was hoping you'd be available sometime to take a look at it."

"Can I go too, Dad?" Annabelle asks, her eyes wide with excitement as she stares at me through the rearview mirror.

"Not this time, Belle. Your mom is expecting you, and this is a work call," I tell the eleven-year-old in the back seat.

"Ahh," she groans, drawing out the word and clearly not happy to hear it.

"Listen, let me run Annabelle inside and then I'll head out to your place. I'll be there in about ten minutes."

A brief hesitation again, before she replies, "Okay, that'd be great. Thank you so much."

"Of course. See you soon," I state, ready to push the button on the steering wheel to end the call.

"Bye, Miss Rutledge!"

"Goodbye, Miss Annabelle. Have a great day with your mom."

"I will, thank you," my daughter practically sings back.

"All right, I'll be to your place shortly."

"Thanks, again, Mr. Pierson," Ava says through the speaker.

"It's Gavin, remember?"

I can hear the smile in her voice as she replies, "Gavin. Right. See you soon."

I hang up the phone and release my seat belt. "Ready?"

"No, I'd rather go with you to Miss Rutledge's house," she grumbles from her seat behind me.

"Not this time. It's a work call, and besides, your mom is expecting you. You're going cosmic bowling later, right?"

She sighs dramatically and slowly gets out of the truck. "I know, but I like seeing Miss Rutledge."

Me too.

I hold open the door while she climbs out and grabs her bag. "Maybe I can go with you for a little bit, and then Mom can pick me up?" she suggests, and I already know how that would go.

"Not this time, sweetheart. I could be pretty busy, if there's a lot of damage to her roof," I reason. It's not Ava's place to watch my kid while I work.

"But...she has a cat! I could help her watch Tabitha," she states pointedly.

My head cocks to the side as I give her a look of sympathy. "Sorry, squirt, but not this time."

She sighs. "Can't blame a girl for trying."

I follow behind as she walks to the front door of her mom's house and twists the knob. "See you tomorrow?" she asks, stepping over the threshold and turning to face me.

"I'll be here at noon," I tell her.

This time of year can be especially wonky. Our custody schedule is shared, and even though we've tried just about every different option for splitting time, we settled on a seven-day schedule for rotation. Every Saturday morning at eight, the parent who just had Annabelle has to drop her off at the other's house. It's difficult to go an entire week without seeing my kid, but in the end, it was just the easiest way to do it. It's way less moving and added stress of the back-and-forth as some of the other schedule options we've tried.

The biggest issue is the holidays.

Technically, since tomorrow is New Year's Day and *my* holiday, I should get her tonight and all day tomorrow. But I try not to be a jerk where my ex-wife is concerned. She's taking Annabelle cosmic bowling tonight with friends and a fun New Year's Eve celebration, and I want her to enjoy her evening without worrying about me. At the end of the day, making sure we're both supportive for Annabelle is what's best for her, so I suggested to Julia she keep her overnight to take advantage of as much fun with her friends as possible. I'm picking her up for lunch and taking her to our favorite pizza joint, which just so happens to be open on New Year's Day.

Sure, I could raise a stink about the event Julia wanted to take Annabelle to cutting into the time I'm supposed to have her, but why? I've seen too many exes fight and bicker, hating on the other so much it just creates stress and uneasiness for the kid or kids involved.

It's not worth it.

I'll never put Annabelle through that.

Despite my feelings toward her mother, I will always put my daughter's well-being first.

That doesn't mean I haven't had to stand my ground a time or two with Julia. You give an inch, she'll take a mile, bat her overly made-up eyelashes, and not give two shits about my feelings on the matter. It's happened plenty, especially in the early days of our split, but once we figured out a custody schedule that worked for everyone, things got a little easier.

"Love you, Dad," Annabelle says, dropping her bag and throwing her arms around me.

I'm so grateful she's not too cool yet to hug. "Love you too, Belle. See you tomorrow."

"'Kay."

"Have fun bowling tonight. Make sure Mom sends me pictures," I add, hoping I'll get at least one at some point during the night. When Annabelle asks for them to be sent to me, Julia does, but it's not something she does out of the goodness of her heart. Not like I do. I want my ex to see our daughter's experiences, even through photos.

"I will," she replies before turning to hang up her coat and take off her boots. "Tell Miss Rutledge I said hello."

"Will do. Bye, kid," I state with a wave before turning and heading back to my truck.

As much as I hate leaving my daughter, duty calls, and the thought of spending some time with the gorgeous Ava goes a long way to ease the ache of missing my kid. Pulling out of Julia's driveway,

I turn my focus on the roadway. The heavier snow has been removed, leaving just remnants of melting slush in its wake. I'm sure the city has been up and working since the snow stopped falling in the early morning hours.

Driving toward Ava's, I spot several driveways already cleaned off. In our small town, you have three options for snow removal. Do it yourself, pay a high schooler who's always looking for cash, or hire Marcus. He isn't just the mechanic and tow truck driver, he plows too. The man is busier than anyone I know, and despite being a little rough around the edges, he's a pretty good dude.

I follow the road to Strawberry Hill, recalling how I found Ava on the side of the road just over a week ago. She looked positively gorgeous in the dress, her hair hanging down in big curls that begged for my fingers. Dropping her off at her doorstep was the easiest, yet hardest, decision I've made in quite some time. Not because the physical act of leaving was hard, but simply because I didn't want to go. I wanted to hang out with her, get to know her better, and maybe steal a kiss or two before I left.

Turns out, this crush is a living, breathing entity that thrives on the sight of her. When she's not around, I don't wonder what she's doing. However, after seeing her somewhere, my brain can't stop thinking about her.

It's like high school again, but worse.

The only positive is the fact I'm not afraid to go after what I want now.

And that just so happens to be more time with Miss Ava Rutledge.

Making a left, I pull onto her road and park in her driveway. The porch is definitely in rough shape. I hadn't even noticed it last Friday when I was here, didn't recognize any warps or sags to the wood. At first glance I'm going to assume either her posts rotted or the braces. I'm really hoping it's the former in this case. If there's brace or truss damage, then a part of the roof may need to come off too.

Just as I climb out of my truck and slip my hammer into the hoop on my jeans, I spot Ava walking through the side door on the front of the garage. She's bundled up beneath a heavy winter coat and a stocking cap, her hands covered in thick gloves. "I was hoping to see you again soon, but not for this reason."

She flashes me a small, pained smile. "Yeah, this wasn't how I planned to spend my New Year's Eve."

I walk toward the front porch, taking a look at the structure. "What happened?" I ask unnecessarily. Really, I can figure it out by looking at the damage, but I love the sound of her voice, so the longer I keep her talking, the better.

Ava goes through what happened, including having her dad come over and help board up the window. I've known Jude Rutledge most of my life. I've done work at his house, as well as his farm a time or two over the years. He's incredibly handy, but there are some things he just won't do himself. Roofing is one of them, as is drywall and flooring. I've been hired to do all three in the last five years, including the roof of his large barn at the farm.

"Well, let's take a look, shall we?" I walk up her stairs and scan the posts that once held her porch roof. "If you want to go inside, I can meet you around back when I'm done."

"I'm all right," she quickly replies, stepping to the side to stay out of the way as I carefully check her fallen porch.

It doesn't take me long to assess the damage from the ground and what I can see from the porch, so when that's complete, I grab my six-foot ladder from my truck. I spend the next several minutes checking the braces, trusses, and the overhang. I climb down and can move the hanging roof enough to see behind it. The storm door might have some damage, but it doesn't appear too bad, and the window will definitely need to be replaced.

"All right," I say, folding up my ladder and carrying it over to my truck. I prop it against the bed, grab my notepad from the cab, and return my attention to Ava. "It's not terrible but does need some attention, sooner rather than later. Can I check the window integrity from the inside?"

"Of course," she replies instantly and turns to head toward the garage.

I follow behind, noting the older blue siding, which is probably the original stuff when they built the house in the eighties. This entire subdivision went up over a fifteen-year span before I was born, but I've learned enough about this town over the last decade to know some history, especially when it comes to dwellings. The old farmhouse at the end of the road was built in the early nineteen hundreds, and when the former owners sold the land in the seventies, a young developer scooped it all up and started erecting houses, fourteen in all.

"Come on in," she says, stepping through the door of the garage. It's a nice two-car unit, with storage shelves along the back wall. She keeps it well organized, but that doesn't surprise me. Ava appears to be the type who appreciates everything in order and in its rightful place.

We walk through the door leading to the mudroom. "You don't have to take off your boots," she says, slipping hers off and placing them on a mat to dry.

No way am I walking through her house with wet boots, so I set my notebook down on the dryer and begin unlacing.

"That's not necessary," she says.

"It is," I insist. The moment my boots are off and not leaving puddles of water on her floor, I grab my notebook and say, "Let's take a look."

We walk through a neat eat-in kitchen to the living room, where a piece of plywood is nailed to the trim. The room is much darker, thanks to the blocked natural light. "I'm going to take this down," I tell her, pulling my hammer out of my jeans.

She nods, while I get to work removing the material used to keep the window from caving in.

When it's down, I'm able to assess the damage. "Well, bad news is you definitely need a new window, but from what I can see, it doesn't appear to have damaged the frame. I can order you a new window," I say, pulling out the tape measure always attached to my hip and taking the measurements I need.

"How much do you think that'll cost?"

My phone vibrates in my pocket, but I ignore it while I grab my notepad and pen and start making rough estimates. "Well, I'll figure on the high end for the window. On Monday, I'll be able to get the real cost for you. Labor and materials may fluctuate a little, but only if we get in there and there's damage beneath the shingles or something."

I hear her sigh and glance up from my notepad. "Sorry, I just wasn't anticipating this expense right now. I just got my car back yesterday from Marcus, and now this. I guess they say when it rains, it pours. Or in this case, it snows," she replies with an awkward chuckle.

"The most cost-effective option would be to replace the posts and rebuild the lean-to porch, but I'll be honest, it's not your best option."

"No, I want to do it right. I was planning to replace that porch when I redid the roof. My inspection when I bought this house said the shingles should be good for another six to seven years, and I was hoping to get another year or two out of them."

"I understand that, and you do have the option to just build the roof. I can send you some drawings to show you what I'm talking about. We could always do the porch now and then the rest of the roof later, but if we do that, you definitely want to pick a roofing color that's common. I'd hate to do the porch and then not be able to get matching shingles or metal to match it."

She takes a seat on the couch, holding my gaze. "What do you recommend? Shingles or steel?"

My phone buzzes a second time in my pocket, but I ignore it again. "That's a tough call. Shingles are cheaper up front, but the metal roof lasts so much longer and holds up better in our weather. I can price both for you and we can go from there."

"All right, thank you," she says, giving me a shy smile that makes my heart speed up.

"Can I text you on the number you called me from?" I ask.

"Yes, that's my cell."

Is that a blush on her cheeks?

"I'll run some numbers and give you a rough estimate later today, just so you know what we're talking about. On Monday, I'll be able to give you a more accurate bid, and I'll break it down for you, so you have the option to do it in two phases if you want."

She nods. "I definitely want to do the better roof. I hated that stupid lean-to one, but I wasn't going to replace it until I was ready."

"I get it," I say as my phone vibrates for a third time. "Will you excuse me? I want to make sure that's not Annabelle."

"Of course," she replies as I pull my phone from my pocket.

A message pops up on my screen, but it's not from my daughter.

Hallie: Hey, Gavin! A bunch of us are getting together tonight for NYE at Gabe and Blair's. Kid-friendly. Food and drinks (both alcoholic and non— whichever you prefer). Any time after seven. Hope you can make it!

I slip my phone back into my pocket without replying.

"Everything okay?"

"Yep," I tell her. "Just an invitation to a gathering tonight."

She nods, that pink blush returning to her cheeks. "Nice."

"Big plans for you tonight?" I ask, mostly because I want to draw out my time with her.

"Oh, I was invited to a gathering, but I'm still undecided. They're not really my thing."

"No, but sometimes, just hanging out with friends is the best medicine."

She chuckles. "That's true, and the way Hallie and Logan bicker, there's always some laughter involved. I'm sure I'll go for a little bit."

I smile widely as she gives me the confirmation I was hoping for. Ava was invited to the same gathering I was, which means I will most definitely be attending now.

Replacing the plywood over the window, I slip my hammer into the loop and hold her gaze. "Expect a text from me this afternoon. The window and the roof are okay as they are, but I wouldn't wait too long to get it fixed. At least have the broken part of the roof taken down so it doesn't put more strain on the braces it's hanging from."

"How is your schedule?"

"For you?" I ask, a grin spreading across my mouth. "Wide open, Miss Rutledge."

She huffs and shakes her head. "I doubt that, but I appreciate it."

"I have a few jobs lined up, but they're not pressing, so if you want me here Monday morning to take it down, I'm yours."

In more ways than one.

"Okay. Let's do that, and then I'll make a decision on what we're going to do about the porch and the roof."

"Sounds good." I make sure I have my things before walking to the mudroom where I left my boots. It takes me a few minutes to get them laced back up, but when I do, I give her my undivided attention. "Enjoy your New Year's Eve tonight, Ava."

"Thanks. You too."

Flashing her a big smile, I can't help but say, "I'm sure I will. My night is suddenly looking up."

Exiting her house, I go out the way I came. The moment I'm in the driver's seat of my truck, I pull up the text from Hallie and fire off a reply.

Me: I'll be there.

CHAPTER
seven

Ava

Hallie: Wear a dress. We're all getting dressed up.

I blink rapidly at the text, hoping it will change. Of course, it doesn't, which leaves me with one big decision to make. I can show up in something casual and comfortable, as I had originally planned, or I can dig in my closet—way to the very back—and find a dress, as requested.

I don't dress up. My work attire might consist of slacks and blouses, but I pick for comfort more than style. Now, my friends are asking me to step out of my comfort zone—*again*—and wear a dress. Off the top of my head, I have the red dress I wore to my cousin's wedding in Florida and the black dress I bought for Blair and Gabe's wedding. Since that was just over a week ago, I may have to go with the red one.

Sighing, I pull my options from the closet and take a hard look at the red dress. It's definitely a summer sundress style, but maybe I could pair it with one of my black sweaters. Then, a memory hits me. I return to my closet and find that black, sparkly sweater I bought a few years back but have never worn. I should have returned it, but I felt guilty, since I bought it at the women's boutique in town. It wasn't her fault I purchased the item and then realized it wasn't really to my taste after I got home.

It has more sequins than I remember, but it's a gorgeous piece. Wearing it over the dress might be the perfect look I was going for. Plus, the sweater is warm, so I don't have to worry about freezing to death in a summer dress on the last day of the year. Knowing I only have two options for shoes, I grab the calf-height black boots and pray it all works together. Though, I suppose if it doesn't, it's my friends' fault for insisting we dress up for a New Year's Eve party that starts in two hours.

Besides, I have no one to dress up for but myself.

My opinion's the only one that matters.

I spend the next hour getting ready. Really, I take short breaks to read between hair, makeup, and wardrobe. That's the real reason it takes me an hour. Otherwise, I'd be done in twenty minutes. Though, I did add a bit more dramatic makeup than I usually wear, as well as curled my hair. I still pulled it all back in a clip to keep it out of my face, but it appears more delicate and elegant than my normal no-fuss ponytail.

Finally, it's time to head over to Gabe and Blair's house. Once my place is locked up, I get in my vehicle and back out of the driveway. I'm super grateful to Marcus and happy to have my small SUV back, but my savings account took a small hit in the process.

Speaking of hits to the bank, my mind goes to the quotes Gavin sent to me earlier. They're not exact, but at least a rough estimate of what it would cost to fix my messed-up roof. As soon as I received the texts, I sent them to Dad for his advice. He suggested I go ahead and do it all at once to ensure the new peak of the porch matched and flowed with the rest of the roof, and while I agree, I cringe when I think about writing that check to cover the expenses.

The biggest decision I have left is shingles verses metal. Personally, I prefer the shingle look better. There's just something about the metal that makes it all look shiny and out of place, and I definitely don't like some of the random colors Gavin sent pictures of. Light blue, green, and even a red color is offered, and I hate every one of them. The only color that truly interested me was the charcoal gray. In fact, I like it for both the metal and the shingled roof. Plus, the darker gray color will look great with the deep blue siding color I dream about purchasing one day.

There are several cars already here when I pull in, which is crazy because I'm always early. Yet, I find TD's truck, Logan's truck, and a few others already here. As soon as I park, I pull out my phone and make sure the text message said seven. Upon confirmation, I slip my phone back into my purse and climb from my vehicle.

Carefully, I make my way up to the front porch of the house Gabe purchased several years ago. It took him a few years, but he slowly remodeled the entire home in his free time—if you can even call it free time when you're a physician.

Before I even take the first step up, the door flies open, and Blair is there. "I'm so glad you came!" she bellows, opening the storm door and waiting for me to step inside.

"Thank you for the invitation," I reply, shrugging out of my winter coat and handing it to Blair, who hangs it in the closet. "You are glowing," I add as I take in her long-sleeved, navy-blue wrap dress that hits just above her knees. It's classic and stunning on the petite brunette, and she's paired it with tan ankle boots.

"Oh my gosh, red is your color," she declares, pulling me in for a quick hug.

I feel my cheeks heat up as I glance down. "Thank you. I admit, I don't have a lot of dresses, so I had to be creative."

She waves off my comment. "You look like a million bucks. This sweater is so great. The boutique?" she asks. When I nod, she adds, "I knew it! They have some amazing pieces in there. Come on, let's get you something to drink." As we step into the gorgeous kitchen, she says, "We have some non-alcoholic drinks, as well as red and white wine and beer."

"There she is," Hallie proclaims, getting up from her stool and walking over to greet us. "Oh my gosh, this sweater is fire."

I look down once more, grateful the red dress beneath it is covering the cleavage the sweater would have shown without the extra layer. "Thank you."

"Come on, Hallie and I made tons of snack food this afternoon," Blair informs me, leading me toward the kitchen island where a massive spread of food waits.

"I told you I would have been more than happy to bring something," I insist.

"Please, there was no reason. I knew we'd have plenty of food," Blair replies.

"These pregnancy cravings are wild, and I can't stop eating. That's why I volunteered to do food," Hallie says with a laugh.

"Ava!"

I turn to find Ellie entering the kitchen from the hallway. She's wearing a bright blue fitted sweater with a sleek pair of black pants and looks absolutely stunning. "Wow, that outfit is gorgeous."

TD walks by. "I know," he practically growls, winking at his wife as he goes.

Ellie blushes a deep shade of red. "He's incorrigible," she mutters, shaking her head.

"He just knows what a smoke show wife he's got," Hallie states, never one to shy away from speaking her mind.

"Damn right he does!" TD hollers from the fridge as he retrieves a beer.

"What would you like to drink, Ava?" Blair asks, waving her hand to the counter by the fridge like Vanna White.

I'm not much of a drinker, but a glass of white wine does sound good right now. Plus, it's early enough in the evening I'll have plenty of time to flush my system with water before I drive home. "White wine, please, but a small glass."

"Coming right up," Blair says, grabbing a wineglass and filling it halfway. "If you don't like that kind, there's a few more bottles we received as wedding gifts in the cabinet."

I take a small sip. "This is great, thank you."

I wave a quick hello to a few other guests I recognize and take a seat at the counter beside Hallie. "How are you feeling?"

"Not too bad," she says, dipping a chunk of Hawaiian bread into spinach dip. "Twenty-four weeks already. On one hand, it's flying by, but on the other, it feels like I've been pregnant for years with no end in sight. I can literally feel my ass getting bigger every day, and by the time I actually make it to the delivery, I'll be as big as a house. Logan will probably run for the hills soon."

I scoff at her in shock. "What? That man is completely in love with you. No amount of weight could ever make him stop looking at you like you hung the moon and the stars."

She rolls her eyes. "That's because I've got some epic level of horny going on. He just loves the sex he gets twice a day."

My mouth drops open as I lean in. "Seriously?"

Hallie nods. "Totally. We've had more sex on his desk at work in the last month than I could count. Like, daily. These hormones are wild. He puts up with my crazy because he gets it so often."

Logan appears out of nowhere and kisses her neck. "I love every bit of your crazy, Cupcake."

"You just love my vagina."

He snorts a laugh. "I do enjoy that part, yes, but I love you. Your vagina's just a spectacular bonus."

"Jesus, what did I just walk in on?" Gabe grumbles, his hand stopping halfway to the chips as he slowly retreats. "I'm going to go give myself amnesia now." Then he spins around and practically runs away in disgust.

Hallie laughs. "I love grossing out my brother."

Logan kisses the tip of her nose, and I look away quickly. The moment feels intimate and private, despite being in the middle of the kitchen, surrounded by friends. "I think he enjoys returning the favor."

She makes a gagging noise. "Please don't talk about my brother and...that."

"Can I talk about it? Because your brother does this thing with his ton—"

"No, no, no, no, no!" Hallie bellows, sticking her fingers in her ears to try to keep from hearing intimate details about her best friend and her older brother. "What the hell is wrong with you?"

Blair giggles. "Nothing. It's quite nice."

My entire face feels like it's on fire as all eyes turn to me. "So, what's been going on with you lately? Seeing anyone?" Hallie asks, a not-so-subtle glint in her eyes that has the hairs on the back of my neck standing up.

"Uhhh, no," I reply hesitantly, just as a knock sounds on the front door.

"I'll get it!" Blair hollers, bolting for the front entrance.

"No one special. Huh. We'll have to find you a partner."

I glance at Ellie, who looks a little embarrassed. "Partner? For what?"

"Euchre," Ellie replies.

"But I don't—"

"Gavin's here!" Hallie bellows, throwing her arms up in celebration.

And that's when it hits me.

I'm being set up.

Everyone welcomes Gavin to the party, and even though I try to look away, my eyes completely betray me. They drink in his dark jeans and black Henley shirt that hugs every muscle he has like he's a glass of water on a hot summer day. His jaw is scruffy, and when he laughs at something Gabe says, his entire face lights up in a way that makes my heartbeat quicken.

My word, this man is simply gorgeous.

Then, his gaze swings toward me, and the grin he once had spreads into a full-watt smile. Not only does my heart feel like it's going to burst from my chest, but it's hard to draw a simple breath into my lungs. Like a moth to a flame, I'm drawn to him in a way I've never experienced before. There's this wild attraction I've never felt. It grabs hold, refusing to let go, and the more I fight it, the tighter the pull.

I clear my throat and look away, trying to get my bearings. I'm certain everyone here just watched me practically drool over one of my student's dad. My gaze returns to Hallie, who's wearing a smug smile on her face, clearly having orchestrated this little setup behind my back.

Looking to Ellie, I whisper, "I smell a rat."

She holds up her hands in surrender. "I had nothing to do with this."

My narrowed eyes return to the guilty party sitting at the island. She flashes me a wide grin, one that speaks of her guilt and the fact she doesn't care. "I don't even know how to play Euchre."

Hallie waves off my comment. "It's, like, the easiest game to learn."

"What?" Ellie bellows with a laugh. "It's so hard!"

"That's what she said!" Blair quips as she rejoins our group.

"Don't think I don't see what you're all doing," I mutter, wishing the floor would open up and swallow me. No way are my friends using a New Year's Eve gathering to set me up.

"We're not doing anything," Hallie insists. "We're not actually playing Euchre, so no partners, but if you just so happen to fall in love with Gavin anyway, then remember who had a hand in bringing you two together."

I groan and shake my head. "You three are terrible."

"Hey, this was all their idea," Ellie states, reaching for the chips and dip.

"Traitor," Hallie grumbles.

"Listen, we're not trying to make you uncomfortable or anything," Blair insists, reaching out and taking my hand. "We just noticed Gavin might have a little crush on you, and since, well, all three us of have found our happily ever after, we just want the same for you. We've not said anything to Gavin or would never push you to do something you don't really want, so if you're not interested in him, we completely understand and will back off immediately."

I open my mouth to say just that, to confirm I'm not interested in him, but nothing comes out. The words just seem to die on my tongue, which might actually be worse than developing a little crush on one of my student's father. The fact I can't even deny it sends me reeling.

When no one says anything, I finally mutter a weak, "Rules."

Hallie rolls her eyes. "Rules are meant to be broken."

"Says the woman who got drunk and slept with the guy she couldn't stand," Blair mutters softly.

"Yes! See? I broke that rule—*twice!* And got myself knocked up! But that rule was definitely meant to be broken, because the sex was..." She whistles low and fans her face.

My face flushes once again as I glance around the room and realize the guys all went into the living room. "What are we playing?" I ask, seeing them sitting around a poker table set up in the middle of the room.

"Thirty-one," Blair replies.

"I love that game. My grandparents taught me and my sister how to play when we were younger," I say.

"Come on. We can all join in. Grab three dollars," Hallie says, reaching into her purse and retrieving the money. She slides off the barstool and lets her belly lead the way. She's so stinking cute, as is Blair. Both have those cute little pregnancy bellies going on, where all you want to do is reach out and touch it. I don't, of course, because that's rude. A lot of women actually don't want you pawing their stomachs, at least without asking permission.

I pull the requested money out of my purse and set it on a chair out of the way.

"Start over! We want to play," Blair tells Gabe as we enter the large space. The fireplace is roaring, making the entire room cozy and adding a soft flickering glow of light.

There are two tables set up, so everyone spreads out and starts finding a seat at one of the two tables. Marcus arrives and agrees to play, making twelve of us. I'm introduced to Naomi, Max's girlfriend. She's from Hudson, a neighboring city, and works at the post office. I know Max, who was a couple years younger than us in school. In fact, I believe he was in Gavin's class.

By the time we get done chatting, I turn and find only one seat left.

Right next to Gavin.

Of course, Hallie just gives me a sweet smile, as if she didn't somehow orchestrate that while I had my back turned.

The moment I take my seat, I'm assaulted with the rich, woodsy scent of his cologne. It tickles my nose and makes my thighs clench just a little tighter. It takes every ounce of self-control I possess not to lean his way and inhale deeply.

Gabe goes over the rules, and everyone agrees to start with three dollars. The loser with the lowest score at each table, of each round, puts a dollar in the middle. The person who wins the final game wins the money.

"Hello, Miss Rutledge," he murmurs softly, the timbre of his voice causing my nipples to pebble.

"Hi," I squeak out, my voice suddenly sounding more like a Muppet than my own.

"You look incredible," he adds, his gaze taking a leisurely stroll down my sweater and dress.

"Oh, uh, thank you," I mumble, wishing I weren't so dang awkward when I'm nervous.

And let's be real. Ever since I started to *notice* Gavin Pierson, I've been nervous, especially when he looks at me the way he is now.

His hazel eyes are full of appreciation and interest, and I can't help but wonder why. What could a handsome man like him see in a nerdy, introverted schoolteacher like me?

I'm only comfortable around kids.

"Ready to win some money?" he asks, his eyes sparkling.

I take a deep breath, not sure how I'm going to survive sitting beside this sexy man all night and not reacting. "I'm ready."

I'm just not sure what exactly I'm ready for.

GAVIN

Jesus, she's so fucking beautiful.

The red dress, black sweater that would give a nice view of cleavage if she weren't wearing something beneath it, and boots. My God, those fucking boots. I'm going to dream about them for the rest of my life. They're nothing fancy, just black leather with little heels, but the way they hug her calves and go with her red dress that hits at her knees and I'm suddenly weak in mine.

"Do you know how to play?" she asks as the first round of cards are dealt.

"I do. I used to play when I was younger with my grandparents," I tell her, collecting my three cards.

"Me too! Maybe it was that generation's game. I think they used to play in a church group," she says, taking a peek at her cards carefully so no one can see.

"I believe you're right," I reply, taking a card off the stack when it's my turn. Ava's to my left, so she'll have the opportunity to take the one I discard or retrieve the top card from the stack. I pull a seven of clubs, and since my original cards contain two clubs, I go ahead and keep it in my hand and discard the offsuit.

"Thank you," she says, scooping up the ten of diamonds and slipping it in her hand. She discards a two of hearts.

"I see you're going for diamonds," I tease quietly, keeping my voice down so the rest of the table doesn't hear.

She flashes me a knowing grin, holding her cards to her chest. "I will neither confirm nor deny."

Playing cards with this group is fun, especially sitting beside Ava. I learn in a short amount of time she's competitive and is most definitely a rule-follower, which doesn't exactly bode well for me with her whole dating a student's dad rule.

But watching her smile and relax with each round of cards we play is what keeps me wanting to try. I was attracted to her before, but now, watching her play cards and relax, I'm all in on my quest to steal a date or two from the lovely Miss Ava Rutledge.

Marcus is declared the winner of the money at our table, and Logan on the other. Before we start another game and change things up, everyone decides to refill drinks and plates of food and use the bathroom. I'm one of the last to use the bathroom and grab a little more food, and as I pile a few chicken wings onto my plate, Ava walks in.

"Thanks again for sending me those quotes," she says, her shy gaze bouncing between me and the food.

"You're welcome. Hopefully I'll have more concrete numbers for you by ten or eleven Monday."

"It's no rush. I'll be home all day," she insists, taking a small scoop of dill pickle dip and placing it on a plate before adding a couple of crackers.

Deciding to jump without a parachute, I say, "Listen, Ava I was wondering—"

"Let's go, you two! We're ready to start the next game!" Blair hollers from the living room where everyone is waiting.

My invitation dies a quick death.

I flash her a smile. "We better get going."

Ava nods and grabs a bottle of water before turning toward the other room with her plate in her other hand. As much as I'd love to have another beer, I opt for a bottle of water myself, knowing I'll be driving home at some point. Plus, I get to spend time with Annabelle tomorrow, which is my main reason not to tie one on tonight to ring in the new year.

When I join the party in the living room, I'm not really surprised to find the final remaining chair next to Ava once more. Something tells me Hallie and Blair have something up their sleeve. I've caught them whispering and have watched Ava blush a thousand shades of red right after they'd all look my way.

Not that I'm opposed to having a little help where Ava's concerned, I just don't want them to push her so hard it has the opposite effect. I want her to *want* to spend more time with me, not be forced into it. That's exactly why I'm being persistent without being overbearing and demanding. It's a fine line, but I refuse to make her feel uncomfortable.

I'm attracted to her, and I think she feels the same toward me.

I just have to take my time and slowly chisel away at that protective wall she's constructed around herself. It feels like tonight I might have chipped away a few small pieces. She's relaxed, laughing, and enjoying herself, and I'd like to think she's comfortable around me. I've caught glimpses of the real Ava, the one she only lets herself be around family and close friends, and I like this side as much as I enjoy her serious, professional one.

We play two more rounds of cards, and I admit, I don't recall when I've laughed this hard. Everyone gets along great, and even though I'm not really part of their group of friends, they've welcomed me and made me feel as if I've always been here. I've always enjoyed visiting with Gabe, TD, Logan, Marcus, and the others, and I know that friendship will continue. They're good people.

"Everyone get a drink. The ball drops in five minutes," Blair says.

Gabe walks over and places his hands on her swollen stomach, a look of awe in his eyes. Both Gabe and Logan have done that throughout the evening, and who can blame them? When Julia was pregnant with Annabelle, I remember always wanting to touch her. Feeling my child move and kick was the one thing that could make the stresses of a long, hard day just fade away.

I head into the kitchen to grab a bottle of water and find Hallie pouring glasses of champagne. "Everyone has to take a sip at midnight to toast the new year," she insists, while pouring two glasses of sparkling grape juice for herself and Blair.

"Champagne is gross," TD says.

"Don't care. Sip it or the New Year's Eve gods will bestow upon you a shitty year. It's the rules," she insists, passing him a little plastic flute of bubbly.

He sighs, takes the glass, and heads into the living room with Ellie at his side.

"You too, Gavin," she states, passing me my own drink.

"Thank you," I reply, even though I'm not really a fan of champagne. I'd much rather have beer or something with a real kick like Tito's and Sprite. But I also don't want the New Year's Eve gods to bestow upon me a shitty year...whatever that means, so I take the offered champagne and return to the living room.

I hang back in the corner, watching as the couples pair up and wait for the countdown to begin. Marcus and James, the fire chief, chat off to the side, not paying any attention to the television or the toast that's about to happen. My eyes glance to the right, and that's when I spot Ava. She's standing back away from everyone else, alone. My feet are moving in her direction before I can even give it a second thought.

"Not feeling the countdown?" I ask when I reach her side.

She shrugs. "It seems a little silly."

"Agreed," I reply, leaning against the wall casually. "I mean, one drink at midnight could determine your entire outcome for the year?"

"Silly," she confirms. "Or a kiss. Why must you kiss someone at the stroke of midnight to ensure good luck in your relationship or to break the cycle of loneliness? I mean, it's a kiss."

My ears perk up and I find myself saying, "Well, I don't know about that. If the kiss could help, it seems like it would be worth a shot."

"Ten...nine...eight..."

I take a step toward her, hearing her sharp inhale of breath at my nearness. If I sense any uneasiness from her, I'll back off instantly. Instead, something flashes in her eyes. Something that looks a lot like excitement.

"Seven...six...five..."

"What do you say, Miss Rutledge? Ring in the new year with some good luck?" I ask.

"Four...three..."

Her eyes widen as the countdown is complete.

"Two...one...Happy New Year!"

Her tongue slips out and wets her lips just as she gives the slightest nod, but as much as I want to kiss this woman, I don't want it to be for this reason, surrounded by friends who may or may not be playing matchmaker.

Leaning in, I catch the subtle scent of her perfume as I press my lips to her cheek, letting them linger a few extra seconds longer than I should. "Happy New Year, Ava."

Her eyes are closed and her mouth slightly puckered. It takes every ounce of control I can muster to not say fuck it and kiss the hell out of her, but again, the first time I truly kiss her isn't going to be here, surrounded by friends.

I feel her shiver as her eyes slowly open. There's a hint of sadness and shock mixed in the depths of those brown eyes, and I can't help but feel happy. Not to see the dejection, but simply because it's confirmation she wanted me to kiss her.

And I will.

"Happy New Year, Gavin," she whispers, clearing her throat and straightening her spine.

Refusing to step back, I hold her gaze as I say, "I just made a New Year's wish. Do you want to hear it?"

She seems a little taken aback by my question, but eventually nods. "I'm going to kiss you, Ava Rutledge. For real. Without everyone else watching us or because it's expected at the stroke of midnight. I'm going to kiss you when the time is right for both of us, when you're ready. But know it's coming, beautiful, and when I kiss you, it'll be just the beginning."

"Toast!"

Ava startles as Hallie hollers for everyone's attention.

I slowly turn, still holding my drink and preparing to face friends. Of course, as expected, several are wearing a knowing smirk, but I'm going to assume they think I kissed her. And I did—just not in the way they're hoping.

Soon, though.

Our time will come.

"All right, I guess I was roped in to the toast," Gabe announces. "Everyone, raise your glass. To the new year. To family and friends," he starts, giving us all a smile. "To expanding families," he says, glancing down to his new wife, whose left hand is resting on her baby belly. "And to falling in love," he adds, making my heart rate kick up a few extra beats. Not because I'm in love, but because I find myself open to the idea for the first time since my divorce. Maybe it's this crazy schoolboy crush I find myself having once more over the woman standing beside me, or maybe it's the fact I'm surrounded by couples who have found their love over the last couple of years. Whatever it is, I won't ignore the hope bubbling in my chest.

Maybe this *is* my year.

"To good health and lots of laughter. May you all find what you're looking for this year, whatever that may be."

"Cheers!" everyone hollers, holding up those plastic glasses and tapping those around us.

Since it's just me and Ava, I tap her glass with my own and say, "To finding happiness."

Her brown eyes hold my gaze, and everyone else in the room fades away. "Happiness," she murmurs before lightly tapping my glass and taking a drink.

The moment is shattered when Blair, Hallie, and Ellie all appear in our little bubble to tap glasses with Ava, and I take a step back, letting them have their time. But my mind is still on our shared moment, on the kiss that didn't happen and the fact we both wanted it to. I'm an incredibly patient man, and if I have to take this slow and steady to prove to her we're worth taking the risk—worth breaking every one of her damn rules—then that's what I'll do.

I told her I was relentless, and it's time to prove it.

I knock on the door and wait for Annabelle. It's a bit warmer today, the sun shining high in the first day of the new year sky. My mind replays everything from last night, as it's done over and over again since I got home. I've thought of nothing but Ava, and the fact I get to work at her house tomorrow morning has me all sorts of excited. I'll start by removing the old porch roof and reinspecting the braces and roof. I'll get the window ordered and the rest of the pricing she needs for her quote, and then hopefully completing the job. A part of me is keeping my fingers crossed she'll hire me to redo the entire roof so I get more time with her, but I'm not holding my breath. I know it's a costly project, and when you're not expecting those costs, it can be hard to pull the trigger.

When no one comes to the door, I knock a second time. It takes a few long seconds but finally the door opens. "Hey, sorry," Julia says, clearly having just got out of the shower. She's wearing a robe, her hair wet and dripping on the floor. "Come in."

I step inside, holding my hands at my sides, and move out of the way.

"We overslept this morning, so she's getting ready now," Julia announces.

Before I can offer to wait in my truck, a man wearing lounge pants walks out of the bedroom I know is my ex-wife's. "Hey, babe. The remote's out of batteries," he grumbles, slapping the remote control against the palm of his hand.

I stare at the man standing in front of me, his eyes narrowed into little slits. "I thought you were getting rid of whoever was at the door?" he mutters, watching me closely.

"This is my ex-husband, Gavin," Julia replies, clearly feeling about as awkward and uncomfortable as the rest of us.

Taking a step toward him, I extend my hand. "Gavin Pierson."

"Mike Gagnon," he states, squeezing my hand firmly. Almost too hard, actually. Like he's trying to prove something or demonstrate his strength.

"Nice to meet you. I wasn't aware Julia was dating anyone," I say, standing my ground.

He shrugs, as if it's none of my business. And in a way, it isn't, but in the other way, it's very much my business. We share a child, and we've always been very firm on talking amongst ourselves when it comes to dating and Annabelle.

"It's new," she replies.

"Not too new," Mike says casually, thumping the remote in his palm again.

I turn my attention to my ex-wife. "Can I have a word?"

She nods, glancing over to Mike. "Give me a minute."

He glances between Julia and me before saying, "Don't forget the batteries," and returning to the bedroom.

The moment he's gone, my gaze zeroes in on my ex-wife. "I thought we had an agreement." Julia rolls her eyes and walks away, heading off toward the kitchen. I follow, determined to get this conversation out of the way before Annabelle emerges from her bedroom. "Julia."

She huffs and pours herself a cup of coffee. "It's not serious."

"Then why are you bringing him around our daughter?" I ask quietly so we're not overheard.

"It's fine. Annabelle knows Mikey, his son."

"How?"

I can tell she's getting annoyed, but I don't care. If someone is going to be around my daughter, clearly sleeping under the same roof as her, in her mom's bed, I have a right to ask questions. I'm one-thousand-percent certain Julia would be doing the exact same thing, if the shoe were on the other foot.

Crossing her arms over her chest, she lifts her chin. "Karate."

I slowly nod, thinking back to the last time I took her to her weekly Tuesday karate class in Hudson, but not remembering Mike. "And you two..."

Julia huffs dramatically. "Listen, we're not getting into the details. We're seeing each other. Mike is a travel agent in Hudson. He's divorced and has one son. Mikey is two years older than Annabelle. Happy?"

Slowly letting out a long exhale, I say, "I don't care that you date, Julia, but do appreciate a heads-up if someone is going to be around our daughter like this."

Her eyes narrow. "You don't trust me? I didn't say a damn word when you dated what's her name with the buck teeth and mousy hair," she counters, instantly going on the defensive.

I hold up my hands. "Actually, you did have plenty to say, but that's beside the point."

"Fine, you want a heads-up? I'm seeing Mike. There."

Sighing, I realize this conversation isn't going anywhere good. She's not understanding my concern, and the fact it has everything to do with our daughter and ensuring she's safe and comes first. "Fine," I reply, turning toward the doorway and hoping Annabelle hurries up so we can get out of here. "And for the record, I never had Samantha around Annabelle. The only reason you knew I was seeing someone was because you guys showed up at the pizza place." Otherwise, she wouldn't have seen us together because I didn't feel it was serious enough to warrant introducing her to our daughter.

"No one will replace me."

I exhale and close my eyes. "You're right, and no one is trying to."

This is how conversations go with Julia. She finds offense in everything I say, always kicking back instead of just listening. It was hard talking to her when we were married and hasn't gotten much better since.

"Ready, Dad," Annabelle hollers as she joins me by the front door.

"Great. Let's go eat. I'm starved," I say, holding up her coat to help her slip it on.

She doesn't have a bag with her, since we're just spending a few hours together and not the entire day, but I do notice she has a book. It's one of the new ones I gave her for Christmas, and by the looks of it, she's already halfway through.

"Bye, Mom. Love you. Be back soon."

"Love you too, Belle," Julia says, bending down and kissing our daughter's head before we step outside.

The moment we get into my truck, she turns to me and says, "I bet you're wondering about Mike."

The right side of my mouth curls up. "A little."

She rolls her eyes in true eleven-year-old preteen fashion. "Let's go have pizza and I'll tell you what I know."

Smiling, I back out of the driveway, praying this closeness I share with my daughter never changes. She can tell me anything, good or bad, and it'll never change the way I feel about her.

"Breadsticks?" I ask, heading toward downtown.

"Duh!"

Laughing, I let the awkward encounter with Julia and Mike go and turn my focus on Annabelle. "Let's do it."

CHAPTER
nine

Ava

I park on the main street through downtown Pine Village and climb from my vehicle. My stomach has been growling, and despite having plenty of food in my fridge to eat, I opted to start the new year off with some comfort food. My plan is to grab a small pizza and salad—you know, to offset the calories from the pizza—and dive into this cute rom-com movie I found on my streaming service. This time of year, there are plenty to choose from, most of which all have the same plotline. Small town, opposites attract, Christmasy, snowed-in vibe.

But I don't care.

I'm here for it.

Most of the businesses in our small downtown are closed today, since it's the first day of the new year, but everyone knows Movie Queue Pizzeria is open all day. They're a huge hit for the early twentysomethings who might have drunk a little too much the night before, ringing in the new year.

Speaking of the night before, I'm still flustered about that kiss. Or almost kiss. Whatever you want to call it. Even the peck on the cheek left me reeling, and worse, made me crave more. I thought of nothing else, replaying every interaction we shared yesterday to the point I was obsessing about it well past the point I should have been sleeping. Then, when I finally did drift off, guess who was starring in my dreams?

Yes, him.

He looked so good last night in his jeans and form-hugging Henley. I've never cared about muscles, but seeing the outline of Gavin's through his shirt had my mind picturing moments where he was removing said shirt so I could get an up close and personal view. It was another reason my dreams were filled with images of him and me together.

And yes, the shirt removal fantasy was the tip of the iceberg.

I woke up wet, aroused, and desperate for relief.

I had to take care of it myself before I could even get out of bed.

Now, I'm taking advantage of the somewhat decent winter day and getting out of my house for a bit to grab lunch. Of course, lunch will also be dinner, since the pizza for two is big enough to cover multiple meals for me.

I hurry into the pizzeria and stomp my boots on their welcome mat to clean off the snow. The scent of Italian sausage and tangy tomatoes fills the air, and my stomach growls. There are many tables filled in the dining room, but my plan is to order my food to-go and take it home. The reason I don't just call in my order ahead of time is because I love this place.

Movie Queue Pizzeria is filled with movie memorabilia. Movie posters and still shots, ticket stubs and props. The walls are covered in it, and I swear, every time I look around, I find new stuff I haven't seen before.

"Good afternoon, Miss Rutledge," Lanita says. The bubbly, hardworking teenager is a former student of mine, having been in my classroom about seven years ago. She's a senior in high school this year and plans to attend cosmetology school after graduation.

"Hello, Lanita. Happy New Year."

"Happy New Year to you too," she replies with a pleasant smile. "Dining in?"

The door opens behind me, but I don't turn around. "No, thank you. I'd like to place an order to go."

"Miss Rutledge!"

I spin around at the familiar voice and grin when I see Annabelle standing there. Of course, she's with her father, who looks gorgeous in a pair of well-worn blue jeans and a beat-up brown leather coat. His hazel eyes are locked on me, and he's wearing a soft, familiar smile on his lips. "Happy New Year, Annabelle," I say when I've finally stopped ogling her dad and find my voice.

"Happy New Year. Are you having pizza too?"

"I was just getting ready to place an order."

Her brown eyes light up. "Will you join us? I got this new book for Christmas, and we can talk about it!" she begs, taking a step forward and holding up her book.

"Oh, I don't know—" I start but am cut off.

"Please, Miss Rutledge?"

I open my mouth to decline her invitation when Gavin moves closer. "We'd love it if you'd join us for lunch."

I want to pass, especially with a restaurant full of patrons who would love nothing more than to tell someone else about me dining with Gavin and Annabelle, but there's something in his eyes that stops the words on my lips. It's a mixture of hope and anticipation, and frankly, I don't want to say no.

"All right," I say, watching as shock registers on his face. It's as if he didn't expect me to actually accept the invitation.

Personally, I wasn't expecting it either.

Annabelle reaches for my hand and guides me toward the dining room. Glancing over at Lanita, I offer a quick, "I guess I'll be dining in today."

She gives me a big smile and grabs menus. "Great. Take whatever's open," she instructs, following behind us as we enter the main dining area.

Annabelle picks the only available booth and slides into one side. "Will you sit with me, Miss Rutledge?"

"I will." That's a much better idea than sharing a booth bench with her father. The rumors would fly faster than the time Mayor Abbott's car "broke down" in front of Shelly Mathers's house the night his wife was away at some book club retreat.

We all slip off our coats and set them aside as Lanita brings the menus and silverware. "What can I get you to drink?"

"Iced tea," Annabelle requests.

Gavin waves to me, indicating I should order next, so I reply, "I'll have the same."

"Make it three, please."

Lanita nods. "Coming right up."

"Dad, we better get extra breadsticks," Annabelle says, passing out napkins from the holder.

"You're probably right," he replies, offering me a wink.

"Breadsticks are my favorite. Do you like them?" she asks, placing her book in front of her.

"I do, but I don't usually get them."

She seems horrified by this revelation. "What? Why?"

I shrug. "When you get older, you'll understand. I usually try to get a salad instead of breadsticks."

Annabelle huffs. "My mom says the same thing, but I'm never trading breadsticks for salad. Breadsticks are life. My butt's just going to have to be big."

I can't help but giggle as Gavin narrows his eyes. "You don't have to worry about watching what you eat for a while."

"I know, but I'm never giving up breadsticks," she replies, opening up her book. "Have you read this one, Miss Rutledge?"

"I have not. Is it good?"

She nods eagerly and starts to tell me all about what she's reading. Listening to her retell the story with excitement makes me smile. I know she was a big reader before my class, but I like to think I've help nurture that passion for reading over the last few months with constant encouragement.

We pause long enough to order a large sausage and pepperoni pizza, with a family salad and breadsticks, and the moment our server walks away to place our order with the kitchen, Annabelle dives right back into her story. I can feel Gavin's eyes on me, but I don't look his way. I'm afraid if I do, I won't be able to return my attention to his daughter, which is the reason I'm sitting here anyway.

Sure, Jan, said in my best Marcia Brady voice.

I refuse to think about the *other* reason I'm here. Yes, a big part of it is simply because I enjoy Annabelle and talking books with her, but there's another reason, and he's sitting directly across from me, and I will not dissect that particular thought at this moment. Especially when his eyes make my stomach flutter and my breathing catch in my throat.

Breadsticks and salad are delivered, and we all dive in. I even decide to have a breadstick with marinara sauce at Annabelle's insistence, and yes, she's correct. They are life.

"Oh! Did you hear about the northern lights?" she asks, her eager eyes wide with anticipation.

"I haven't heard about them," I reply between bites.

"They're called aurora borealis, and it's predicted we'll be able to see them this Friday night," she informs me, dipping her breadstick in sauce and taking a big bite. "I asked Mom to take me to see them."

"They're supposed to be visible any time after ten o'clock Friday through early morning on Saturday," Gavin adds. "They were talking about it on the news earlier today."

"Yes! And Mom says we can go to the Bluff Preserves to see them," Annabelle adds.

"That sounds amazing," I reply. "Maybe we should do a classroom activity around them," I add, my mind already spinning.

"That would be so fun. We can do an art project too, drawing and coloring the sky."

"I like the way you think," I inform the eleven-year-old beside me. "I'll do some checking and see what kind of information I can find on it. We'll dedicate Thursday and Friday to learning all about the northern lights."

Our pizza is delivered, and even though I'm already a little full on bread and salad, I take a small slice of the cheesy goodness.

"Are you going to watch them?" Annabelle asks.

I give her a shrug. "I'll have to see if I can stay awake long enough," I answer with a chuckle.

"You sound like my dad," she replies. "He goes to bed early too."

"I get up early for work," Gavin defends.

She rolls her eyes. "Not on the weeks I'm living with you."

He shakes his head and smiles, clearly enjoying letting her monopolize the conversation. "I still get up early. I just don't leave until you're off to school."

Considering his statement, she replies, "I guess that's accurate."

He snorts and finishes off his first slice of pizza.

"If you go to watch them, you should go to the Bluff Preserves too. I'm going to tell all my friends to come out and see them with me."

"I don't think my students want to hang out with me on a Friday night," I quip.

Annabelle shrugs. "I like spending time with you. You talk books with me."

I lean over and gently bump her shoulder with my own. "Us book lovers have to stick together."

Something crosses her face as she smiles up at me. "Yes, we do."

I don't have time to consider what she was thinking about because one of my students from last year comes up to our table. "Hi, Miss Rutledge."

"Good afternoon, Vic. Did you have a good Christmas?"

He nods, his eyes dancing with excitement. "I got a new game system for my room."

"That sounds like a great gift," I reply, making sure I give my former student my complete attention.

Vic glances over his shoulder and says, "We're getting ready to leave now. I just wanted to say hi."

"I'm glad you stopped by. Enjoy the last of your winter break."

"Thanks, Miss R. Bye!" he hollers, taking off to join his parents and younger sisters. Both of the young girls wave as they pass, and I give them friendly smiles and return their waves. I'll have the middle daughter, Evelyn, next year in fifth grade.

"Kids love you."

I look over and find Gavin's smiling eyes watching me. My cheeks start to heat up at the compliment, and I do my best to shrug it off. "They make it easy. We have great kids in our school system."

"Except Damian. He's a nut," Annabelle chimes in, still enjoying her lunch.

I want to argue, but she's not wrong. Damian doesn't come from the best home life and often acts out in class. He's getting better about it, especially since he knows it won't be tolerated, but he definitely pushes the boundaries in class. I don't have to send him to the office nearly as much as I used to, which is a huge plus, but it does happen on occasion.

We finish up our meal, and I pull out my wallet to pay.

"I've got it," Gavin insists, grabbing the check as it's deposited on our table.

"I can pay half," I reply, pulling out some cash.

He looks up with a penetrating gaze that makes my heart skip a beat. "I said I've got it. Thank you for joining us, Miss Rutledge."

Trying to ignore the purr of my professional name on his lips, I divert my eyes and dig a few smaller bills from my wallet. "At least allow me to pay the tip."

He seems like he wants to argue, but eventually nods. "Fine."

I set ten dollars down on the table, tipping well over twenty percent, but that doesn't matter to me. Lanita is a senior in high school this year and will be looking forward to college in the fall. A few extra bucks won't completely cover those expenses, but every little bit helps.

As I stand to put on my coat, I feel his hands as he helps. Gavin holds up my coat while I slip my arms into the sleeves, and even though it's warm in the restaurant, I know that's not the reason I'm feeling a bit flush. Having him close, smelling his clean scent, does something to me. It instantly makes me think about the feel of his lips against my cheek, which only causes my blush to burn even darker. I've always hated that particular trait of being a redhead, and it still holds true today. I blush way too easily and often. There's no hiding my emotions.

Annabelle slips her hand inside mine as we walk through the restaurant. Some of the tables have cleared out, but there are several still occupied. We wave or say hello to everyone we pass, and there's no missing the questions they have in their eyes. They're all curious as to our relationship status, especially with Annabelle's hand tucked inside mine.

The rumors will start soon, if they haven't already.

I notice Gavin staying a few feet behind us, as if sensing my uneasiness and worry. I know I shouldn't care about everyone else and what they think, but I can't help it. I've always been that person, the one who wants everyone to like them and never tries to cause a problem. That's why the whole incident from several years back is always fresh in my mind.

It's a reminder.

It's why I have rules.

"Have you seen this one, Miss Rutledge?"

I turn to Annabelle, who's pointing at a movie poster for the original *Ghostbusters* movie from 1984. "I have. It's one of my favorites," I tell her.

"I want to watch it. I've seen *Ghostbusters: Afterlife* and can't wait for the next one to come out on DVD."

"I've not seen that one yet either." When she seems shocked, I add, "I'll have to add it to my to-be-watched list."

"Yes, definitely. Paul Rudd is in it, and my mom says he's the hottest man on Earth."

I glance at Gavin, who shakes his head.

I mean, she's not wrong.

"Maybe some time we can watch it together. I have it on DVD," Annabelle states, her eyes full of hope.

"Come on, Belle. Let's leave Miss Rutledge to her day. We've monopolized enough of her time," Gavin says, a welcome reprieve. It's not I wouldn't enjoy watching the movie or hanging out with her, but I just don't do that with students.

Ever.

"All right," she grumbles. "See you on Wednesday?"

I nod. "I'll be there," I reply, referring to the first day back to school following break.

"I'm sure I'll have this book finished by then, so I'll tell you about it in class."

I can't help but smile. "Sounds good. I look forward to hearing about it." Lifting my gaze, I meet Gavin's. "Thank you for lunch. You didn't have to pay for my half."

"I didn't mind," he says, his lips looking completely kissable. "See you in the morning?"

"Yes."

"Can I come?" Annabelle asks eagerly, making her dad grunt.

"No, Annabelle. I have to work, and you're at your mom's for the week."

"Fine, but if you ever need help watching Tabitha, I'm your girl, Miss Rutledge," she insists.

"I'll keep that in mind," I say, fighting the smile threatening to spread across my lips. "Enjoy the rest of your day, and Happy New Year."

"Happy New Year!" Annabelle hollers as she starts to head for her dad's truck.

Gavin steps back, slowly retreating, but his eyes remain on me. The smile he offers practically brings me to my knees. It's potent, sexy, and promises things I have no business picturing.

"See you tomorrow, Ava."

I wave, the words seeming to freeze on my tongue, and make a beeline for my vehicle. How in the world am I going to survive having him in my house while he completes the repairs? The good news is he won't actually be inside for a big portion of it, but still. He'll be near.

And I have to somehow figure out how to get through the day like it's no big deal, even when I find it hard to breathe and think straight around him.

Shouldn't be too difficult.

Sure, Jan. Sure.

CHAPTER Ten

GAVIN

Max and I carefully lower the mangled piece of porch roof to the ground. "I've got it," he says, dragging the metal toward the driveway.

While he carries away the old material, I take a closer look at how the old structure was attached to the house. It definitely wasn't the best option for adding coverage to the front door, but it got the job done. And considering it was probably built shortly after the house, I'm sure it was completed on a budget.

I spend a little time checking things over before climbing down from the ladder. "The good news is everything seems to be in decent shape up there," I say to Max as he approaches.

"Good news for the client."

"Yep," I reply, covering the exposed roofing with some heavy plastic. It'll keep the moisture from seeping down until Ava decides which route we're taking to fix and replace.

We're getting everything buttoned up when my phone rings. I pull the device from my pocket and head for the notebook in my truck cab. I've been waiting for Logan Johnson to put together the numbers I'd need to finish my quote for Ava. "Hello?"

"Hey, Gavin, it's Logan. I got some pricing for you," he says.

"Shoot."

He gives me two prices for double-paned window styles and says he's already emailed me images I can show Ava. He also shares the current cost of shingles and metal for the square footage I'm looking for, which is the final pieces I need to figure her quotes. "Thanks, man. Appreciate it."

"Let me know what you want me to order. Both of those windows are in stock, so I can have it here in forty-eight hours."

"Perfect. I'll be in touch," I inform him, hanging up and grabbing my laptop.

"You need anything else, boss?" Max asks, making sure our equipment is picked up and put away in one of our trucks.

"All good. I'm going to input these numbers and go meet with the client. Tomorrow we'll start at the Henderson place, and then probably be back over here after lunch."

"Sounds good. I'll see you tomorrow," he replies before hopping in his truck and heading back to the shop to unload.

I spend the next few minutes updating the numbers in the quotes I had already drafted and shared with Ava on Saturday. Now, I have more concrete numbers to present so she can make her decision.

When I'm ready, I take my laptop, notepad, and phone and head for her front door. She hasn't been able to use it since the roof fell Friday night, and I'm sure she'll feel much better about having the eyesore gone from the front of her house.

Before I can knock, she opens the door and gives me a smile. "Hi. Hello. Come on in," she rambles, seeming a little flustered.

"Thanks. I heard from Logan and have numbers for you," I tell her, stopping inside the living room to take off my boots.

"You don't have to do that," she insists, but again, I take them off anyway. No way am I walking on her carpet with wet boots.

With my boots off and set aside, I join her in the living room and open my laptop. "I'll send these to your email, but I wanted you to see them now so we can go over them and I can answer any questions you may have. There are several different options. The first is for the window replacement. Logan recommended two different windows, both double-paned for better insulation." I pull out my phone and retrieve the pictures he sent to me. "Here are the two options. The first one is a double hung window, which means both top and bottom pieces slide up and down. The second option is a sliding window, and that one opens from side to side. I didn't have him price them with grids, or grilles as some call them, because none of your other windows have them. I should have asked your preference, but if you're not looking into replacing windows anytime soon, I thought you'd want them to be more uniform."

"I do," she quickly replies, taking my phone and looking over the two options. "I'm not looking to replace windows right now, especially if I have to redo the roof, so I don't want the grids." She looks over at the old window that's boarded up before turning to the one on the south side of the room. "I think the ones I have must be single pane."

"Yes, they are. Single pane is an option, but there are several advantages to a double hung. Cleaning and venting are a huge plus to this window. They're very easy to use."

She looks them both over again before saying, "I think I like the double hung more than the sliding option."

"All right, I'll have Logan get that ordered. He said it'll be in in about forty-eight hours, so if he can get it ordered today, we should have the window sometime Wednesday."

"Wow, that's fast."

"Now, let's talk roof."

We spend the next several minutes going over all the different options. Between deciding on how much of a porch to rebuild and if she wants to redo the entire roof now or wait, plus the cost difference between shingled or metal roof, she has big decisions to make. "If you want to take a day or two to think about it, that's fine. We put a thick piece of plastic over the roof where the old lean-to porch was attached, just to ensure you don't get snow down in there, but it should be okay for a few days. I wouldn't leave the exposed part open too long though. We still have a lot of winter left, and sometimes Mother Nature isn't very nice to us up here," I say with a smile. She's lived here her entire life too. She knows we can get snow all the way through March, often into April.

She sighs. "I talked to my dad yesterday afternoon after we had lunch. Your ballpark numbers aren't too far off from what we discussed. I think it would be best to go ahead and just do it all now. Roof and porch, as you drew up."

"Okay, sounds good. Shingles or metal?" I ask.

Ava sighs and closes her eyes. I enjoy a few seconds and take in her appearance. She's wearing thick leggings and an oversized crewneck sweatshirt. It hangs off one shoulder, but her skin is covered by an undershirt. She has thick, fuzzy socks on her feet, and I can tell she's the type of woman who prefers coziness over style. She's casual and comfortable in her space, with her hair pulled up in a ponytail at the top of her head. Frankly, I prefer this laid-back version of this woman more than the gussied up one. Yes, those dresses were very nice, but this is the Ava I want to get to know.

"I think I want to do the metal roof. As long as you promise it's not going to look bad."

Chuckling, I lean forward and reach for my phone. Our fingers touch as I do, and a shock wave of lust bolts through my veins. I don't need to wonder if she felt it too, because her reaction to the touch says it all. Her beautiful brown eyes widen, her mouth falls open, and she jerks back as if she's been zapped.

It takes the patience of a saint not to reach for her right here and now.

But I don't. I set my phone back down on the coffee table beside my laptop and pretend that touch didn't just send all the blood in my body to one concentrated area south of my belt. "I think you'll like the end results of the charcoal roof you looked at."

She nods. "I believe you. It's just so much money not to like it."

"I totally agree, Ava. You have to be able to live with this purchase for a long time, and just know, if it were me looking to replace my roof—which I will probably have to do in the next five to seven years—I'd be going with the metal one. The longevity and durability of the product is a huge selling point for me."

Exhaling, she sags back in her seat. "Let's do it."

"Okay. I'll get the material ordered. It should be in within a week or so. Logan said that's a pretty popular color, so availability is always good. He's got the material for the new porch in stock, so I'll have that delivered tomorrow, and Max and I will start tomorrow afternoon."

"Wow, okay," she says. "Is it safe to be on a roof in the middle of winter?"

I flash her a smile. "Well, it's not always ideal, but it is what it is. Yours is not the first winter roof I've had to take care of. We just need to take extra precautions if it's slick or wet, and if it's snowing, we won't go up there."

She nods in understanding. "What about payment?"

We go over the details, and even though I had already included in my bid that a portion of the bill is due when the job starts, I make sure to mention it again.

"Not a problem. I'll go to the bank in the morning and transfer the first half. You'll have a check right away. Insurance will work with me for reimbursement after I submit the paperwork."

"Let me know if you need help with that part. Do you have any other questions?" I ask, not really wanting our time together to end.

"No, I don't think so," she says, standing up.

That's my cue to leave.

I head over to put my boots back on, taking my laptop, notepad, and phone with me. Just when I have no other reason to stay, I open my mouth and just start talking. "So, I was thinking,

Friday night is that northern lights thing Annabelle was talking about. Even though it'll be way past our bedtimes, it might be pretty cool to see. Interested in going with me?"

She worries her bottom lip with her teeth. "Like...a date?"

I lift my shoulders. "We can call it whatever you want."

"I don't know. I don't date pare—" she starts, and before I can give her a chance to turn me down, I cut her off and continue.

"Hear me out. There's this really cool scientific event happening on Friday, one you're going to be discussing and teaching in class, and this is an amazing opportunity to see it in person. We wouldn't go to the Bluff Preserves, where I'm sure the rest of the town will go to view it. I know a spot where no one else will be, so no one will see us."

The corner of her mouth ticks. "You know a spot, huh?"

A full-watt smile breaks out across my mouth. "Yep. Completely secluded, and not in a creepy way. You're totally safe with me."

"I don't know, Gavin," she replies softly, and I can tell I'm wearing her down.

"Come on, Miss Rutledge. Live a little."

She narrows her eyes a bit and purses her lips. "I did that once, and it came back to bite me in the butt years later."

I'm certain I know what she's referring to, the infamous keg stand photo that surfaced and almost caused her to lose her job, but I don't want her to always think of the bad. "I promise. There'll be nothing that could cause you problems. This night will be...educational, if you will."

A faint smile crosses her lips as she shakes her head. "I might regret this," she says, almost absently to herself.

"Never. I'd never risk doing something that could cause you to regret spending time with me, and I'd never push you. I just, well, want to get to know you better, and if I have to subject myself to fifth grade science to do so, then so be it," I say with a grin, hoping to earn one in return.

It works because the gentlest smile spreads across her lips. Lips I dream about ravishing until they're swollen and chapped. Then I might do it again.

"I do appreciate the offer, and it would be cool to see it in person. I know I've said this multiple times, but I don't date dads of my students."

Knowing this is such a big step for her, I decide to add a little more humor to the conversation. "Well, I don't usually date my daughter's teachers so we're even."

Unable to fight her chuckle, she asks, "Didn't she have Mr. Parmelee last year?"

"She did, and as much as age is just a number, the whole silver fox thing isn't my jam." Mr. Parmelee is in his fifties and divorced, and I've heard plenty of women talk about how good-looking he is for his age. I don't think he lacks for the company of women.

"Mine either," Ava replies with a blush. She takes a deep breath. "But I think seeing the aurora borealis in person would be phenomenal. If the offer still stands, I'd love to join you...as a friend."

Friends...that's a start.

But it's not my endgame.

I can't stop my wolfish grin. "Of course it stands. There's no one else I'd rather enjoy the view with than you, Miss Rutledge."

Even though she's blushing a dark fuchsia, I don't miss the anticipation on her face. "All right. Where would you like to meet?"

"Here. I'll pick you up," I tell her, grabbing my stuff to leave.

"I don't mind meeting you," she offers.

"And I don't mind picking you up. It'll be easier to get where we're going in my truck."

"Oh boy. I'm not sure I like the sound of that," she grumbles.

Pulling open the door, I step through the storm door and reiterate, "You're safe with me, Ava. Always."

"I know," she whispers, the words barely audible. But I catch them, nonetheless.

"See you tomorrow afternoon," I tell her. "Your new porch, window, and roof will be done before you know it."

"Thank you."

"Of course." I lift my arm and wave, walking to my truck and resisting the urge to look back at her.

I set my stuff on the passenger seat before climbing inside. Only when I have my seat belt fastened and the truck started do I finally glance back at the house. She's standing at the door, watching, and something in my chest cracks. It's a tidal wave mixture of excitement, longing, and desire, all swirling together with enough force to level a skyscraper.

That's what she does to me.

Makes me feel wild and a little reckless.

This is more than just a crush.

I just hope I don't end up devastated in the end.

I pull out of her driveway and head for the shop. Since I don't have Annabelle, I can spend a little extra time getting caught up. There are a few quotes I need to finish and send off, and the business side of things, such as taxes and end of year crap is always waiting. Might not hurt to dive in and get ahead of some of the office bullshit. At least if I'm there, working, I won't be home and thinking about Ava.

Now I can just think about her at my office.

I pull into the alley and park in one of the available spaces. I don't have a storefront for my business. Instead, I rent the small warehouse and connected office space on the back of an old industrial company in town. That business has long-ago closed. The whole front is used by two different shops, while I rent the back for a fair price, since neither business needed it.

At first, I didn't want the added expense of renting a spot, but after only a short time of storing work-related tools and materials at my own house and cluttering up my garage to the point I couldn't use it, it became apparent it was worth my while. Now, I don't have to worry about it. Everything is here, in one central location, and it's secured.

However, as soon as I let in, I realize I don't want to stay. My thoughts return to the beauty I just saw in her oversized sweatshirt and leggings. I want to drive back over there, to hang out. I want to get to know her better.

But I'd be lying if I said I didn't want more too.

I know it won't be easy. She's got rules, and that's why I'm hoping this Friday is the start of me slowly breaking down those walls.

I only have to wait four days to find out.

CHAPTER
eleven

Ava

"You all have my email address in your Chromebook and on the paper in your take-home folder, so if you send me a picture of the aurora borealis this weekend, you get extra credit points," I remind the class as the bell gets ready to ring on Friday afternoon.

Several of the students already have cell phones, and the rest agreed they can use a parents' device to email in a picture or two after tonight's big event. I'm going to print them all off and hang them on the bulletin board at the back of the class. I'm sure they'll get a kick out of seeing their photos displayed proudly.

We've spent the last two days learning all about the aurora borealis, or northern lights. I found a video online from National Geographic, as well as other educational and informational materials. We also completed an art project, thanks to a tutorial I found on YouTube. It was a great few days, and I truly think each student learned something new and is eager to witness the event firsthand.

I'm excited too for a variety of reasons. Yes, to see the lights, but also because of the company I'll keep. I've only talked to Gavin a few times since he asked me to join him on Monday, and each interaction was related to the job he's completing for me. My window arrived yesterday and is being installed today, and the front of my house has already been transformed, thanks to the beautiful new roof he's framed and covered. The metal was in stock and has shipped, and as long as there aren't any transit delays, it's expected to be delivered to Logan's hardware store tomorrow.

Despite the expense, I'm eager to see what the finished project will look like.

"Miss Rutledge, are you going to see the lights?" Annabelle asks as everyone finishes picking up their supplies and straightening their desks.

I open my mouth but hesitate. Do I answer her honestly? What if she asks me where I'm watching it or with who? I don't make a habit of lying to my students, but this definitely feels like something I can't really talk about.

"I believe I'll watch them," I finally answer, hoping she doesn't ask any more questions.

"I'm super excited. My dad says he's going to see them too, but I don't know where. I invited him to come to the Bluff Preserves with me and Mom, but I don't think he wants to. It might be weird, because Mom has a new boyfriend. Mike's nice, but he's way different than Daddy."

The corner of my mouth ticks. "Oh yeah?"

Annabelle nods. "First off, Mike has a hairy back and it's really gross," she informs me, making a face and sticking out her tongue. "My dad just has a hairy chest, not a back."

I have to fight from laughing.

"Plus, he wears fancy clothes for his work and gets manicures. Mom was telling me she goes with him, and he pays. Dad's hands are all rough, and he sometimes gets cuts and splinters."

"Well, there are many different types of jobs, each one just as vital as the next."

She nods in understanding. "Mike wants to take Mom on a trip. He gets good deals through his work, and she wants to go on a cruise. I don't get to go though, but that's okay. I get motion sickness when we go out on the water."

"I get motion sickness too," I tell her, recalling the last time I went out on the lake. Five minutes into the ride, I was throwing up over the side. It was not an experience I'd ever want to repeat.

"I like to go on the pontoon though. That's different because it's bigger and we go slow. You don't feel the waves as much. Do you like pontoon boats?" she asks, her brown eyes so focused and interested.

"I've never been on one," I confess. I'm not a huge fan of large bodies of water, and since taking risks are at the bottom of my to-do list, I've always chosen to keep my feet on dry land. The one time I let a few friends talk me into taking a Jonboat out was the very last time I was on the water.

"We have one at my dad's. Maybe this summer you can come with us. He usually gives me pills so I don't throw up, but even when we forget them, I don't feel icky like I do on the other boats."

The bell rings, cutting off any further conversation. Annabelle darts off to get her coat and book bag, while I move to the door. The students are mostly lined up, ready to get out of school for the weekend. "Make sure coats are zipped up," I remind them, even though I know most of them won't listen.

I have to try.

"Bus riders, you guys keep to the left side of the hallway, and those going to the pickup line, stay to the right," I say, as I do every afternoon.

We all walk out into the hallway and join the students already filing out of the neighboring classrooms. I stand in the middle of the hall and watch as my class moves to the exit. Everyone seems eager to go, not that I blame them. There aren't many kids who actually like going to school as much as I did.

"Have a good weekend, Miss Rutledge," Annabelle says as she nears.

"Thank you, Annabelle. You too. Make sure you take a picture of the sky tonight," I remind.

Her brown eyes light up. "Oh, I will! I've already told my mom I need to use her phone to send you some pictures."

Giving her an easy smile, I reply, "I look forward to receiving them. Have a great weekend."

"You too," she hollers with a wave as she moves through the hallway and out the door. I know her grandma is here to pick her up, as she is every day. The only exception is when Gavin gets her, but I never see that part, since I'm inside.

When everyone has exited the building, I return to my classroom and prepare to leave for the day. A few teachers pop their head in to wish me a happy weekend or to ask about the aurora borealis tonight. It sounds like everyone from the school is excited to see the event and willing to stay up and try to catch the gorgeous lighting.

I'm more anxious to leave today than normal. Even though I'm not considering this evening a date, I'm feeling a little nervous as if it were. Dating is outside my comfort bubble; despite the fact I have done it on occasion. I'm an introvert. I enjoy books. Finding someone who understands that and doesn't try to drag me along to every social event they can is difficult.

That's what caused me problems a few years ago, when the infamous keg stand photo surfaced on social media.

Yet, despite having a bit of anxiety over something like that happening again, I still feel safe with Gavin. And like my friends have reminded me, I can't stress about things out of my control. I couldn't control someone else's actions or words, but I can control how I react to them. I can also control the situations I put myself in as best as possible, which is why I don't go to bars, and if I do, I don't drink. My friends also know not to put any photos of me on social media and respect my wishes.

I grab the papers I have to grade over the weekend and slip them into my satchel bag. When I have what I need, I put on my coat and gloves, lock my room, and make my way out to my vehicle, throwing a wave goodbye to any staff member still lingering.

The early January air is crisp, and while a shiver runs through my veins, I don't let the cold temperatures bother me. Instead, I let it invigorate me and excite me for what's to come.

Of course, I'm sure it's because I'm seeing the northern lights for the first time, and not simply for the man who's taking me to witness the event.

That's my story, and I'm sticking to it.

At precisely nine o'clock, I hear Gavin's truck pull into my driveway. I lock the back door of my house and move through the slight breezeway to the garage, ensuring everything is secured there too. Then, I exit the side door into the night air.

Gavin is climbing from his truck and makes his way toward me. "Can I carry that for you?" he asks once he reaches my side, hand extended.

"All right," I agree, handing over my bag. It's packed with my older digital camera, extra batteries and memory card, and a blanket. "Thank you."

When we reach his truck, he places my bag in the seat behind me and opens the passenger door. "Great minds think alike," he says, pointing to the large, fluffy blanket on the seat.

"It's not terrible out, but it could get chilly the longer we have to wait for the lights," I reason, climbing into the cab.

"Ready?" he asks, holding the door while I get situated and belted in.

"Yes."

He flashes me a grin and says, "You look great, by the way."

Even though I blush at the compliment, I shake my head. "You can't even see me." The fact I'm wearing my thickest winter coat, snow boots, gloves, a scarf, and my warmest beanie makes it a little difficult to see past the layers.

A slow smile spreads across his face. One that makes my breath catch and my thighs clench. "I think you're adorable just like this," he says, tapping me on the nose.

Unable to formulate a response, I offer a small grin and wait while he closes my door. Glancing around the truck, I note the items that seem work-related, but what catches my attention is the beaded flower hanging from the rearview mirror.

Gavin climbs in and catches my line of sight. "I know, it's not very manly, but Annabelle made that for me a few years ago and told me it was for my work truck. She said I needed some color."

"I agree. It's perfect," I reply.

"It is." He clicks his seat belt into place. "So, are you ready?"

To see the lights? To spend time with him? The answer is a surprising yes to both.

"I am."

"Good," he replies, throwing the truck into reverse and slowly backing out of my driveway. "How did the kids like the science lessons this week?"

"They all seemed to enjoy it," I tell him honestly. "I found a lot of great material on it, and I've given them all a chance to grab a few extra credit points if they email me a photo of the lights. I know everyone doesn't have a cell phone, but I figured most would have access to a parents' phone for something like this. But I did send home an information sheet with each student, so parents know what's going on."

"Smart. Annabelle doesn't have a cell phone yet, but I'm sure she can use her mom's," he says, heading farther out of town, away from the Bluff Preserves and city streetlights.

"That's what she said, and it's perfectly acceptable. I want as many kids as possible to take advantage of a few extra credit points. They get to see something beautiful and learn a little too."

He gives me a quick grin before returning his eyes to the road. "Like I've said before, you're an amazing teacher. Annabelle won't want to move on to sixth grade next year."

"Are you kidding? Of course she will. Most of my students are excited about the lockers and switching classes throughout the day. It's a big deal, like coming of age."

Gavin starts to slow down, flipping on his blinker. I realize we're nearing the private lane for Hanson Tree Farm. As he starts to turn left onto the gravel roadway, he says, "She's always loved school, but one of the main reasons she's having such a great year is because of you. You have been able to pinpoint her interests and strengths, while helping her work on the weaknesses. She's growing as a student *and* a person, and a big part of that is you. She's going to be incredibly sad to leave your classroom, Ava." He glances my way for a few seconds before returning his gaze to driving.

"She's a remarkable child," I find myself mumbling, a little overwhelmed with his compliment. Each student is unique and learns differently. They have strengths and weaknesses, and it's my goal—my job—to help them realize both and work through it.

Clearing my throat, I turn my attention to our location. "This is the back side of the tree farm."

He nods, slowly moving around the large barn at the back of the property and parking near the back door. "It is. I worked here when I was in high school for two seasons. I helped cut down trees at Christmastime and loaded them for customers. It was cold, but a pretty neat gig. Old man Hanson is great. I still visit with him every chance I get."

"And I'm assuming he gave you permission to be on his property," I state, looking around at this part of the farm I've never seen.

"Well, I've learned over the years it's easier to ask for forgiveness than permission, Miss Rutledge."

My eyes widen as I gape over at him.

He looks my way and cracks up laughing. "I'm joking. I called Norman earlier in the week, and he agreed to let us come out here." Sobering, he adds, "I'd never risk you like that, okay? Some rules are meant to be broken, but I draw the line at trespassing."

"Oh," I reply, feeling a little silly by my response. "Of course," I add.

Is it hot in here?

Gavin turns off the truck and shifts to face me. "Norman turned over the day-to-day side of the business to his granddaughter, August. She runs the farm, but he still lives here and works in the payment hut. Annabelle and I came out to get our tree last month, and he's still handing out candy canes to the kids, just as he did when I was a kid. Hell, he's done it well before I was born. He's a cool ol' bird.

"Anyway, he's always offered to let me bring Annabelle back here and take her on the trails, so when I called him up to ask about coming out here tonight, he said yes. In fact, he offered to let us use the tractor."

I feel my eyes widen. "A tractor?"

"Yep," he replies, taking his keys out of the ignition. "We could take my truck, but we're going down into the pasture by the creek. You up for it?" There's a hint of challenge in his hazel eyes as he gazes at me from across the truck cab.

A wave of excitement rushes through my veins. I've never been one to take risks, but something warm and caring in his eyes brings me comfort. I know I'm in good hands.

And speaking of his hands...

Pushing all thoughts of what it could possibly feel like with his big, strong hands on me, I decide to keep taking small steps outside my comfort zone. They might be tiny little baby steps, but movement, nonetheless. I'm not saying I'm always going to be a risk-taker, but these little strides with Gavin might be just what I need.

My life is good, content, but being around him makes me want to take chances.

Good or bad, for the first time in my life, I want more.

And that scares the ever-loving hell out of me too.

I'm already here, sitting in his truck and preparing to go see the northern lights, so why not take another risk. Climbing on a tractor in the middle of winter doesn't exactly sound like a good time, but I'll trust him that to take this next step, we need to experience the tractor ride. What could it hurt?

Well, you could fall off and break your leg.

Or worse, your entire body.

Someone needs to put her big girl panties on and give it a whirl.

Looking over, I find Gavin watching me. He's not rushing me or making me feel bad for considering my options. He's patiently waiting for me to decide, and I'm certain he'd be fine with whatever decision I came up with. He seems completely at ease, and frankly, a little gorgeous in his winterwear. Heavy coat, thick flannel shirt, and a Carhartt stocking cap on his head, he's incredibly handsome in a rugged, lumberjack way. He even smells like the outdoors. Woodsy, clean, and fresh. Exactly how I would expect a man like him to smell.

Again, a jolt of anticipation races through me.

Reaching for the door handle, I take a deep breath and give him a big smile.

"All right, let's do it."

CHAPTER Twelve

GAVIN

I hop out of the truck like my ass is on fire and do it with a huge grin on my face.

The first thing I do is meet her around at the passenger door and make sure she gets through the snow with ease. I guide her to the back of the barn and push open the sliding door. It's unlocked, just as Norman said it would be, so as soon as she's inside, I turn to grab the rest of the supplies from the truck.

Slipping both blankets under my arm and her bag over my shoulder, I retrieve the picnic basket I packed and join her in the barn. "What's all of that?" There's a bit of appreciation reflecting back at me in the depths of her brown eyes.

"This is a surprise," I tell her, setting the basket and bag on the fender of the tractor, along with the blankets. "Come on, Ava. Up you go." Extending my hand, I wait anxiously for her to place hers within mine. The moment she does, I swear I feel the spark. Yes, she's wearing gloves, but it's there, alive and bright like the moon shining brilliantly in the midnight sky.

She climbs up on the step. "Where do I sit?" she asks, glancing around.

"Hold up," I inform her, moving around to the other side and hoisting myself up. The moment I have a seat on the only chair, I position my leg so it's sticking out and gently slap the top of my knee.

"Seriously?" Her eyes are big and filled with worry.

"Trust me, Ava."

She holds my gaze once more before turning around and having a seat on my leg. The moment she sits, I reach around her and grab the fuzzy blanket. Opening it up, I place it over her legs to help keep her warm.

"You may have to hold on to the basket. It'll bounce around if we don't. I can try to bungie strap it in place if needed."

"I got it," she insists, sliding the basket and her blanket a little closer so it's positioned better between the seat and the fender.

"Ready?"

"As I'll ever be." There's no missing the hint of nervousness in her voice, but she doesn't say a word as I fire up the old tractor and slowly back out of the barn.

I gently maneuver the machinery, trying not to jolt or scare her, as I head for the clearing not too far from here. The pasture is rough, but not too terrible, and eventually, we make it down to the creek. It's frozen over, but I keep the tractor on the path running along the water. Driving about two hundred yards, I turn away from the water's edge and into the large clearing where we should have a great view of the night sky.

Steering the tractor toward the tree line, I park it out of the way, yet close enough we don't have to hike too far to get to our destination. When the engine is shut off, I ask, "This okay?"

Ava looks around, the entire area dimly lit by the stars and the moon in the sky. "It's beautiful."

"Come on," I say, helping her stand so I can dismount the tractor. Once I get two feet on the ground, I extend my hands and hold her waist while she climbs down.

When we're laden with the blankets, bags, and picnic basket, we set off toward the spot I had in mind when I asked Norman if I could come back here. The trees are to the south, and we have a perfect unobstructed view of the north sky. We stop at the huge bolder in the middle of the clearing. No one knows how it got here, but it's large and flat and can easily fit two people comfortably.

If you consider sitting on a rock as comfortable.

I wipe off what little snow is there and spread out the large, fluffy blanket. "Have a seat."

She does, wrapping her blanket around her shoulders. "We should have a spectacular view," she states, looking up.

"Should." I hope, anyway. She likely knows more about the aurora borealis than I do, since she has been discussing it in class. The extent of my knowledge is the tips I found on the internet Tuesday night.

I open the picnic basket, which admittedly, I had to borrow from my mom, and retrieve the thermos of hot cocoa. I fill two of the insulated tumblers I had in my cabinet with the warm liquid and pass the first one her way.

"Is this cocoa?"

"It is," I confirm, replacing the thermos in the basket and pulling out the container of snacks. "I also have cheese sticks wrapped in meat, as well as a fruit and nut mix."

"Yum. I wasn't expecting snacks with the show."

I give her a wink and a slow grin. "This is a full-service non-date date."

"Non-date date, huh?"

I shrug and hold out the container of meat and cheese. "We can call it whatever you want, Ava. You said it wasn't a date, but it feels a little like one, so we'll go with a non-date date." I pop a cashew in my mouth and give her a big, cheesy grin.

Her beautiful eyes narrow just a bit as she brings the cocoa to her lips. "It feels like a date because you've made it one."

Lifting my shoulders, I reply, "A man has to use every tool in his arsenal to achieve his goals."

She looks at me from beneath her lashes as she asks, "And what are your goals?"

"To get to know you, and maybe, someday, take you on a date date."

Her brown eyes watch me, assessing my seriousness and intent. After what feels like forever, she finally rewards me with a little grin. "You're relentless."

It's not the first time she's called me that, but the fact there's a sparkle in her eyes and she's wearing a smile while she says it lets me know she's not completely put off by my persistence.

"That I am. Now, sit back and relax. We'll enjoy some snacks and cocoa and wait for the show to begin."

Reaching for a piece of cheese wrapped in ham, she takes a bite and leans back in contentment. I take my own piece of salami wrapped in mozzarella and join her on the rock. There's plenty of room for two people, but I don't shy away from sitting nice and close. If she makes a comment, I'll insist it's for warmth. You know, sharing body heat and all.

What I'm not expecting is for her to adjust the blanket and wrap it around me too. Now, we're sharing it, sitting close. My left leg is pressed against her right one and she leans just a bit against my side. On instinct, I slip my arm around her shoulder and hold her, fully aware she may pull back. When she doesn't, I mentally throw my arms up in the air in celebration, because this seems like something monumental.

Plus, it feels pretty fucking amazing to have her with me, against my side. Despite the fact we're both wearing enough layers to keep an Eskimo warm, I can still feel the heat of her body, and I know this was a big step for her. I'm content to just sit here, holding her close, and watching the night sky.

Beautiful woman.

Beautiful surroundings.

Beautiful night.

It doesn't get much better than this.

I can't stop smiling while I watch her take photos.

The sky most definitely has a different hue to it, but it's not the bright pink I was expecting. However, when she showed me the view through her camera, it's every bit as beautiful as I've heard. I even went as far as to take a few pictures with my phone.

Now, I'm using said device to take pictures of Ava. She hasn't caught me yet, her focus on the aurora borealis, but I've managed to snap a handful of images of her smiling up at the majestic sky.

"I can't believe how beautiful it is," she practically sings, smiling widely as she gazes heavenward.

"Stunning."

But my eyes aren't on the sky. They're on her.

She's simply breathtaking.

Her nose and cheeks are red from the cold, but she hasn't once complained. Considering we've been outside for more than an hour, waiting for the time when we can see these amazing lights, she seems completely at ease. We've talked about work, Annabelle, and growing up in Pine Village. We've spent the last hour snacking and keeping warm under the blanket, and yes, have remained very close, perched on our rock.

"You're not even looking at the lights."

I give her a quick grin, realizing she's caught me watching her. "I saw them, and you're more beautiful."

Her cheeks turn a darker shade of pink, and she averts her gaze. I watch as she licks her lips and wonder what she's thinking. "I don't think that's possible, but thank you."

She spends the next twenty or so minutes snapping pictures from different angles and just enjoying the view. I do the same, though we're not exactly looking at the same thing. Yes, I grab a couple of pictures of the pink sky, which I do admit is pretty cool, but for the most part my eyes are on her. That crush I had in high school comes back, if it ever truly left. Maybe it just sat dormant, waiting for the opportunity to reemerge and grow. Well, the moment I saw her in the bar wearing that damn red dress, that crush exploded like a bomb in my chest, and I've lusted after her since.

From a distance.

Until that Friday night of Blair and Gabe's wedding where I found her on the side of the road.

Since then, I realized these feelings aren't going anywhere, and I want to explore them, and while she seems hesitant—for good reason—she's not pushing me away. I'll continue to show her I'm interested, while respecting her boundaries and distance. Stealing time with her, like tonight, is the perfect way to demonstrate my intent and sincerity.

"I'm freezing," she says when she joins me over by the big rock.

"There's a little more cocoa left in the thermos," I tell her, digging into the basket and retrieving the insulated device. "I use this a lot for work. During the winter, I'll keep extra coffee in it, and throughout the hot summer months, we store ice to dump into our individual insulated tumblers."

She takes the remaining cocoa and sips. "You sure you don't want any of this?"

"No, I'm good. You enjoy it."

Ava takes a seat on the rock and retrieves the blanket, carefully covering her legs and waist without spilling. When I slide in beside her, she tosses the blanket over my legs too. Together, we just stare up at the sky. I'm not sure I've ever felt this content, this relaxed in my life.

Ava is so completely different than Julia. Julia was all passion, full of energy, and hated sitting idle. Ava, on the other hand, seems completely satisfied to sit, whether with a book or gazing up at the night sky. It's nice to just...be, sometimes. No running, no expectations, no worries. Just sitting on a rock, watching the beauty of the world around us.

She shivers and leans into me a little more. As much as I like having her pressed against me and could sit like this for hours, I don't want her to catch pneumonia. "Are you ready to go?"

Without looking away from the sky, she replies, "A few more minutes."

So I do my part to help keep her warm and slip my arm around her. She fits like a glove, her perfect body against my own. We sit like this for a while, continuing to enjoy the view, when another idea hits me. I carefully pull my cell phone out of my coat pocket, slip one of my gloves off my hand, and bring up the photo app.

"What do you say, Miss Rutledge? Care to commemorate this night with a picture?"

There's slight hesitation in her response, but she nods. I hold up the camera, the screen pointed at us so we can see, and prepare to snap the picture. Only, you can't see much of the pink sky, since we're facing it. "Let's stand," she suggests.

I wrap the blanket around her shoulders, and we turn so we're facing south. I step behind her and hold the phone out. Angling it up so we get the northern lights behind us, I snap a few shots. Her scent hangs in the air, all sweet and alluring. It tickles my nose and makes me want to bury it in her neck. Or her hair. Or somewhere else I have no business thinking about right now.

When our little selfie photo session is complete, I slip my phone back into my pocket as Ava lets out a yawn. It's late, and even though I'm having one of the best nights of my life just because she's here, I know the time has come to take her home. "Do you have all the pictures you want?" I ask.

She's still standing close, and when she turns to face me, our chests touch. With coats, we can't exactly feel anything, but it's still electrifying. A zing of a current slides through my veins and I reach out. My right hand caresses her cold cheek, and I swear she leans into my touch just a bit. Ava licks her lips once more, and my eyes zero in on them. Lush, plump, and ripe for kissing.

I want to taste her so damn bad.

My thumb traces a gentle line across her lower lip and her eyes flutter closed. Her mouth is slightly open, and the warm puffs of air have stopped. She's holding her breath, waiting.

She's waiting for me to kiss her.

Slowly, as to give her plenty of time to stop me, I lower my head and lightly brush my lips across hers. Again, I allow her the chance to pull back or end the kiss, but when I feel her gloved hands grip my coat, anchoring herself to me, all bets are off. My lips are a little more urgent as I gently deepen the kiss. Her mouth opens, allowing my tongue the opportunity to delve inside, to taste her.

Ava leans closer as I shift my hand to the back of her neck. The angle allows me to deepen the kiss without letting it get carried away. Her grip on my coat is tight, and I feel the gentle sway of her body into mine. I realize right here and now, standing in the middle of an open space, the northern lights beautifully on display above us, this is the perfect kiss.

The first of what I hope will be many.

Even though I don't want to, I slow my lips and slightly pull back. Resting my forehead against hers, we both suck in deep, greedy breaths of oxygen. The cold of night long forgotten, at least for now. The feel of her body pressed against mine, her face touching me, has my blood in my veins hotter than the Fourth of July.

"Wow," she whispers, her breath warming my face.

"Yeah," I reply, clearing my throat and trying to get my bearings. Just one kiss from this woman has completely scrambled my brain.

Her face is flush, and I hope it's from the heat of the moment and not from embarrassment. There'd be nothing worse than her regretting the kiss I thought was outstanding. "We should probably get back," she whispers, gazing up at me under her eyelashes.

"It's late."

She nods and slowly releases her grip on my coat. When she takes a small step back, I let her go, hating the instant wave of longing and coldness washing over me. I want her back in my arms, my lips pressed to hers.

But I'm in no rush.

Where's she's concerned, I have all the time in the world to make sure I get this right.

I pack up the picnic basket and set it up on the tractor fender, while Ava folds the large blanket from the rock. When I have it added to the tractor load, I turn and extend my hand to assist Ava.

"Thank you," she says, her bag and blanket thrown over her arm.

I take them both while she climbs up the steps and gets herself situated. Handing off her items, I climb up and take the seat. Ava sits on my leg, just as she did on our trip out here, and wraps the smaller blanket around her legs. I start the tractor and let it warm up a few moments before putting it in gear.

The return trip to the barn is uneventful, and I'm pulling the tractor inside before I'm ready. Now that I've had my lips pressed to hers, there's a heavy buzz of desire swirling through the air. Plus, I'm enjoying the hell out of getting to know her, and I'm just not ready for our night to end.

As I lock up the barn, she places our belongings into the back seat of my truck, and before I know it, we're heading back to town. I can't help but steal glances her way, because she's wearing a content little smile on her lips as she watches the scenery pass us by. Sadly, I'm pulling into her driveway when I'd much rather take a drive around town—hell, the county—just to draw out our night a little more, but I know I can't.

Our time together has come to an end.

"I'll walk you to your door," I offer, releasing my seat belt and climbing out. I retrieve her bag and blanket from the seat and walk beside her as she makes her way to the front door.

"Thank you," she says after releasing the locks. Brown eyes sparkle up at me. "I had an amazing night."

"I'm glad," I reply, rocking back on my heels.

She turns to step inside the house but pauses just before crossing the threshold. "Gavin?"

"Yes?"

Can she hear how loud my heart is pounding right now?

Without saying a word, she goes up on her tiptoes and presses a light kiss on my lips. Before I have an opportunity to respond, she pulls back and grabs her belongings from my hands. Then, she slips inside and shuts the door, leaving me standing on the porch.

I stand here for a few long moments, lost in the memory of that kiss. A smile spreads across my lips as I return to my truck, feeling lighter and full of hope. Just as I'm ready to climb back into the cab, I spot a silhouette in the window, the one I just installed.

Knowing she's watching, I slip into my truck and throw it in reverse. You couldn't peel my smile off my face with a putty knife as I head home from one of the best nights I've ever had.

"Best non-date date ever."

CHAPTER
Thirteen

Ava

I'm securing one of the last few pictures onto my bulletin board at the end of the school day on Friday. The school day ended thirty minutes ago, and most of the staff has headed out for the weekend. My students have been anxious to see the finished bulletin board project with the photos they submitted last weekend.

I only had two not complete the extra credit assignment. One girl didn't have access to a phone. She seemed embarrassed as she told me her mom was gone Friday night, leaving her at home to watch her seven-year-old little sister, and even though she went outside and wanted to submit a photo, she didn't have access. I could tell she was upset by her lack of participation, and even though she really doesn't need the extra credit points, it meant something to her to partake.

That's when I asked her if she could draw it. Her eyes lit up in a way that gets to me. The disappointment and shame that once filled her blue eyes was gone. She nodded, insisting she could draw the aurora borealis, just as she saw it Friday night, and now that drawing will accompany the rest of the photographs I've received and printed, right in the middle of the bulletin board.

Extra credit earned.

The other student flat-out told me Monday morning he didn't do it. Keeping his interest in the classroom setting is a huge challenge, so asking him to "do schoolwork on Friday" wasn't in the cards. I appreciate his honesty though, and while he could use those extra ten points toward his grade, I can't force him.

My mind returns to my own Friday night, as it seemed to do an awful lot this last week. I still can't believe I kissed him. It was...incredible. I might not have a lot of experience when it comes to the opposite sex, but it felt like a pretty amazing moment. Not just the first one, which blew my socks off, but even the light press of our lips together at the very end of our evening. The entire night was unbelievably wonderful, and I didn't want it to end.

Which is why I'm glad it did.

Even though I was comfortable and enjoyed his company, I was still aware of the fact he's Annabelle's father. My student. Yet, as he made me feel at ease as our non-date went on, I knew I was in trouble.

Why?

Because I wanted it to be a date.

It felt like a real one too.

That's why I've tried to avoid him this week, but considering he's finishing up my roof, it's been a little difficult. He's still there, wrapping things up, when I get home from work. Whether it's intentional or not, I'm unsure, but Max is usually gone and Gavin's packing up the last of their tools when I pull into my driveway.

Perhaps that's why I'm still here.

Delaying my return home, hoping he's already gone. Which sucks, because I really want to see him.

When the last photo is hung, I pull the last few pictures from the envelope. The ones I slipped in in a moment of weakness Sunday evening when I submitted my online picture printing order. The shots

Gavin texted me once he got home Friday night. The selfies of us, standing super close with the gorgeous view of the night sky behind us.

I dissect the picture. Everything from the intimate way we're standing to the genuine smiles on our faces. Our noses and cheeks are red, and we're both wearing enough layers of clothing and winter gear to the point we resemble marshmallows, but the overall picture is serenity. We look so...natural and happy.

So coupley.

And it's really conflicting to feel this way about him when I've been doing everything in my power not to.

"Hey, that looks great."

I glance up with a startle, almost dropping the photos in my hand. Evelyn Valero, the second-grade teacher, is standing in my doorway with a friendly smile and her bag thrown over her shoulder.

"Sorry, didn't mean to surprise you."

I wave it off. "It's fine. I was lost in my own world," I tell her, taking the photos over to my desk and slipping them into the top drawer.

She steps inside my classroom and looks over the bulletin board. "This really turned out great. The students took all the photos?"

I nod. "They did," I state proudly.

"What an experience for them. Well done."

I feel my cheeks heat at the compliment. Even though I'm a fourteen-year veteran here, it still feels good to have my efforts recognized by someone who's spent her entire almost-forty-year teaching career at this exact location. In fact, she was *my* second-grade teacher way back when. "Thank you."

"I won't keep you," she says. "I'm sure you're ready to head home. It's been a week," she adds with a chuckle.

"Agreed."

She turns to exit my classroom when she pauses. "Oh, by the way, not that it's any of my business, but I think it's great about you and Gavin Pierson. He's such a nice young man."

The hairs on the back of my neck stand up and my throat is suddenly dry. "What?"

"You and Gavin."

Blood swooshes in my ears. "I'm not...we're not...dating."

"Oh. You're not?"

"No. Where did you hear that?" I ask, unable to keep my irritation out of my voice.

She tries to wave it off with her hand. "You know how the rumor mill is in the teachers' lounge. Someone said they saw you and him at the pizzeria on New Year's Day, and I'm sure someone took it and ran with it."

I nod. "We just happened to be at the same place at the same time, and his daughter asked me to join them. I wasn't going to, but she was insistent."

"Don't fret about it, Ava. I know you don't like to be associated with gossip, but I promise you, anything I heard was all positive. We all think it's a wonderful thing you're dating him. Or at least someone thought you were dating him."

"Oh." That's all I've got.

She's absolutely correct. I hate being the center of any attention, especially gossip. I know you can't help it when people talk, but I much prefer their chatter not to be about me. After the photo incident, in which I thought I was going to lose my job, it felt like my name was on everyone's lips forever. Most of the staff were supportive, publicly stating they've all done things in our youthful years they're not proud of and pledging their support of me in my position.

It was a terrible time in my life, one I wish to never ever repeat.

"I didn't mean to upset you. If I hear any more comments about you and Gavin, I'll be sure to put a kibosh on it right away."

"Thank you," I mutter, my mind reeling.

"Of course," she replies, clearly feeling a little uneasy as she prepares to leave. "For what it's worth, you have a right to live your life, Ava. This is a small town, and with that comes good and bad. You know everyone already, so the chances of you finding and spending time with someone you may not know can be difficult. Don't be afraid to live your life, just because a few people were jerks a few years back and tried to sabotage your career. You're so much stronger and braver than you think." She pauses, giving her words time to penetrate my brain before she adds, "Have a wonderful weekend. See you Monday."

And with that, she's gone, leaving me standing at my desk with what can only be considered a dumbfounded look on my face.

Did that really just happen?

I've always liked Mrs. Valero, as a teacher and a mentor. She's incredibly kind, knowledgeable, and fair, and for the most part, like me, keeps to herself. But she's always offering an encouraging comment or sound piece of advice when you didn't even realize you needed it.

Like now.

I have rules in place for a reason, and for the first time, I'm actually entertaining the idea of breaking one. Well, not breaking it, exactly. Bending it, maybe?

My heart starts to quicken in my chest at the thought.

But if I'm going to bend or break a rule as important to me as the no-dating-a-student's-dad rule, shouldn't it be for good reason?

For someone who makes my heart pound and butteries flutter in my stomach?

Someone who makes me feel all swoony every time he looks at me with those intoxicating hazel eyes?

A man who seems patient and willing to take things slow simply *because* he knows of my rule, and while wanting me to break it, is supportive with my boundaries?

There's only one person who checks off each and every one of those questions, and I've been avoiding him this week because he makes me feel things that scare me.

And that's exactly what it boils down to.

I'm scared.

Carefully, I pull the photos out of my desk drawer. I printed out all five he sent me, and while each one is basically the same, the last one holds my attention. Gavin isn't looking at the camera. He's looking down at me. The same gentle smile on his lips, and even though I can't see his eyes, I can feel the sparkle, the heat. Those orbs hold so much power it almost knocks me on my ass.

I slip the photos back into my desk drawer except for that one. Grabbing my coat and my purse from the bottom drawer, I carefully place the photo inside and make a dash for the door. Usually, I'd put my snow boots on, since my flats don't have the traction or warmth I seek, but there's no time. If I hurry, I might make it to my house before he leaves.

As soon as my classroom door is locked, I quickly make my way to the exit. I'm one of the last ones here, and darkness is setting in, despite the fact it's only about four thirty. Fortunately, it hasn't snowed for a few days, so the lot is mostly clear, with the exception of a few icy spots. I'm careful not to slip and bust my rear, shuffling over to my vehicle and climbing inside.

Driving a little faster than normal, I wind my way through Pine Village until I get to Eldridge Road. I'm not too far now. Tempted to press a little harder on the accelerator, I refrain. The last thing I need is to wreck my car. Between the previous car expenses and my porch and roof, my savings is quite depleted.

When I turn into my subdivision, the excitement coursing through me is dashed. The spot Gavin has been parking his work truck is empty. Worse, I look at the front of my house, and my roof appears complete, the porch beautiful and inviting.

Maybe this is a sign...

I slowly pull into my driveway and press the button to raise my garage door. Just as I reach the entrance, something catches my eye. There's a bag sitting in front of the garage door, one I didn't leave there. After closing the large door, I carefully climb from my small SUV and make my way to the door leading outside. I pull it open and reach for the bag, peeking inside to see the contents.

That's when a huge smile spreads across my face.

Even though I want to open it now, I return to my vehicle and grab my stuff. When I have everything I need, I let myself in the house and go straight to the kitchen table. Reaching into the bag, I pull out what's inside and smile. There's an old hardback book and a bouquet of fresh flowers. Bringing the blooms to my noise, I inhale their rich, fragrant scent.

Next, I examine the book. I can tell it's well loved, the cover slightly marred and the pages turning yellow. The old National Geographic hardback has a gorgeous starry night sky on the cover and a title referring to the exploration of it. I'm intrigued instantly, already knowing what I'll be reading later this evening.

My eyes land on the envelope, and I carefully pull the contents out. The large sheet of paper is a bill. Not just any bill, but the balance I owe for the job he completed. This sheet confirms what I had suspected when I pulled in. The job is finished.

There's no longer a reason for him to be here.

The disappointment I suddenly feel is almost overwhelming.

With the bill is a handwritten note. My fingers are slightly shaky as I open it up and scan. It's written on a smaller lined sheet of paper, probably one from the notebook he carries with him. My heart skips in my chest as I start to read his words.

Ava,

The bill is separate from the rest of what's in this bag. I was planning to give it to you first, so business was completed before everything else. On the business side, your roof is complete. I hope you like it, and the metal isn't too ugly. I really think you'll be happy with the quality and life of the product. Also, if I do say so myself, your porch looks amazing. It really changes the curb appeal of your house and will provide plenty of shelter to you when needed. If you have any questions or concerns, please call me. Usually, I'd take a homeowner around and explain everything we did, but I wasn't sure what time you'd be home. I am available any time after 8 tomorrow morning and can swing by after I drop Annabelle off at her mom's.

Now, the rest of it. I know you have rules and I respect that. I was in the bookstore with Annabelle earlier in the week and browsed the used section. I saw this one and smiled. I couldn't help but think of you and our non-date date. Then, I was grabbing something from the deli at the supermarket for lunch and saw this bouquet. The pinks and oranges reminded me of the sky that night, and suddenly, I found myself purchasing them.

Turns out, you're everywhere I look and all I think about.

I hope you enjoy them, and maybe we'll try for another non-date date.

Although, that's such a long thing to write, so maybe we'll just go with date to save my hand from cramping.

I'm out of room on both sides of the paper now.

Thinking of you,

G

After I finish the note, I turn it over and reread it. And again. Each time, I grin even more, and by the time I've completed a third pass, my cheeks hurt.

He's been thinking of me.

I take a few moments to remove my coat and shoes, slipping my feet into a pair of slippers I keep by the back door. After retrieving my phone from my purse, I pull up the texting app and find his name.

Me: I just got home. I'll get you a check ASAP for the balance.

The bubbles appear instantly, so I wait for his reply.

Gavin: No rush. I know where you live if you try to ghost me. *insert winky emoji*

Me: I'd never.

Gavin: I know, I was teasing. But seriously, I'm in no rush.

I take a deep breath and let it out before typing again. It's now or never, and frankly he left the door cracked open. All I need to do is be brave enough to step through.

Me: I was thinking, maybe you could stop by tomorrow and show me what you did?

Gavin: Absolutely. Name the time.

Me: How about in the afternoon? And then perhaps, if you don't have plans, you could join me? For dinner?

My heart is pounding so hard in my chest as I tap the send button, I swear the neighbors can hear it.

He doesn't reply right away, which only causes my nervous anxiety to amp up to the point I could give myself a stroke if I don't see those bubbles appear soon. I might not have a lot of dating or guy experience, but I know I haven't misread the room. He's made it very clear he's interested in me.

Finally, bubbles.

Gavin: Sorry for the delay. Annabelle and I are cooking dinner. And to answer your question, I'd love to join you. I have no plans at all, and even if I did, I'd cancel in a heartbeat to spend time with you.

Swoon.

Me: All right. How about 4? Will that give you enough time to show me everything before dark?

Gavin: That's perfect. What can I bring?

Me: Nothing.

Gavin: I'll bring a bottle of wine. White, right?

He remembers.

Me: Thank you.

Gavin: See you tomorrow.

Gavin: Oh, and Ava? I'm glad you messaged me, and for the record, I was going to wait until later, but my plan was to text you and see if you were interested in another non-date date.

Me: I would have accepted.

Gavin: Good to know…See you soon.

Me: Bye

I'm smiling from ear to ear as I place my phone on my table and do a shimmy. It's only when I start to mentally replay our conversation that I realize I didn't thank him for the book and flowers. But that's okay. I can tell him tomorrow. Since he'll be joining me for dinner, I can properly express my gratitude for his gifts.

Maybe with a kiss.

I still can't believe I messaged him and asked him to dinner. I've never been one to go after something—or someone—I want.

You're braver than you think.

Evelyn's words come back to me as I take a deep, calming breath.

It's time I go after what I want, to be brave.

Do I want Gavin?

The answer is a resounding yes.

Rules be damned.

CHAPTER *fourteen*

GAVIN

After dropping Annabelle off with her mom for the next week, I head to the grocery store to stock up on food. I'm a pretty simple guy during the weeks I don't have my daughter. Hell, I keep it simple on the weeks I have her. When it's just me though, I tend to cook only a few larger meals, making enough to eat the leftovers a day or two afterward. My favorite is in the summer when I can grill, preparing plenty of meat for a few days at a time, and since Annabelle is a huge fan of hamburgers and hot dogs, they're a staple for us anytime I can fire up the ol' gas grill.

Today, however, I stick to just a few of the basics, mostly because my mind is on Ava, not prepping for lunches and dinners for this week. Besides, I'm an optimistic guy, so I can't help but wonder how much of my time I'll get to spend with Ava. I mean, there's no sense in buying for the whole week if I'm going to be able to enjoy her company a night or two.

I grab bread, lunch meat, and cheese since sandwiches are quick and easy lunches while I'm working, and then head over to the fresh meat section. Even though our grocery store is small and family owned, the meat comes from area farms. It may cost a bit more to support local, but the benefits outweigh a few extra cents per pound. Plus, we know exactly where the meat is coming from, not being shipped in like the big box chains in Hudson.

I find a package of ground beef, sausage, and a couple of pork chops that don't expire right away and toss them into the cart. Just as I'm turning into the aisle with the alcohol, I hear a familiar voice from behind.

"Well, if it isn't my handsome son."

I stop, making sure my cart is out of the way for anyone passing, and give my mom a big smile. "Well, hello, beautiful," I greet, leaning forward and pressing a kiss to her cheek.

"I was just grabbing everything for beef and noodles and mashed potatoes for dinner tonight. Would you like to join us?" she asks.

"Uhh, I can't." I don't know why, but my heart is starting to beat a little harder in my chest. It's not like I'm doing anything wrong, but I know how private Ava is, and I don't want to be the one blurting it out in the middle of the grocery store on a Saturday morning.

Mom watches me for a few seconds before a slow smile spreads across her lips. She leans toward me and whispers, "Do you have a date?"

I barely get the confirmation out of my mouth when her eyes widen with delight and she asks, "Who?"

"None of your business, Nosy Nelly," I tease, glancing around to make sure anyone nearby can't overhear.

Her hazel eyes the same color as my own narrow. "Don't hold out on your mother. That's just rude."

Chuckling, I lean forward and rest my elbows on the handle of the shopping cart. "It's pretty new, Mom."

Holding up her hands, she replies, "Okay, okay, I get it. New means you're going to keep private about it. Fine. Have your secrets."

"It's not that it's a secret, really; just new."

"Well, I think it's great, nonetheless. You don't put yourself out there very much when it comes to the opposite sex."

My eyebrows draw up. "Seriously?"

She shrugs her delicate shoulders and smiles. "You're always having a beer with that nice young man who works for you, Max. Not that there's anything wrong with that, but it's nice to know you're slipping in the occasional female variety."

"Jesus," I grumble.

"I'm not saying you can't be gay!"

My eyes widen, because she sure as shit said that a hell of a lot louder than she should have.

"I would support you," she insists.

"Mom," I whisper-yell.

"I'm saying I would support and love you despite your sexuality," she states, nodding toward old Mrs. Perkins who rounds the corner and stares at me and Mom.

Mrs. Perkins takes her sweet-ass time walking past us. Could be because she's pushing eighty and doesn't get around as easily as she used to, or it's the more likely scenario and she's being nosy and hoping to catch the moment I come out of the closet in the middle of the supermarket.

When the older woman finally gets down the aisle, I lean in close and whisper, "I'm not gay."

"I know," she replies back just as quietly. "I'm just showing my support if you were."

"Thank you, really, but we're off topic."

"Yes, we are. So, about this woman..."

I hold up my hands in defeat. "I'll tell you more when there's more to tell."

She sighs. "Fine, but if this doesn't work out, I'd like to set you up."

"What? No."

"Hear me out," she starts. "Betty's granddaughter that drove her to our house on Christmas Eve. What was her name?"

My throat goes completely dry. "Ava?"

"Yes, Ava. She's Annabelle's teacher, right?" She knows the answer to this, so I don't reply. "Anyway, Grandma Zelda was chatting with Betty about, you know, dating, and Zelda may have mentioned Ava isn't seeing anyone right now."

I don't even want to know why my grandma was talking to Ava's grandma about dating. "Mom—" I start, but she cuts me off.

"All I'm saying is that bit of information might be worth looking into."

"Fine," I tell her, ready to get the hell out of the beer and wine aisle and away from the inquisition.

"Oh goodie! You two would make beautiful grandbabies."

If I were drinking, I would have choked on the liquid. "Love you, but I'm out," I tell her, slapping a chaste kiss on her cheek before grabbing my cart and spinning it around. Of course, when I do, I almost slam the front of my cart into Mrs. Perkins, who apparently returned without me realizing and happens to be browsing the alcohol selection.

"Let me know if you want her number," Mom hollers behind me. All I do is lift my arm and wave.

She did this on purpose, I know. Mom has never been quiet or shy about making her feelings for anything known. She may bite her tongue to allow us to work through our problems, but she's not afraid to give us a nudge or advice.

Funny she was suggesting I date Ava. I kept wondering if those around the table could pick up on the sparks I felt flying while we enjoyed dessert. I was sure everyone would be able to see the way my eyes couldn't be pulled away from her, despite how hard I tried. Maybe Mom noticed. She is the most observant person I know, so I wouldn't put it past her to pick up on the way I felt and so desperately tried to hide from the room. Of course, my brother could have said something too. He figured out really quick who I was crushing on. The moment she walked into the house; I was a goner.

Either he blabbed to my mom, or she was able to figure it out too.

Chances are she knew exactly what she was doing when she mentioned Ava to me. The only difference is she isn't aware of who I'm actually seeing tonight, because if she knew she would have had something to say.

I make my way to the checkout, without grabbing the bottle of wine. It's fine though. I'll just stop somewhere else and buy one on my way to Ava's. There might not be the variety at the old gas station owned by Jeb, but I'm sure I can grab a bottle of something before I wind my way toward Ava's house.

I just have to make it until four.

Maybe a few minutes before.

We'll get the work part out of the way first, and then we can enjoy the rest of our non-date date.

No, fuck that.

It's a date, and it's up to me to show her.

I pull into her driveway, and that familiar spike of adrenaline I tend to get when I'm near Ava sweeps through my veins. I haven't seen her since our Friday night together, and I'm ready. We've texted a few times since her invitation to dinner, mostly because I wanted her to know I was thinking of her. What started off as a simple message asking about her day turned into chatting for an extended period of time. And even though I would have preferred just to call her to hear the sound of her voice, I kept it to texting.

I didn't want to overwhelm her.

I can be relentless in my pursuit of the beautiful Ava Rutledge while still letting her feel at ease and comfortable.

I shut off my truck, leaving it parked in the same place I used when I was working on her house. It's directly in front of her property along the street, so she had access to her driveway. As I climb from the driver's seat, my gaze is drawn to the front door. She's standing there, her hand wrapped around the new pole I installed at the very beginning of her home improvement project.

Grabbing the bottle of white wine and small gift I found at Jeb's, I shut my door and head her way. "Hi."

She flashes me a shy grin and slowly makes her way down her front steps. "Hello. Thanks for coming."

"Of course." I meet her on the sidewalk and add, "You look gorgeous."

Her red hair is down, hanging loosely beneath a warm stocking cap, and her eyes are a bit darker with makeup. She's wearing jeans, a somewhat rarity, and a long sweater that hits just below the bottom of her coat. Her cheeks are already rosy, after only a few moments outside, and her brown eyes sparkle under the late afternoon sky.

She's simply breathtaking. The most beautiful woman I've ever seen.

"Thank you," she murmurs gently, pushing a strand of hair off her shoulder.

"This is for you," I tell her, holding out my hand and earning the chuckle I was hoping for. "I know it might be silly, but I've already given you flowers this week, and not that you don't deserve flowers twice, because really, you deserve them every day, but I thought I'd think outside the box."

Take a breath, you goon.

She smiles widely, palming the candy bar. "You remembered."

I'd do anything to keep seeing that smile on her face. "Of course I remembered. You said they were your favorite," I reply, speaking of the Twix bar in her gloved hand.

She gazes up at me beneath her lashes. "And yours is a Reese's. Cup, not Pieces."

"Why would they even make those little things?"

She shrugs, still holding the candy bar. "Possibly to compete with M&M's."

I give her a nod. "Makes sense." I look up at her roof. Even though I'd much rather stare at her for the next few hours, I'm here for a reason, so we might as well get the first part out of the way. "Shall we take a look around?"

"Yes," she says, falling in beside me as we make our way up on the porch first. I set the bottle of wine down on the steps so I don't have to carry it, and Ava slips the candy bar into her coat pocket.

I go through everything we did, and even though I'm certain she doesn't know some of the terminology, she nods in understanding. As we step off the porch and into the snow-covered yard, I offer her my elbow. Yes, to be gentlemanly and try to offer her stability, but also because I flat-out like the way my body feels when she's pressed against it. Her fingers, albeit being covered in warm material, are wrapped around my arm, and it only takes a few moments before the heat of her touch seeps through the layers between us.

"All right," I start, after going over a few details of her new roof, "Tell me the truth. What do you think of the metal?"

She looks up at it and grins. "I like it. I wasn't sure until I came home last night and saw the completed product. Okay, that's not true. It was starting to get dark, and I wasn't able to see it properly until this morning, but when I got a clear view in the daylight, I realized I didn't mind it at all. Yes, it's shiny, but the charcoal coloring fits the house. Even my dad likes it."

"I'm glad. And I do appreciate praise from Jude Rutledge."

"He's always singing your praises," she tells me as we start to make our way to the front porch once more. "He insisted I call you after my porch fell. He said you're the best."

I grab the bottle of wine I had set down earlier and we move inside her house. Even though I've been here before, I take in the living room with fresh eyes. It's warm and comfortable, with throw blankets and books. There're a few pictures I missed the first time around, some of the faces I recognize. Her sister and her family pose in one of the photographs and Ava with her grandma are in another. There's a group shot of her entire family together and what looks like a kid's birthday party, and an anniversary photo of her parents.

"I know I said this before, but you have a great home," I tell her, slipping off my coat.

"Thank you. My dad and I have put a lot of work into it, and I love it. Can I get you something to drink?" she offers when her coat is hanging in the front closet beside mine. We both carry our boots into the small mudroom that leads to the garage, placing them on the boot mats she has to catch the melting snow.

"May I open the bottle of wine?" I suggest.

"Please." She retrieves a bottle opener from the drawer and hands it over. Our fingers graze and that now-familiar spark of electricity zings through me.

"I'm not sure how good this'll be. There weren't too many options available at Jeb's," I tell her, popping the old cork. I stopped at the gas station and browsed his small selection of bottled alcohol, settling on this sweet white wine with a name I couldn't pronounce.

"I've never bought wine from his place."

My conversation with my mom flashes through my mind. "Well, I was planning to get it at the grocery store, but there was some Nosy Nellys watching, so I just decided to skip it. No reason to give them something to wonder about," I tell her, even though my mom is probably at home, doing just that.

Wondering.

There's gratitude in her brown eyes. I know she has a fear of being talked about in a negative light, so if I can help keep that worry from bothering her, I'll do it in a heartbeat.

I pour the moscato into two glasses she retrieves from a cabinet, hoping this stuff doesn't taste like shit. When she takes her glass, I hold mine up for a quick toast. "To a wonderful evening amongst new friends."

A faint blush burns her cheeks as she taps my glass with her own and takes a small sip. I watch her intently, studying the curves of her face and the way her lips form around the glass. I can't help but notice she doesn't grimace when the cold liquid hits her tongue, so that's a plus. Taking my own taste, I instantly catch the hint of floral mixed with the sweetness of the wine, and I realize it's not terrible. Definitely not the worst I've had.

Of course, the company's pretty fucking fantastic, so the wine could taste like goat piss and I'd still drink it as if it were the best thing I've ever had. Seeing her drop her guard minute by minute has me relaxing a bit more. I'm completely entranced with her movements, her smile, and watching the change in her eyes.

Forcing myself to stop watching her, I ask, "What smells so amazing in here?"

"Oh, uh, I found this recipe online a few weeks back and have been wanting to try it," she informs me as she sets her glass down and moves to the Crock-Pot.

"So I'm your guinea pig?"

Her cheeks blush again. "It makes so much. I can't just prepare it for myself," she insists, glancing down at the lidded Crock-Pot. "I probably should have asked what you prefer."

Propping my hip against the counter, I cross my ankles and watch her. "We discussed this early this morning when we talked about food." We texted into the wee hours of the morning, and it's not the first time. Since our non-date date last Friday, we've talked quite a bit, getting to know each other.

She sighs. "I know. You said you like everything but candied yams and bananas, which is so weird, by the way."

"They're mushy," I reason with a smile.

"Well, I'm hoping you like sausage tortellini."

"Love it." My reply is instant.

She shakes her head and grins. "I haven't even told you what's in it yet."

I lift my shoulders and take another sip of my wine. "Doesn't matter. I like about everything, and if I don't, I'll pick it out."

"Spinach?"

"Yep."

"Sun-dried tomatoes?"

"Absolutely."

"Cheese?"

"Who doesn't?"

She giggles the sweetest sound. "Well, then you should like this. It has all of the above."

"Perfect," I tell her, continuing to watch her move about her kitchen.

When she pulls two plates from the cabinet, I step forward. "Let me."

Ava retrieves a covered container of sliced bread that smells freshly baked, while I find the silverware for the table. When she places hotpot holders on the table and goes to lift the Crock-Pot bowl out of the base, I'm there to help. "Let me."

When the amazing smelling food is on the table, we take our seats. "This looks delicious, Ava. Thank you."

She gives me a small grin. "Thanks. I don't cook a lot because it's just me, but I do enjoy it."

Placing my hand on my belly, I add, "Well, I love to eat, so anytime you want to try a new recipe, I'm your guy."

Her cheeks stain pink as she nibbles on her bottom lip. My cock notices right away, but I will him into submission. No way does she need to know I could get hard just by watching her teeth bite into her plump lip. She'll probably think I'm a sex fiend and kick me out.

Yes, I'm a guy who enjoys sex, but my reaction is simple.

It's her.

I clear my throat, ready to dig into this delicious meal she prepared for me. "Let's eat."

CHAPTER *fifteen*

"So, Denny and I invited a few girls to tag along, and we all went swimming in the pool. Denny and I dared each other to strip down to nothing, but the girls decided to keep on their undergarments. It was fine for about five minutes, and we were all having a great time. I had just dared Denny to jump off the diving board when a security light turned on. Turns out, they were home and not away for the weekend like Denny was told. When they heard us splashing around at close to midnight, Mr. Zecker came outside in his tighty-whities, carrying a shotgun because he thought a bear had gotten trapped in his yard," Gavin says, trying not to smile while telling his story.

I, on the other hand, am grinning from ear to ear as he recounts the story I had heard long ago while away at college. A group of five or six students climbed over the fence surrounding Principal Zecker's backyard and went skinny-dipping, but I guess I didn't realize it was Gavin who did it. "I bet that was a sight."

He shivers. "Sometimes, late at night, it pops in my head like a scene from a horror movie you just can't stop thinking about, and I have to cry myself to sleep."

Giggling, I reach over and rest my hand on top of his. Upon contact, a flash of electricity races through me. The zap startles me, but I'm not sure why. I've felt it every time we've touched, even with the most basic contact through layers of winter weather gear. Clearing my throat and trying to catch my breath, I reply, "The stuff nightmares are made of."

"You have no idea. Especially when he realized it wasn't a black bear frolicking around in his yard and pool, but his students, he made us boys get out of the pool—naked, covering ourselves with only our hands—while he proceeded to hand out detentions like throwing confetti. It wasn't until he was done with his lecture that he realized he was in his underwear. His face went beet red, and as much as he tried to...*cover* himself, it was no use. The damage had been done. He was so embarrassed, he told us if we never speak of this again, we could skip those detentions, but thanks to the giggling girls and their big mouths, it got around town faster than Saul's meatloaf announcements, and by Monday morning, those detentions were back on."

I'm laughing now, unable to stop myself. "Oh my God, I heard about this when I was at college, but didn't know the specifics. This is horribly funny. I'm so sorry for laughing at your expense."

"Yeah, yeah."

"Did you at least get a date out of your experience?" I ask, even though I'm not sure I really want to know. Gavin is incredibly gorgeous. I'm sure he's had plenty of *dates* in his time.

Way more than me.

His smile is slow and to the point. Without saying a word, I already know the answer. "Perhaps, but only because I was a true gentleman and turned around while the ladies got out of the pool and put their clothes back on."

Shaking my head, I beam at him, at the story he shared. I've been told Gavin was a wild one when he was younger, and while he was three years younger than me in school, it's a small enough town to hear the stories over the years. Sure, I'm certain a few have been embellished, but I have no doubt that Gavin Pierson, with his charming smile and charismatic personality, was every bit of the gorgeous troublemaker I heard about.

We sit and stare at each other for several seconds, enjoying the conversation and getting to know each other. The meal is long consumed, the dishes already in the dishwasher and the leftovers in the fridge. We've been sitting here, talking, for almost two hours, and neither seems to be ready to part ways. It's comfortable having him here, and I find the more I learn about him, the more I like. I want to know more.

Clearing my throat, I blurt out, "Would you like a tour?" I feel my face flush a thousand shades of red and wish I could reel the invitation back in. It's much bolder and more brazen than I'm used to.

"I'd love one. Tell me what you and your dad have done to the house since you purchased it," he says, standing up and reaching for my chair.

"Well, there hasn't been too much, just some cosmetic updates here and there. We pulled up the flooring in the kitchen and bathroom and repainted the cabinets. They were a horrible shade of yellow when I bought this place."

"You have a great color scheme with the lighter color on the top cabinets and the darker one on the bottom," he says, taking it all in.

"Pinterest is my favorite site. I love to craft and create, and you can find so much on there. I spent hours and hours looking over kitchen designs and color schemes."

"You did well," he informs me.

When we move from the kitchen to the living room, I feel his hand on my lower back. It's warm and inviting and causes butterflies to flutter in my belly. "Umm, we painted in here. The original walls had three gray ones and a dark red accent. It was...I don't know, but it wasn't the comforting feel you'd want when relaxing in the living room. It was overwhelming to me. I guess I prefer more soothing earth tones, which is probably why I chose the ivory and sage green colors for the cabinets."

"It fits you," he says as we walk down the short hallway.

Pushing open the first door, I reveal my playroom, as I like to call it. It's a combination library and craft room and was the first project my dad and I tackled when I received possession of the house.

"Impressive," Gavin states, glancing around the clear, organized space.

"Thank you. Dad built me the shelves, workstation, and organizers. It took some time, but I couldn't imagine what it would have been like without it. I use the workstation for nearly everything, and thanks to the organizers, I have bins and spaces for materials."

"Maybe he should have gone into carpentry and construction instead of farming and insurance," he says, taking a few extra minutes to look around.

"Farming has always been his love. Well, after my mom and family. Insurance kept a steady income rolling in, especially when the farm had a rough year for whatever reason."

When he seems to have his fill of checking out my playroom, we move on to the small bathroom. We don't hang around too long because, well, if you've seen one bathroom, you've pretty much seen them all, so we move on to the final doorway in this part of the house.

My bedroom.

The master bedroom is a nice-sized room with two big windows on the back wall that face the timber behind me. I love to keep the window shades open during the day to enjoy the view and let in the natural light, but now that it's dark, they'll need to be closed before I get ready for bed.

I take in the space, trying to put myself in Gavin's shoes. There's plenty of room to move around. My queen-sized bed is positioned against one wall, while my dresser and standing jewelry box I received following my mother's passing are opposite. I do most of my reading in the living room, but I do have an old rocking chair that belonged to my grandma in the corner, along with a small table with a reading lamp and a couple of books.

"This suits you."

I glance around. "How so?"

He steps forward until he's directly in front of my bed before he turns around and looks at me. I'm very much aware of the fact we're inside my bedroom, so close to my bed, my body starting to hum with desire. I feel my nipples pebble against my bra, and a low tingle starts to swirl between my legs. My breathing quickens into short little pants and my head feels like I'm floating. Memories of that kiss from last Friday night flash through my mind, and all I want to do is repeat it.

"Well, it's relaxing and inviting, with the tans and soft pinks. There's a mix of newer pieces of furniture, as well as a few things that are most likely sentimental items you'll never part with. You have a few throw pillows to add comfort, but not so many they overwhelm the bed, and the carpet is thick and plush, just like the socks you tend to wear on your feet. It's welcoming and very...you."

My throat goes dry at the thought of *welcoming* Gavin into my bedroom. Not because I don't want him here, but simply because I do. Having him standing beside my bed makes me picture things I have no business imagining, yet can't seem to stop myself. I see him standing here at the end of a long day, climbing beneath the covers, and snuggling up against me as I drift off to sleep.

That's relaxing.

The thought of him being here.

With me.

My feet move before I can even reconsider. I stop when I'm directly in front of him, our socked feet toe to toe. He doesn't move a muscle, just watches me, waiting for me to make the first move.

So I do.

Going up on my tiptoes, I press my lips against his. It's not the light brush of our lips from last Friday, but one packed with heat and hope. Wrapping my hands around his arms, I lean into his chest just as his arms snake around me. His hands sit low on my back as his tongue slips across the seam of my lips. My mouth opens, granting him access. His tongue slides against mine, taking the lead in this incredible dance we seem to engage in.

Hesitantly, I move my hands. They glide up his back, around his shoulders, and to his neck. My fingers dive into his hair as I crush my chest against his. I ignore the ache in my feet as I climb higher, to get closer.

More.

I don't even realize I'm moving backward until I gently meet the wall. His hands dive down to my rear. Long, firm fingers grip the globes of my butt, gently squeezing moments before he lifts. A yelp of surprise erupts from my mouth, and my legs instinctively wrap around his waist.

With my back against the wall and his strong arms helping hold me in place, he deepens the kiss. Tongues duel, lips nip at lips. When he sucks on my tongue, I almost orgasm right here, right now, my body pressed firmly against his. I can feel the firmness and thickness of his erection between my legs, and while that might usually embarrass me, I don't give it a thought. Instead, all I want to do is grind against him until I explode like a bomb.

I've had sex. I may not be super experienced, since I spent my college years actually learning instead of partying and sleeping around, but I'm not unfamiliar with desire. But any desire I've felt in the last fifteen years has paled in comparison to how I feel right now. My body is hot, tingly, and craving more.

His touch.

His mouth.

His ability to make me feel wild and free.

For the first time in I don't even know how long, I want to experience everything I didn't even realize I was missing in my life.

And I want it with Gavin.

He kneads my butt with his big hands and my hips rock forward. The only air in the room is what we share. What he breathes, I breathe. This kiss is ravenous, desperate, natural.

Ours.

And I never want it to end.

A soft meow breaks the moment. "There's something brushing against my leg," he murmurs.

"Tabitha. She's very jealous, but I'm not sure why. Half the time, I don't think she likes me."

He gives me a lazy smile. One that makes it hard to catch my breath. I'm not exactly sure if it's from the epic kiss or the way he makes me feel when he grins at me like that. His hazel eyes brim with the desire conveyed, and all I want to do is kiss him again. By the feel of his erection pressed firmly against my core, I think he'd be game for it too.

But that's not what happens.

He carefully starts to lower my legs down, holding me against him as my feet touch the floor. While his hands remain firmly on my ass, his front pressed to me, he rests his forehead against mine and murmurs, "I really want to continue that kiss."

My heart is pounding a million beats per second. "I sense a but coming…"

His smile is gentle as his right hand moves to caress my cheek. He brushes his thumb over my bottom lip. "I've dreamt of kissing these lips since I was fifteen."

Okay. I wasn't expecting that.

"What?" I whisper, my mind spinning a little. Clearly the power of his kisses has knocked me for a loop, because there's no way he just said he's wanted to kiss me for eighteen years.

He smiles again, leaning forward, brushing his lips across my forehead. "True story, Ava. I had the biggest crush on you when we were in high school."

All I can do is gape at him, trying to process.

His gritty chuckle is a balm to my soul, one I didn't even know I needed. "Freshman year, I saw you walking down the hallway with your friends. You were holding this big stack of books, laughing at something one of them said. I literally stopped in my tracks in the hallway and just watched you. You were the most beautiful girl I'd ever seen."

My face flames red. "I'm not so sure about that," I insist. "No one thought I was beautiful. I was a nerd."

His lips caress my cheek as he inhales, breathing in the scent of my hair. "The most beautiful nerd in the world," he confirms. "I was smitten with you that entire year."

I blink several times before replying, "I don't know what to say."

"You don't have to say anything, just listen." He pauses and holds my gaze. "Call it a crush or whatever, but I've been attracted to you for as long as I can remember. I probably should have made a move and asked you out before now, but I was afraid it was just that. A crush. But the more I saw you, the more I wanted to know you, and my timing might not be the greatest because of your rule about dating a student's father, but I think this chemistry I feel when we're together is worth exploring."

He takes a deep breath before continuing, "That's why I'm not taking you to bed like I want to. This isn't just sex for me. This is...more, Ava. I feel it in my bones, and I'm going to prove it to you. When we're finally together, when you're in bed with me, naked, it's going to be because you're all in. You and me. We can keep it quiet though the rest of the school year or however long you need to feel comfortable, but when the time comes, I'm going to tell the world how I feel about you."

My mind is spinning from his words, his declaration, but more importantly, from the way they make me feel. For the first time in my adult life, I realize I want more. Not just a relationship. Someone to come home to, chat about my day with, and hold me while I fall asleep, but more with Gavin. Call it rushed or too soon, but I don't want to ignore these feelings I have. I want to find out where they lead.

But I'm also scared. I'm not one who usually takes risks. I prefer the comfort in familiarity, and while I'm a pro at dealing with change on a professional level, I'm not so good with it personally.

Maybe that's exactly why I need someone like Gavin in my life.

Someone who not only makes me *want* to step out of that comfort zone, but who's willing to catch me if and when I fall.

He presses his lips to my forehead once more, as if he can't stop himself. Frankly, I hope he never stops wanting to kiss me. "Can I see you again?"

I nod instantly. "Yes."

He gives me a slow smile that makes my thighs clench. "What are you doing tomorrow?"

"Tomorrow? Usually just grocery shopping and catching up on laundry and cleaning."

"How are you with heights?"

That question gives me pause. "Uhh, okay, I guess."

"Good. I'll be here at two. Comfortable shoes and clothes." He presses his lips to my own in a chaste, yet sweetly perfect kiss.

I want to ask him to stay, to tell him I'm ready, but deep down, I know I need just a little more time. And the fact he knows it is all the more reason to put my trust and faith in Gavin Pierson. Why this man is still single is beyond me, but I'm damn glad he is.

Tabitha jumps up on my bed and gets comfortable, while Gavin takes my hand and walks me to the front door. While he slips on his coat and hat, I grab his boots from the mat in the mudroom. It doesn't freak me out when I see them beside my own boots. In fact, it's as if that one little picture is the most natural sight in the world.

What is this man doing to me?

When he's ready to go, he takes me in his arms, slipping his hands into my hair. "Thank you for dinner. It was delicious."

"You're welcome," I murmur right before his lips swipe gently across mine.

"Tonight has been incredible," he whispers before releasing his hold on my head and stepping back.

I miss his touch already.

"It has," I confirm, my throat dry and my lips tingly.

"See you tomorrow, Ava." He flashes me a happy, yet somewhat cocky smile before stepping through my front door and onto the porch. "Lock up behind me."

"I will," I reply.

He waves goodbye before walking to his truck. Even when he climbs inside and starts it, I can feel his eyes on me. My fingers automatically go to my lips, tracing the still-swollen flesh he just spent the better part of several minutes devouring.

A wave of excitement sweeps through me as he slowly pulls away, leaving me with the memories of his amazing kisses, the hardness of his body against mine, and the desire for more.

Gavin Pierson might very well be my Kryptonite.

And the wild part is, I don't seem to be as worried as I used to be.

In fact, I'm anxious to find out more.

Excited to spend more time with him tomorrow.

Elated at the prospect of jumping into this relationship with him.

Hoping and praying it doesn't all come crashing down around me.

CHAPTER
sixteen

GAVIN

"I'm not so sure about this," Ava states, the hesitation evident in her voice as she gazes up at the twenty-five-foot rock wall in front of us.

"No sweat, sweets. You got this," I insist, trying to ease her worry. "We're harnessed so you won't fall, and you have proper grippy shoes. Annabelle and I have been coming here for a few years now. It's fun."

She continues to stare up at the brightly colored pegs on five thousand square feet of climbing space. "This doesn't scream fun to me, Gavin," she mutters, turning worried eyes my way.

I step forward, placing my hands around her upper arms and kiss her soft lips. "You look so stinkin' adorable. If you don't want to, we won't. But I promise, it's not as difficult as you think. We're starting on the beginner's side, which isn't as tall, and the pegs are larger and closer together."

She sighs and meets my gaze. "I haven't done physical activity since PE in high school, and even then, I was the least athletic and coordinated person in the class."

I snort a laugh and kiss her forehead. "And look at you now. A total badass, who's about to climb a rock wall."

Ava rolls her eyes and glances back up at the wall, reaching up and straightening her helmet. "All right, I'll give it a try, but if I fall to my death, I'll be haunting you for the rest of your life."

"I'm certain it won't come to that, but I would look forward to seeing you in ghostlike form," I tease.

Of course, my mind goes to the haunting she's already doing. She has no clue, but she was with me last night when I went home, the memory of her mouth against mine, her body wrapped tightly around me, the desire swirling in her brown eyes, kept me hard and wanting the entire way. She was right there when I tried to take a cold shower and the reason I ended up taking my cock in my hand and getting myself off. I couldn't stop thinking about her.

About our non-date date.

Same thing again from the second I woke. Okay, if I'm being honest, she was in my dreams too, but from the moment I got up this morning, she's been on my mind, so when I say she's been haunting me since last night, I speak the facts.

Her memory is right there.

Ava reaches up and grabs two of the larger pegs and places her right foot on one about a foot off the ground. Slowly, she pulls herself up, setting her left foot down on a peg. She sighs and glances over her shoulder at me. She's barely a foot off the ground. "You know, maybe you should go again so I can see how you do it."

Before I can say a word, a young boy rushes over to the wall about ten feet from where we're at and scurries up to the top like it's nothing. "See? Easy," I retort, trying not to smile.

"He looked like Spider-Man," she mutters, adjusting her hands and glancing toward the top. "You're sure I'm not going to die?"

Grinning from ear to ear, I reassure her, "I'm sure. Take your time. There's no need to try to outdo Spidey over there."

Placing my hands on her hips, I watch as she readjusts her hands, takes a deep, calming breath, and starts to climb. She starts off slowly and with a bit of uncertainty, but by the time she's at my head level, she seems more confident. Ava reaches up, grabs a peg, and climbs higher and higher.

"You're doing great," I say, hoping it doesn't distract her.

Catching movement out of the corner of my eye, I look over to find the employee holding her rope staring up at her. Or, more specifically, starring at her ass. He's gotta be in his early twenties, probably barely old enough to drink, and checking her out like she's a popsicle on a summer July day.

Not that I blame him, of course. She has an amazing ass. I had my hands all over it last night and hope for a repeat very soon, but if Junior over there doesn't peel his eyes off her backside soon, I might have to remove them for him.

"I did it!"

I look up and smile widely, feeling a huge sense of pride in her accomplishment. "Look at you, beautiful," I reply, beaming up at her as she does the same back down to me. "Great job."

"I can't believe I did it," she says, mostly to herself, taking a risk by looking around the massive room.

"When you're ready, you can push off the wall and they'll bring you down."

It must have just hit her how's she's getting down. "You mean...just...let go?"

"Yes, just let go. Remember, you're in a harness that's secured through the pully on the ceiling. Your rope is here, and they have the brake on," I remind her, pointing to the nearby employee ready to lower her to the ground. "You won't fall."

She closes her eyes for a few seconds and inhales. "This is like one of those trust-fall things."

"Yep. Let go and trust me."

Her brown eyes zero in on me and remain locked while she slowly begins the process of letting go of the wall. First, both her feet, and then her hands. She's suspended from the ceiling, tethered by the security device, and slowly lowered to the ground, while wearing the most brilliant smile ever.

The moment she's unhooked, she's in my arms. "That was amazing."

"I knew you could do it," I tell her, squeezing her a little tighter than I should, because I love the feel of her against me.

"I'm so glad I did it," she beams up at me.

"See? Stepping out of your comfort zone isn't so bad, is it?" I whisper.

Her answer is to go up on her tiptoes and press her lips to mine. I fucking love it when she does that.

"Wanna go again, or would you like to grab something to eat?"

She looks up at the climbing wall. "Food. Definitely food. As fun as that was, I think I'll keep my rock-climbing record at one and oh and call it a success."

I snort a laugh and reach for her hand. As I lead her toward the counter where we can turn in our gear, I notice the young guy checking her out once more. Bringing her hand to my mouth, I place a kiss on her knuckles, and the moment he looks up and finds me watching him, I throw him a wink and a smirk.

He glances away quickly, winding up the rope in his hand and preparing for the next climber.

"Where do you want to eat?" I ask after we return our gear and pull our boots and coats out of our assigned lockers.

She shrugs. "I'm not picky."

Before stepping outside and heading to my truck, I turn and face her. "Well, if you could be picky, what would you choose?"

She nibbles that bottom lip again and contemplates. My eyes zero in on the action, like they always do. "Well, there *is* this really great seafood place not too far from here, down by the river."

"Done," I insist, guiding her through the parking lot to my truck. As she climbs in, I add, "I love seafood."

"Me too, though I don't get over here too often."

We make small talk as I drive to the seafood place she wants, and I can't get over how easy it is being around her. Julia was always indecisive when it came to eating. She'd tell me all the time she didn't care where we ate, but no matter where I picked, she'd complained. It got to the point, I'd always go to one of her known favorites, because at least I knew she'd find something she liked. After a year or two of doing that, then she'd complain I always went to the same spot.

It was exhausting.

But Ava picked. She may have said she didn't care, but when I asked her to pick anyway, she did. It wasn't a fight. It wasn't a game. She chose something she enjoyed eating, despite worrying if I'd like it or not.

She's a breath of fresh air.

One I can definitely get used to.

We find the restaurant and park. As soon as we're out of the truck, the scent of fresh seafood fills the air, making my mouth water. I wasn't super hungry until just now, with the delicious aroma of buttery fish and savory shrimp filling the air.

I take her hand and lead her to the front entrance. It's an old building, one you'd probably not give a second glance at if you were to pass it on the street, but by the way the seats are mostly filled in the middle of the afternoon, I can tell this place is a hidden gem. One known by the locals and probably not frequented by many out-of-towners.

"Have a seat wherever," a server hollers the moment we step inside the building.

My eyes start to scan the walls, taking in the nautical décor and old boat pieces. "There's a booth available," I state.

"Let's grab it," Ava replies, heading in that direction.

We claim the booth and sit side by side after taking off coats and laying them across the unused bench. Warmth spreads through my veins as our arms brush against each other, despite the fact it's not skin on skin. Ava's wearing a pair of blue jeans, comfortable ankle boots, and a souvenir sweatshirt from Bluff Preserves.

Scanning the menu, I ask, "What looks good?"

"I can't decide between the butterfly shrimp and scampi meal or the fish and shrimp combo," she replies, giving some serious consideration to both options.

"How about you get one and I'll get the other, and we'll share."

Her eyes twinkle with happiness. "Okay."

When our server stops by the table, we order drinks and both meals. "So, tell me about your family. I think your sister, Analise, and my sister, Ginger, were in the same class."

She nods. "They were. I remember going to watch Analise's basketball games and seeing your sister. She had the most beautiful curly brown hair. I always wished mine was like hers."

"I bet most girls said the same about yours. Still do."

Shaking her head, she takes a sip of water when it's delivered to the table. "No way. Growing up with red hair, freckles, *and* glasses wasn't any fun. Kids always made fun of the kids with red hair and freckles."

"Three of my favorite features," I assure her. Her hair is a darker red color and her freckles are a light dusting over her nose and cheeks.

She blushes, just as I predicted. "Well, thank you. Now, everyone loves redheads, but back in school, it wasn't the case. Anyway, your sister had the best curls. I envied them."

"She gets them from my mom," I tell her. "But she hated them back then. Curls aren't easy to tame, that's for sure, so Ging keeps her hair shorter now. Her youngest, Bethany, has them."

Ava gives me a gentle smile. "I remember her from Christmas Eve. She's adorable. How many nieces and nephews?"

"Five. My brother, Paul, has two and Ginger has three. Your sister has the twins, right?"

"She does. They're almost fourteen and in eighth grade."

"I bet it's nice having your sister here," I state, referring to the fact Analise is still in town.

"It is." Something passes through her gaze as she adds, "Especially when Mom got sick. She was able to be here and help as much as possible."

My hand is covering hers before she's even done talking. "I'm sorry for your loss. I remember your mom from the pharmacy. She was incredibly kind and friendly."

She visibly swallows. "Thank you. We all miss her every day."

"I'm sure you do." I squeeze her hand before bringing it to my mouth and kissing her knuckle. She turns to face me, her eyes holding so much sadness and pain, and all I want to do is take it away from her. Even if I can't, I want to try. I'd much rather see her smile than what's on her face now.

She clears her throat as our food is brought to the table, and while I'd love to get to know more about her childhood and her mom, the moment has passed. We dive into the meals, sharing what's in both baskets.

"I think the hushpuppies are my favorite," she tells me between bites.

"Agreed. It's all amazing, but these little suckers are to die for. I'll have to bring Annabelle sometime. She'd love it here," I say, wanting to invite her along, but not wanting to push her too far. It's a huge step being out just the two of us, and the last thing I need to do is remind her of the fact she's my daughter's teacher. Not that she'll forget that fact, but I'm sure she's not going to be in too much of a hurry to make our relationship known, especially while we're still in this school year.

"So, can I ask you something?"

She seems a bit hesitant with her question, so I quickly put her at ease. "Of course. Open book."

"You and Julia. You seem to have an unusual custody arrangement," she comments.

I nod and swallow the piece of popcorn shrimp I was chewing. "We do. We tried them all. It took quite a while to settle on this one. It's not easy to go a week without her, but it was the one that was the least stressful for her. Neither of us wanted to lose any time and there was a lot of bickering and stress for a while. But in the end, Annabelle came first and mattered the most, so we agreed to one week on, one off. We exchange every Saturday morning at eight and we split holidays."

"I'm sure it's not easy at all, but kudos to you both for putting her above your personal feelings."

"Like I said, it's not always easy, but she comes first. Always."

She gives me a small smile. "You're a great dad."

"She makes it easy. She's a great kid."

Ava nods. "She is."

When our food is gone and our check is paid, we slip from the booth and walk toward the exit. The sky is now dark, the air crisp and chilled, as we make our way to my truck. I hold the door while she climbs into the passenger seat, and the moment she's buckled in, I take the opportunity to lean in and kiss her lips. It's much quicker and gentler than I'd like to give her, but even though it's dark, we're not exactly in the location to make out like teenagers.

"I've had the best day," I tell her.

"Me too," she says softly, nibbling on her bottom lip.

My fingers instantly trace over the plump skin, my thumb gently pulling her lip from within her teeth. "When you do that, it makes me want to lick the exact spot your teeth just bit." My voice is deep and husky, the lust I feel for her evident with each word.

She blushes, of course, and smiles. "I might like that."

Flashing my own devious grin, I lower my voice and practically growl, "Oh, you'll most definitely like it, Miss Rutledge. I'll make sure of it." With a wink, I step back and close her door. When I reach the tailgate of my truck, I adjust my growing cock in my jeans, hoping it's not a painfully hard ride back to Pine Village.

Climbing into the driver's seat, we set out to return home, and unfortunately, the thirty or so minute drive back seems to only take about five. I'm pulling into her driveway way too soon, wishing I could drive somewhere else, just to spend a few more minutes in her company.

"I had an amazing time," she says, the moment I put the car into park.

"I'm glad. Next time you can pick where we go or what we do."

"And you can pick where we eat," she insists with a happy little grin on her face.

"Deal." Taking a deep breath and releasing my seat belt, I add, "I'll walk you up."

"Wait!" she practically hollers, catching me by surprise. I remain where I am, waiting to hear what she has to say.

But she doesn't say a damn word.

Ava releases her own seat belt and moves, climbing over the console and onto my lap. Before I can even process what's happening, she slams her mouth against mine, throwing caution to the wind, taking a risk, and kisses me.

And managing to steal not only my sanity, but my damn heart too in the process.

CHAPTER
seventeen

Ava

Don't ask me what possessed me to do what I'm doing right now, but I'm not fighting it. Not stopping it. Not asking.

Taking.

Stepping so far out of my comfort zone and just taking exactly what I want.

Gavin.

I want Gavin.

Despite the fact I'm his daughter's teacher. Despite the fact I have rules that have always kept me moving forward and between the lines my entire life. Despite the fact I've tried to fight my attraction to him.

I'm tired of pretending.

I'm tired of taking it slow.

I. Want. Gavin.

The kiss is powerful. It's consuming, intoxicating, and everything a kiss should be. My hands dive into his hair, and as his tongue delves into my mouth, caressing my own, all I can do is hang on and enjoy the ride. Gavin can kiss. My word, he's potent and pure sex. He makes me want to do things I've never done—*feel* things I've never felt. And the wild part is, I'm not scared.

I mean, I am, but not of him.

Never of him.

His large, rough hands gently slide under my sweatshirt and caress my back. But they don't stop there, I'm very much aware of the fact they're moving to my side. The right one keeps going around to my front. My grip on his brown hair tightens as his fingers dance across the bottom of my simple cotton bra. Then, those long fingers swipe across my hard nipple, and I almost detonate like a bomb.

My blood is swooshing through my veins, reckless and uninhibited. I've never felt as alive, as desired as I do right now. His erection is pressed firmly against my core, hard and ready, and my hips automatically rock against it, needing more.

"Gavin," I groan his name, a plea dripping from my lips.

"Take what you need, Ava," he murmurs, his words so heady and full of his own desire.

My body moves, chasing the need for release. He slides his tongue against mine, in and out of my mouth, mimicking sex to the same rhythm as his hips. Pleasure floods my entire body, my mind does nothing but focus on the way he makes me feel. Through my bra, he rolls my nipple between his index finger and thumb, and the wave of euphoria is almost too much. Especially when he grinds his hard length through my jeans against my clit.

Squeezing my eyes closed, I try to fight the onslaught of rapture, but it's no use. Not when he seems hell-bent on making me come right here, right now.

"Let go, beautiful," he murmurs against my lips.

The fierceness, the determination in his voice, paired with the expert manipulation of his hands, mouth, and groin, is enough to send me over the edge. I'm flying, riding the waves of my release, crying out his name as my hips rock against him. I can feel him tense beneath me, his hands pausing, fingers flexing.

Leaning forward, I rest my face against his headrest as the embarrassment starts to replace the bliss. *Did that really just happen? Sitting in my driveway, in his truck?*

"Ava," he murmurs, turning his head into my neck. "Look at me."

After a few breaths, I answer, "I'm not sure I want to."

He kisses my face and shifts me until we're looking at each other again. "Why are you embarrassed?" he asks, gently reaching up and caressing my cheek.

"Umm, well, that was...*not* something I've done before. Ever." I wait for the laughter, the smile, something. I'm a little on the inexperienced side when it comes to sex. I've *had* sex before, just not a lot.

He doesn't react the way I expect though. There's confusion in his eyes, but the hazel orbs are void of humor. "And that makes you embarrassed?"

I shrug, knowing this discussion has been coming, but feeling uncomfortable having it nonetheless. "Yeah. I mean, I've had sex and orgasms. Most of them done by my own hands," I state, watching as his eyes suddenly darken with desire and his cock starts to get hard once more.

"We're going to come back to that, because I definitely want to watch," he says before clearing his throat. "And as far as the other, you have no reason to be ashamed. If something felt good and we were both into it, what's to be embarrassed about? I know I'm not."

I wiggle, which causes his half-mast erection to jolt in excitement. "Sorry."

His grin is wolfish. "I've had that problem since last summer when I saw you at the bar. You were celebrating Hallie's birthday and wearing that amazing red dress."

My mouth might fall open just a bit. "You remember what I was wearing?"

"Of course I do. I couldn't take my eyes off you. And I hope this confession doesn't make me sound too much like a horny dog, but I jacked off for a week straight with those images of you in that dress."

My face flames redder than my hair and my hand covers my mouth. "Really?"

"Totally." Leaning forward and pressing his mouth against my ear, he whispers, "Sexiest. Fucking. Dress. Ever."

My heart is pounding in my chest as I stare into his heated eyes. "I wore it on New Year's Eve," I blurt out like the dork I am.

"I figured. It took me a bit to figure out it was the red dress with a black sweater over the top, but rest assured, the result was the same. Jacked off before I could fall asleep." His confession is heady and does wonders for my confidence level and calming my nerves. "You are the sexiest, most beautiful woman I've ever seen, and the fact you haven't dry humped anyone before actually makes me happy, because not only was it a first I get to share with you, but I don't have to kill some poor asshole because, apparently, I'm a jealous fucker when it comes to you. I really like you."

A smile cracks across my lips as I lean forward and press them to his. "I really like you too."

Again, he strokes his finger over my bottom lip. "Good. And I don't want you to ever feel embarrassed when we're together. Every moment I spend with you is perfect, because it's just you and me. We're getting to know each other and doing things that make us both feel good. There's nothing wrong with either, especially when I get to watch you come undone the way you just did."

Feeling myself relax, I hug him as best as I can, considering our positions in the truck. "You're too good to be true," I whisper.

"No, I'm not. I'm just a man doing his best to learn from past mistakes and do right by the people around me, especially those I care about."

You couldn't pry my smile off my face with a putty knife. Glancing down, I notice the wet spot on the front of his jeans. "Ummm…"

He snorts, looking down after noticing where my eyes are. "Occupational hazard?" he jokes.

Knowing how messy I feel right now in my own pants, I can't imagine what he's dealing with. "Do you want to come inside? You know, get cleaned up?"

His smile is the sweetest, most gentle one I've ever seen. "Yes," he says, placing a chaste kiss on my lips. "Which is why I'm not."

There must be confusion written all over my face.

"We're not quite there yet, despite what might have just happened, but we're close. When I take you to bed, it's all night, Ava. You and me with nothing between us, literally and figuratively."

"I want that too," I murmur.

"And we'll get there. I'm not rushing this. I'm not rushing *you*."

My lips find his once more in a leisurely kiss. I realize I could kiss this man all day, every day, and never tire. He has the most amazing mouth and evokes feelings I've never experienced.

When we finally pull apart, it's with a sigh. "I'll walk you up."

Again, I glance down at the wet spot between us. "I'm sure that wouldn't be very comfortable. I can manage."

He opens his mouth, most likely to argue, but I silence him with a finger to his lips. "I'll be fine."

Seeming annoyed, he insists, "Text me when you get inside, and be sure to lock the door."

"I will," I agree, reaching for my purse.

Carefully, I climb off his lap and out the door, only to be stopped the moment my feet hit the pavement. "Thank you for an amazing day. And just so you know, this was definitely a date date."

Nodding, I concur. "It was definitely a date date."

Pressing one final kiss to his lips, I make my way to my house, smiling the entire way.

By the time I'm inside, my panties are soaked from my orgasm, but it doesn't stop me from spinning around in a circle in elation. I quickly fire off a text message, realizing Gavin is still sitting in my driveway, most likely waiting for the sign to leave. His reply is instant and makes me smile once more.

Gavin: Good night, beautiful. Talk to you very soon.

Best date date ever.

"I have a question for you," Ellie says the moment she reaches my table.

"Well, good evening to you too," I tease as she delivers a glass of water.

"Do you want something besides water?" she asks.

"This is perfect, thank you."

"Can I put in an order?" she offers.

I turn and look at the specials board, happy to see Saul's bacon-wrapped meatloaf listed. "You still have some left?"

She nods. "He's been making double batches lately, so we've actually been making it through the day."

"Green beans?" I nod as she scurries off to the kitchen to put in my order. When that's done, she takes off her apron and drops down onto the bench across from me. "What a day," she says, leaning her head back against the wall behind the booth.

"We can do this another time," I suggest.

Ellie waves off my comment. "It's okay. TD should be here shortly, and then we'll head home. He had team lift and a leadership council meeting for the team," she informs me, referring to the football team her husband coaches.

"If you're sure," I start, hating to keep her here if she's ready to go home and put her feet up.

"I'm sure. The reason I asked you to stop by is to see if you were interested in helping me with a baby shower. Well, two baby showers, actually," she says, her eyes bright with excitement.

"I'd love to help," I insist without needing to hear a single detail.

"Really? Oh, thank you so much. Both Blair and Hallie said they'd help throw the other's shower, but that just seems silly. I mean, I know they're best friends and sisters-in-law, but they shouldn't have to lift a finger to do anything, especially if we combine their showers into one."

"Oh, I like that," I tell her, taking a drink of water.

"At first, I wasn't sure about that. They both deserve their own day to be showered, but once Hallie suggested it, the idea didn't seem so bad."

"Those two have been best friends forever," I agree, knowing they'd love to have their showers together. Their babies—who will be cousins—are due a month apart.

"Agreed. Patience offered to host the showers at their house, but I was afraid that might be too uncomfortable for Blair's mom."

Blair's mom and dad split up the summer between our junior and senior year of high school, thanks to her dad's affair with his much younger nurse, Patience. Once Frank and Donna's divorce was finalized, Donna and Blair moved to Merrillville, Indiana, while Frank and Patience got married one week after the divorce. They also had a daughter, Aggie, who is eight now, and even though it's taken a long time to get to a place of common ground, that wasn't always the case, so I can understand Ellie's worry where the exes are concerned.

"We could rent the community center," I suggest.

"I think that might be the easiest," she agrees. "I called this morning to see what dates are available next month. February twenty-sixth is a Sunday."

My brain starts to do the math. "Yikes. That doesn't give us a lot of time." About six weeks to be exact.

"No, but we can totally do it. We just need to confirm the venue and date. Once we have that, we can finalize invites and get those in the mail. Blair and Hallie are both working on a registry, and what I was hoping you'd help me with is the decorations. You're so crafty and creative, I think you could come up with some cute stuff."

I nod. "I'd love to," I tell her enthusiastically. "Blair is having a girl, so that's easy. The tricky one is going to be Hallie, since they want to be surprised."

"Hallie and Logan are doing a forest animals theme in very neutral, light colors, and Gabe and Blair are doing everything pink and girly," she confirms.

"Well, I'll figure something out," I state, ready to go home and start planning. "I can help with invites and whatever else you need."

"Thank you. All the moms have volunteered to help too, so we'll have plenty of hands." There are several, including Donna, Blair's mom, Patience, her stepmom, Debbie, Hallie and Gabe's mom, and Patty, Logan's mom. Not to mention the grandmas.

"Well, you tell me what you want me to do, and I'll do it."

The bell chimes, signaling a server to the kitchen for a completed order. When Ellie glances over there and sees the to-go bag, she jumps up and goes to retrieve it. "Here's your food."

"Thank you," I reply, pulling out a twenty from my wallet. "Keep the change."

She gives me a grateful smile. "Thanks. I'll call and book the community center tomorrow and text you."

"Are we sure Hallie and Blair are available that day?"

"They both told me they'd make whatever date we picked work. Gabe may have to be on-call for the clinic, but he promised to cover for Blair so she had nothing on her calendar," she adds.

"All right, well, let's get to planning a double baby shower."

She grins as I stand up and give her a hug. When she pulls back, I whisper, "How are you doing?"

It's no secret Ellie and TD have been trying to have a baby since they got married last summer, and unfortunately, it hasn't happened for them yet. I know she's anxious and worried, since we're all in our mid to late thirties now. Pregnancies are considered high risk, and statistically speaking, the more time that passes without getting pregnant, the harder it becomes.

She shrugs. "I'm okay. TD keeps telling me to stop stressing, but that's easier said than done. I just...what if I can't give him a baby? We wasted so many years being just friends, and now that we're married, what if I can't get pregnant? He wants to be a dad so bad."

Food forgotten, I step forward and wrap my arms around her. "He *is* a dad. He's been Brody's dad for most of that boy's life. It doesn't matter what name is on the birth certificate or whose blood runs through his veins. TD is the only dad who matters to Brody."

"I know," Ellie whispers, her eyes filling with tears.

"And if and when you're able to have a baby, he will be the best dad ever, I know it. I also know he would happily spend the rest of his life just the three of you. That man only needs you to be happy, Ellie. You and Brody."

Tears start to fall down her cheeks. "I know. He tells me that all the time."

"Believe him," I insist. The bell over the door chimes, but neither of us pays any attention. "He loves you so much. Always has."

"Ellie."

We turn to see TD making his way toward us. He's zeroed in on the fact she's crying, and the look on his face is part pain, part concern, as if the mere sight of her with tears streaming down her cheeks could bring him to his knees.

He's such a good guy.

"Hi," she whispers, smiling as he approaches and takes her in his arms.

"What's wrong?" he asks, looking her over after he kisses her lips.

"I'm just being silly. Girly emotions and all that stuff," she says, trying to wave off his concern.

As realization sets in, he pulls her against his broad chest and holds her close. "You ready to go home, love?"

"Yes. Let me grab my bag from the office," Ellie replies, swiping at the remaining moisture on her cheeks and giving him a small grin. "Be right back."

As soon as she leaves the table to retrieve her bag, TD turns to me with pain in his eyes. "This is killing her."

"I know," I reply quietly, not really knowing what else to say.

"We'll keep trying. We'll try until we're eighty if we have to."

I don't have the heart to tell him that probably won't work. Once menopause sets in, their chances of having a baby the old-fashioned way will come to an end. "Is this double baby shower going to be too much for her?"

TD sighs. "I asked her if it was necessary, and she said it was. She insisted if the shoes were on the other foot, both Blair and Hallie would demand on hosting her shower."

I nod, knowing he's right. "I'll do whatever I can to help. If you think it's too much for her, let me know and I'll take over."

"Thanks, Ava," he says, the relief evident in his voice, as Ellie appears from the back.

"Ready to go," she says, slipping under his extended arm. "I'll text you after I get the confirmation."

"Sounds good."

I watch as they leave together, feeling their overwhelming love for one another, as well as the added worries of not conceiving yet. I know he wants to help and protect her, which is one of the things I admire most about TD. He's such a great man, father to Brody, and husband.

He reminds me a bit of Gavin.

Speaking of the amazing man, I grab my to-go order of Sal's meatloaf and head for home. We haven't spoken since he dropped me off last night, but he's all I've thought about. Throughout the day, while I'm teaching my class, he randomly pops into my head at the most inopportune times. I can't help but wonder if he's thinking about me as often as I've been thinking about him. Day and night, Gavin Pierson has taken over my every thought, and I just don't know what to do about it.

I'm afraid, at this point, there's nothing I can do.

He's in my brain—and on my heart—like a tattoo.

And what's surprising is the fact I like him there.

GAVIN

It's been about two weeks.

Two whole weeks in which I've only been able to steal texts, late-night phone calls, and one surprise drop-off to her house when she was resting. After our date to St. Paul with the rock climbing and dinner, we planned to sneak away Wednesday night, but that was foiled when she got sick. She spent three days at home, completely under the weather, which was why I made the surprise drop-off on Thursday night. I wanted to go in. I wanted to take care of her and hold her in my arms, but I refrained. Instead, I left her blue Gatorade, ibuprofen, chicken noodle soup, and Kleenex.

By the time she was feeling better, it was Saturday and the kickoff to my week with Annabelle. Unfortunately, by mid-afternoon on Saturday, my daughter started feeling bad. This started the cycle of sickness that then passed from her to me. I tried to stick it out at work but ended up taking two days off myself. Ava ended up reciprocating, dropping off a homemade potato soup, along with electrolytes and cold medicine while Annabelle was sleeping. I wanted to go outside, to see her and hold her in my arms, but I didn't want to risk reinfecting her with this aggressive sickness that seemed to make its way through the streets and buildings of Pine Village at a rapid pace.

Fortunately, it's now Saturday again, almost two weeks after our date, and my daughter is with her mother. I have big plans for tonight. Ava will be coming over shortly for dinner, and we're planning to watch a new documentary just released on a streaming site. It's the first time she'll be here, in my house, and I honestly can't wait. I've made arrangements for her to pull her car into my garage bay, so nosy neighbors won't be staring at her car, trying to figure out who's at my house.

As the clock approaches five, I turn my attention to watching the driveway. I told her I'd open the door, so the moment I spot her slowly pulling in, I press the button on the automatic door opener by my back door. Then, I head out to greet her, anxious to steal my first kiss in almost two weeks.

"Hi," I say the moment her door opens.

She gives me a smile that makes my heart beat a little faster and my cock start to thicken in my jeans. She takes my offered hand and starts to climb from her little SUV. "Hello."

There it is.

That faint blush I can't get enough of. I knew I missed her, but seeing her now, pulling her into my arms, makes me realize to what extent. The moment my lips connect with hers, I feel...lighter. Freer. Happier than I have any right to be.

"I've been needing that for almost two weeks," I confess, wanting to deepen the kiss, but knowing this isn't the right spot. "Let's go inside," I add, shutting her car door and reaching for her hand.

"Hold on," she replies, opening the back door and pulling a container from the seat. "I made cookies."

"Chocolate chip?"

"Is there any other kind?" she teases with a grin. In one of our many text conversations, we discussed sweet treats, and both concur there's nothing better than fresh, chewy chocolate chip cookies. Except maybe warm ones with a scoop of vanilla ice cream on top.

"Come on," I say, pressing the button to lower the garage door.

"How about a quick tour while dinner finishes?" I offer the moment coats are hung up and boots are off.

"Absolutely," she agrees, setting the container of cookies on the counter by the Crock-Pot and following me through the house.

"You did these cabinets, didn't you?" she asks before we even leave the first room.

"I did."

"They're stunning," she replies, touching the smooth oak wood.

"I love using white oak, but wanted to avoid the traditional honey coloring, so I used a darker Jacobean stain with a lighter backsplash to add contrast."

"Beautiful," she insists. "You do amazing work."

"Thank you." I clear my throat and take her hand once more. "Come on. We've got more to cover."

She points out her favorite features in each room we visit, and it's not lost on me they're all things I've built. Bookcases, Annabelle's bed, tables, and more. All projects I've worked on in my free time, mostly when Annabelle was with her mom. Creating stuff was the perfect way to keep my mind busy while I was alone, and even though I don't consider myself a furniture builder by any stretch of the imagination, I'm proud of the pieces I've created.

Construction is my passion.

Furniture is a fun hobby.

When we reach the final room on the tour, I stand back and allow her to enter my bedroom first. She walks in slowly, taking it all in for the first time. The massive California king-sized bed takes up most of the space, and I can't help but picture her lying in it. With me. Naked.

Ava walks to the dresser, where I have a photograph of Annabelle and me from when she was little. She holds the picture, smiling at the love I always feel from the image. It's my favorite one, taken when my daughter was about eighteen months. She's got a big, drooly, toothy grin on her face, and my head is thrown back in laughter. I don't even remember what she did or said, but I'll never forget the way I felt in that moment.

When she returns the frame to the dresser, she takes in the wall of art, as I like to call it. Things Annabelle's made for me over the years are taped to the wall opposite my bed. Obviously, I can't save every drawing or piece of art she creates, but I do keep my favorites. At first, I'd put them on the fridge, but that space was quickly filled, so when Annabelle was in second grade, she suggested I hang them on my bare wall so I could see them every day. In the last three years, that tradition has continued, and my wall is now home to a few dozen of her best art pieces.

"I love this," Ava murmurs, taking her time and scanning each picture.

"I wanted to keep some of her work, so she suggested we hang them here. We add to it a few times throughout the year."

She turns and gazes at me, her eyes full of awe and excitement. "You're such a great dad."

I shrug casually, even though the compliment is the greatest I could receive. "Thank you. I try hard."

"It shows," she replies.

"There's a walk-in closet and a bathroom through there," I tell her, pointing to the two other doors in the room.

"You have a great home," she states, turning her attention back to me.

"Thanks. It's quiet and a bit lonely when she's with her mom, but when she's here, it's filled with laughter and happiness." I keep my feet rooted to the floor instead of going to her and taking her in my arms the way I want.

She takes a few steps toward me. "I couldn't help but notice how big your bed is." A faint pink coloring stains her cheeks.

"I like to spread out," I tell her, now vividly picturing her curled up in my blankets.

"Me too," she confesses, turning her attention to the bed. "Though, I've never really had much opportunity to try the whole cuddle thing, so I don't know if I prefer that."

"No? Maybe we should try it sometime. I've always preferred my space, but maybe if I had the right cuddle partner, I wouldn't mind snuggling close."

She's fighting a grin. "Makes sense. We could give it a test sometime, you know, to see what all the fuss is about. Come to think of it, I don't have anything going on later tonight."

My cock is now fully erect and ready to go. "No?" I'm able to keep my excitement and anticipation out of that one word.

"Nope," she says, stepping into my personal space and placing her hands on my chest. "I might have brought an overnight bag."

My dick kicks at my zipper, desperately trying to get out. "Really? I don't recall seeing it," I reply, wrapping my arms around her waist and pulling her against me.

She lifts her shoulders gently. "I wasn't sure you were on board for a potential snuggle buddy tonight, so I left it in my trunk."

Placing my hands on her arms, I hold her gaze as I say, "I'm always on board, but not until you're ready."

Going up on her tiptoes, she brushes her mouth against mine. "I'm ready."

My heart is trying to burst from my chest, and my cock is all but pulling a Kool-Aid Man from its denim confines, but as excited as I am, I'm doing this right. "All right, let's table this discussion for a bit later. First up, dinner. Then, that true crime documentary. What happens after, happens. We'll talk about it when the time comes."

Something flashes through her eyes, but before I can dissect the look, it's gone. "So what did you make for dinner?" she asks, taking a step back and putting space between us. I hate it but know it's necessary. Otherwise, I'm liable to throw my timetable right out the window and take her to bed right now.

"I cheated and pulled something from the freezer," I confess, taking her hand and leading her back to the kitchen.

"Well, it smells amazing, whatever it is."

"Lasagna and garlic bread. My mom insists on making freezer meals all winter long, and I benefit from her obsession. I was going to make something myself, but this seemed simpler and allows me to spend more time with you without worrying about cooking. Plus, let's be honest, my mom's meals—even her freezer ones—are much better than anything I could fix," I say. "Have a seat at the table, while I finish up. Are you thirsty? I have white wine, water, juice, and Sprite."

"I'll have a Sprite for now. Maybe some wine later," she replies.

While I grab the French bread I prepped before she arrived and place it in the preheated oven, I take out two cans of Sprite and put them on the table, where two place settings are ready.

"Oh, how was the movie last night with Annabelle? She was so excited to go see it," Ava asks, opening her drink and taking a sip.

"She loved it. I never would have thought she'd be so into the *Ghostbusters* series. She loves the new ones, and when she heard the original was turning forty and coming back to theaters for the anniversary, she insisted on going to see it."

"I love it. *Ghostbusters* was one of my favorites when I was young. My dad and I used to watch it a lot. That and *The Karate Kid*."

"Classics," I reply, pulling the baked bread and lasagna out of the oven. Carefully, I take them both to the table and cut servings. "I was a huge fan of *Days of Thunder* and *Top Gun* when I was little." I scoop a piece of lasagna for Ava and take two for myself. The bread I cut into thin strips, which is Annabelle's preferred way of eating it. It takes longer to cut but it's so much easier to eat.

"Oh, my dad definitely watched those. This looks and smells so good," she replies, placing a napkin on her lap.

Joining her at the table, I prepare to dig in. "Let's eat."

I'm not paying an ounce of attention to the show. Don't get me wrong, I'm staring at the TV, but instead of watching the drama unfold on the screen, I'm thinking about the woman currently sitting beside me, snuggled into my side, and resting comfortably beneath my arm. We fit together so easily, naturally, contentedly.

I could get used to this feeling every night at the end of a long day.

About an hour into the program, Ava shifts against me. "Gavin?"

"Yeah?"

"Are you watching this?"

I open my mouth to lie, to tell her I am, but that's not what comes out. "Well..."

Our eyes meet, and I can not only see the fire blazing in those brown orbs, but I can feel their heat. She's moving, crawling on my lap and straddling my thighs, just as she did in my truck a couple weeks back. Only this time, we have plenty of freedom to move. "I wasn't really watching it either," she confesses.

"Why not? I thought you really wanted to see it," I reply, my hands flexing against her hips as I hold her in place. I'm certain she can feel my quickly growing erection pressed between her thighs.

"I was, but then..."

"Then..." I repeat, wanting to hear her say the words. The last thing I want is to make wrong assumptions, so if she wants this thing between us to move to the next step, she's going to have to ask.

She exhales slowly and whispers, "And then I was snuggled against you, and I couldn't stop thinking about that bed."

The corner of my mouth ticks. "My bed, huh? What about it?" I ask.

Ava rocks her hips, grinding on my cock, that invisible thread tethering us together tightening. "It looked so big and inviting when we were in there earlier. Perfect for cuddling."

Her short nails dig into my chest through my long-sleeved T-shirt. "Definitely worth exploring," I bite out through gritted teeth as she wiggles on my lap.

Leaning forward, she brushes her lips across my own. "I'm ready, Gavin. I don't want to wait any longer."

"Are you sure?"

"Positive," she murmurs before pressing her mouth firmly against mine and opening.

My tongue slips inside, tasting, as it glides with hers, and my hands cup her ass, holding on tight as she rocks against me. She whimpers as our movements create sweet friction between us, driving us both absolutely wild. And while I'd love nothing more than to hear her come, feel her let go above me, I have more planned for the rest of our night.

Pulling back, I ask again, "You're sure? We can do other things without sex."

Her fingers slip into my hair as she presses her chest firmly against mine. "I want to be with you, Gavin. I've thought about nothing but feeling you inside of me all day. Well, all week really."

I can't help but smile at her confession. "I like this bolder version of you, Miss Rutledge."

She gives me a sassy little grin herself. "I'm becoming rather fond of her myself, Mr. Pierson."

And with that, I'm moving. I stand up, holding her against my chest. Ava wraps her legs around my waist as I head toward my bedroom. The moment I cross the threshold, I walk to my bed and gently lay her on top of my comforter. She looks like a fucking goddess, her red hair splayed out across my pillow and her breasts rising and falling as she breathes deeply. Her eyes are filled with desire, with hope, excitement, and maybe a hint of nervousness.

I know I have to make her feel at ease, to feel good, give her pleasure, and there's nothing I want more than to do all of the above. To be the man who makes her forget her own name and leaves her completely spent and boneless. To make her come so hard, she'll never remember what it was like to be with anyone but me.

I'm the man for the job.

"May I take these off?" I ask, waiting for her to nod yes before I remove her clothes. I start with her jeans and sweater, leaving her lying on my bed in her light blue bra and panty set. They're silky and soft, with a thin layer of lace over the top, and I've never seen anything sexier in my life.

I get on my knees and lean over her. She watches me with wide eyes as I lower my head and kiss directly between her breasts. She shudders a breath as I kiss my way up her neck. Her scent wraps around me, a mixture of her desire and a subtle floral lotion. I keep my mouth moving, kissing back down her chest. When I return to her breasts, I meet her gaze and wait in silent question. She nods without hesitation, giving me permission to continue my exploration.

Gently, I pull the material to the side, exposing dark, hard nipples. They're small and perfect and make my mouth water. I swipe my tongue over the first peak, watching her shiver. Then, I draw her nipple into my mouth and suck. She arches off my bed, moaning, as her hands dive into my hair, anchoring her to me.

I lap at the first nipple before giving the second a little attention too. "Please, Gavin," she mutters with a gasp. "Please."

"Do you want some relief, beautiful?"

"Yes, please," she begs, drawing out the last word as if it had four syllables.

I move between her spread legs and lie on my stomach. She's wet, the panties soaked with her arousal, and all I want to do now is taste it. Taste *her.* I feel like I've waited a lifetime for this moment, for the chance to be with this woman.

Now, we're here.

Her and me.

Together.

And I know I'm never going to be the same.

CHAPTER
nineteen

Ava

I'm barely breathing as I wait for what's to come. Every moment of being with Gavin so far has been mind-altering, and we've only just begun. The anticipation is almost too much to bear.

He pushes aside my panties, exposing a part of me only a few have ever seen. I wasn't kidding when I said I didn't have much experience, but with Gavin, I'm not scared. I'm not afraid to be with him, to give him my body for pleasure. It just means only a couple have ever seen me naked, and none have ever been as close as he is right now.

But I don't have time to dwell on the fact no one has ever gone down on me before, because Gavin is there, licking my clit and causing my mind to go completely blank. All I can do is feel, and my word, does it feel amazing. He sucks my clit into his mouth, almost causing me to jackknife off the bed. A groan fills the room, and I'm completely oblivious to the fact it came from me.

I gasp when I feel one finger press into me. My muscles are tight but slowly start to relax as he slides in and out. He laps at my clit, licking and sucking it between his warm lips. A part of me wants to cover myself up, but I refuse to let my shyness get the best of me right now. All I want to do is feel.

And let go.

My body starts to tighten like a coil, and when he adds a second finger, the tension and pleasure is almost too much to take. My nipples ache, my limbs are taut, and my orgasm is building. With his mouth on my clit, his fingers buried inside me, he reaches up and pinches one of my hard nipples. The sensations are overwhelming as my hips rock, seeking more.

No, *needing* more.

Gavin hums against my swollen flesh. "Let go, Ava. I can feel how close you are. Just. Let. Go."

His words help push me the rest of the way over the edge. My release explodes through me, blinding my sight and sending me orbiting through space. It feels like I'm floating, my body weightless, as waves of pleasure wash over me. I cry out as he draws out every ounce of euphoria from me until I'm left spent and boneless on top of his bed.

I feel him shift, removing his fingers and crawling up my body. He slides his lips across my chin, my cheek, until they finally land on my lips. He tastes like me, and while it's new, I don't completely hate it. In fact, it's a little...erotic.

"More?" he murmurs against my mouth, his big, warm hand slipping up my side and landing on my breast.

"Yes," I whisper, arching my chest into his palm and groaning as he swipes his thumb over my sensitive nipple, rekindling the pleasure.

"Are you sure?"

Forcing my eyes open, I stare into his lust-drunk gaze. I take a page from his playbook and run my finger over his bottom lip. He puckers, kissing the tip before sucking it into his mouth. His tongue swirls around my finger, causing warmth to flood my core once more. "More than sure, Gavin. I need you."

His smile is slow and sultry as he turns his attention to his bedside table. He pulls a new box of condoms out of the drawer and rips the first one out of the package. "I bought these with you in mind. I don't want you to think I had any other reason to use them."

"I trust you," I insist, understanding the immediate truth in the statement.

He reaches down and cups my jaw. "I will never break that trust, Ava."

He climbs from the bed and starts to remove his clothes. In the past, the act of disrobing always seemed to be done in total darkness, but I'm grateful for a little light coming into Gavin's bedroom. Watching him take off his clothes is like watching the sunset or ocean waves crash against the sandy beach. It's beautiful, mesmerizing, and heady. His chest is a work of art, but not as if he spends an obscene amount of time in the gym. You can tell he takes care of his body, both with a physical job and the occasional workout in a gym setting.

Then, his hands move to his jeans. The belt comes off first, followed quickly by a flick of the button and lowering of the zipper. He shimmies out of his jeans, standing in front of me in a pair of boxer briefs. They're tented in front of him, his erection standing tall and proud and ready. My mouth waters at the sight, and all I can think about is getting my hands and mouth on him.

As if knowing exactly where my mind is at, he says, "Later, beautiful. Right now, I need to be inside your pussy. I want to feel it gripping my cock when you come a second time."

I shiver at the heat in his voice, at the naughtiness dripping from his words. The moment he drops his boxers, my mouth goes dry. How in the hell is that supposed to fit inside me? Seriously, I'm having my doubts on the logistics of that monster fitting without tearing me apart.

He moves toward me, touching the side of my face. "Don't worry, Ava. I've got you."

I nod, my tongue heavy and dry in my mouth. With wide eyes, I take in the act of him sheathing himself in protection before climbing back onto the bed. My legs wrap around his hips.

Tenderly, he takes my lips in a slow, sensual kiss as he shifts his weight and lines himself up at my entrance. "Yes?" he asks, making eye contact as he waits for my final confirmation.

"Yes," I assure him.

He gently starts to enter me. The stretch is...wow. Intense. Full. A little painful. "Deep breath, sweetheart," he murmurs against my ear. Then, he trails his lips across the tender skin just behind my ear and runs his tongue over the rapidly beating pulse point on my neck. "That's it, Ava. You feel so fucking good."

My back arches on its own as he pushes deeper, filling me completely. My nipples brush against the coarse hair on his chest. The contact sends shock waves of pleasure jolting through me. I hitch my ankles higher on his hips, opening myself up wider. That slight change in angle hits different.

"Oh God," I mutter.

It's like a caress, but so much better.

He kisses my neck, all while his hips continue to move. Masterfully. I can feel a second release building. My hands start to move, exploring his skin, caressing his back, shoulders, and chest. When he claims my lips once more, there's an urgency in the kiss. The heat pours from us, that sweet ache from when he first entered me completely gone. It's replaced with a drive for more, a need only Gavin can fulfill.

His hips start to buck against me, as if he's lost his ability to control his movements. He thrusts forward, hitting this magical spot deep inside me. With every stroke, I cry out, rocking against him and racing toward the finish line.

"I need you to come again, Ava," he insists.

"I'm so...close," I mutter with a gasp.

"Thank Christ. I don't know how much longer I can hang on. You feel too fucking good," he tells me, pistoning his hips forward.

Stroking my G-spot, the dam bursts once more and I'm flying. His name falls from my lips as my body grips his erection so tightly it triggers spasms in my limbs. "Fuck," he groans, going completely still before he slams forward, grinding himself against me and riding out his own release.

I feel him go tight, his erection swelling as he comes. His mouth smashes against mine, his tongue slips inside as he rides out his orgasm. His continual movement just draws mine out until I fall limp against the bed, sated and spent.

Gavin hums in satisfaction as he rolls to his side, taking me with him. We're pressed chest to chest, my right leg still thrown over his hip, as we both try to catch our breath. "You okay?" he whispers, turning his focus on me.

"I'm excellent. You?"

He grins gently. "I'm perfect. Did I hurt you?" he asks, running his thumb over my bottom lip.

"No. I feel...amazing."

"You *do* feel pretty amazing," he insists with a cocky smirk, running his hand down my arm. He sobers quickly. "I should probably go take care of this condom."

I nod. "And I need to use the bathroom."

"You go first," he offers, but I shake my head.

"No, you. I can wait a few extra minutes."

"All right." He leans over and kisses my forehead. "I'll be quick."

He's up and shutting the door to the en suite bathroom, leaving me lying in the middle of his big bed. My muscles are weak as I stretch, and you couldn't wipe the smile off my face. I can't believe we just had amazing sex.

No, check that.

I *can* believe it, because everything seems *different* when it comes to Gavin. He's so much more attentive and caring than the few guys I've been with in my past, so it doesn't surprise me the sex would be phenomenal.

My history with men is pretty limited. I didn't lose my virginity until I was in college, and that experience was more about two people who had never engaged in sex, fumbling through the act. It wasn't pleasurable, that's for sure.

My second experience was also in college. It was with my then-boyfriend, Colton. He was a soccer player in my English class, and we paired up for studying. He wasn't the typical jock, caring just as much about his classes and degree as he did perfecting his craft on the field, so when he asked me out, I readily agreed. We dated for several months before I finally agreed to sleep with him. It was better than my first time, but wasn't what all the girls had been bragging about. Colton was fumbly and...well, fast. The whole thing was over in about two minutes, and all he wanted to hear was how good he was.

Colton was the guy I was with the night of the college party. You know, the infamous keg stand photo? He convinced me to go to this party at a fraternity one Saturday night. It's not that I didn't like parties, but the ones at the frat houses weren't my scene. I much preferred hanging out in someone's dorm, a group of friends having a few drinks and talking. Frat parties are full of obscenely drunk people, too-loud music, and bad decisions.

Case in point, Colton did a keg stand. It didn't look fun at all, really. First off, I'm not a fan of beer, and why someone would find enjoyment in chugging it upside down is beyond me. Once he did it, he begged me to. I didn't want to, but everyone was watching and chanting my name. I gave in to peer pressure, just to shut them all up.

I hated every second of it. It was nasty and it went up my nose, but everyone cheered when it was over, so what harm did it do?

A lot.

Seven years ago, a photo from that night appeared on social media. There I was, performing my one and only keg stand, and yes, I was only twenty. Word spread quickly around town. The schoolteacher who was caught underage drinking. It didn't matter if it was nine years later or that it hadn't happened again. It was as if I was the only person in this town to ever engage in underaged drinking while off at college. In the court of public opinion, I was a terrible person, and probably providing alcohol to my young fifth-grade students.

It was ridiculous.

And almost ruined me, both professionally and personally.

Over the years, I've dated a few other guys, but only two of them made it to the bedroom. I've just never felt that connection. The soul deep connection you feel clean down to your toes. The feeling you get when you're with someone you know is special, and how you can't remember what your life was like before you met them.

Gavin's image fills my mind, and I smile.

The door opens, and despite the fact I'd much rather stay curled up on his bed, I need to use the bathroom. I always go after sex, thanks to the insistence of my gynecologist back when I was sixteen. Urinary tract infection and all that, and even though I wasn't having sex at that time in my life, the message she shared stuck with me.

I climb from the bed, my legs feeling a little wobbly. As much as I'd rather stand in the middle of the room and stare at the breathtakingly beautiful naked man in front of me, I need to take care of my own business. Plus, I'm not one who usually stands in the middle of a room without clothes on and lets someone gawk at me. Even though it doesn't exactly feel like gawking when it's Gavin. There's so much appreciation and desire in his eyes.

"I'll be...just a few minutes," I blurt out, quickly walking past him and closing myself inside the bathroom.

The first thing I do is take a look at myself in the mirror. My cheeks are rosy and appear to have a scruff burn, which makes me grin. I study my appearance, from my tussled hair to my smudged mascara and find myself...glowing. Is that what good sex does to a person, because if so, I like it.

A lot.

I use the toilet and wash my hands. Only when that's done and there's nothing left for me to do but return to where Gavin waits, I get nervous. Am I supposed to leave now? I brought a bag, but maybe he's not the type to do sleepovers. I know he talked about cuddling and whatnot, but that could have been just that. Talk.

Knowing I can't just stand in here and fret, I slowly open the door and flip off the light. Gavin is sitting in bed, the bedside lamp on and illuminating the room. His eyes follow my every move as I make my way toward him. It's not lost on me the fact I'm still naked, wishing I had a shirt or something to cover up with.

"Don't do that," he says.

"Do what?" I stop in front of the bed.

"Worry about being naked. You're stunning."

My cheeks flush as I avert my gaze. "I, uh, I'm not sure what happens next."

"Well," he starts, flipping open the comforter beside him, "next, you climb into bed with me, and we give the whole snuggling thing a try. It's important to see if it rivals spreading out."

My heart does this weird swooning thing as I watch him. "I wasn't sure if we were doing the whole spend the night part."

His eyebrows creep up. "Why wouldn't we? Plus, you brought a bag, right? I'll go get it from your car in the morning, since you're not going to need the clothes or whatever's in there until tomorrow."

I slowly walk to the available side of the bed and slip beneath the blankets. As soon as I'm there, he throws the comforter back over me, bathing me in warmth, and then moves in close. We shift to our sides, his front pressed to my back, and yes, his erection is already growing hard between us.

"This is nice," he whispers, kissing the side of my head before getting comfortable on the pillow we're now sharing.

"It is," I reply with a yawn.

"I've had the best time tonight," he murmurs, his deep voice soothing and calming as my eyelids grow heavy.

"Me too. I don't want to be presumptuous, but I'd like to do it again."

He flexes his hips, pressing himself into the cleft of my rear. "Oh, we will *definitely* do it again."

Snickering, I glance over my shoulder and hold his gaze. "That's a given, but I was referring to the entire night. The dinner, hanging out, and yes, the sex."

Cue the massive blush.

"All of the above, sweetheart. I've loved every moment I've spent with you, and I want to keep going. I want more moments."

Grinning, I snuggle into his warm arms. "I'd like that too."

"Good. Tomorrow we can deal with figuring out what's next. Tonight, we're going to fall asleep together. Having you in my arms is pretty much my favorite thing in the world." Before I can comment, he reiterates, "Wait, let me correct. My favorite thing is holding you in my arms *after* I've been inside you. Excuse my bluntness, but your pussy is fucking magic."

That familiar warmth spreads all over my body as the memories reappear. Even though it only happened a short time ago, I'm certain it's been a night I won't ever forget.

"Good night, Ava," he whispers, kissing my cheek before resettling on the pillow.

"Night, Gavin. Thank you for an amazing night."

"You're welcome, even though there's no need to thank me. It was amazing because of you, not me."

I could argue, because it was both of us, not just one, but I let it go. We're both exhausted, and sleep is calling. Closing my eyes, I wiggle deeper into his embrace as I feel myself relax against him. His breathing is slow and even, and although I'm certain he's not sleeping yet, I like this.

I like being in his arms.

I like lying naked together.

I like the way he makes me feel.

Yeah, there's definitely something to this whole snuggling thing.

It's spectacular.

GAVIN

I slowly rouse from the best night of sleep I've ever had. My body is warm and comfortable, my cock hard and wet.

Wait, what?

I crack open my eyes and find Ava kneeling beside me, holding my dick. Her tongue swirls around the head before slowly lowering her mouth around it. She goes down about halfway before coming back up. My eyes are riveted in place, glued to the action in front of me. Ava seems a bit uncertain, but that's not stopping her from taking what she wants. She's told me she doesn't have much experience sexually, so to watch her come out of her shell, to explore what feels good and what she likes, is a heady feeling.

She takes a bit more of my cock into her mouth, adding just a touch of suction. "Jesus," I grumble, my hips wanting to flex. I reach out and hold her hair, pulling it to the side so I can watch the show. "That feels so fucking good."

Turning her head, I notice the blush creeping up her neck. "Am I doing it right?"

Forcing myself to lie still, I reply, "There's nothing you could do that wouldn't be right, Ava. Trust your instincts. I promise you; I'll love it."

She seems to take my words to heart and shifts herself into a slightly more comfortable position. Then, she uses my cock as her personal learning device, sucking and licking my dick until my eyes are crossing and I'm ready to explode.

When I notice she still seems a little unsure of what to do with her hand, I reach down and move it to the base of my cock. Her fingers flex against the hard skin, which is the equivalent to a bolt of lightning through my veins. Her touch is a shot of adrenaline.

"Apply gentle pressure and move your hand," I instruct, showing her how to do it.

"Like this?" she asks when I pull my hand away.

My response is a moan. "Yes, beautiful. Just like that."

She leans down again, adding her mouth to the mix, and I realize now the error of my ways. Showing her how to give pleasure, to get me off, is going to cause this to end way too soon. My balls tighten, and I know my release is imminent. Her touch is better than anything in this world, except the feel of her pussy strangling my cock as she comes.

"That's enough," I blurt out, reaching for her hand and pulling her off me.

Her face registers a little shock, as well as worry. "Did I do it wrong?"

I reach for a condom in my bedside table. "Nope, you did it completely right, and that's the problem. I was two seconds away from exploding down your throat."

That sexy as fuck blush returns. "That would have been all right."

"Next time, sweetheart. Right now, I need to be inside you," I state, wrapping my dick in rubber and reaching for her hips.

Guiding her over my lap, she gets in position. "Umm, I'm not sure I can do this."

"You can," I tell her. "Let your body do the talking. Just do what feels good. I'll love every second of it."

I wait for her to tell me she's not interested in being on top, but that never comes. Instead, she reaches between her legs and takes my cock in her hand. She rubs the head of me through the wetness dripping from her pussy before positioning it at her entrance. She slowly starts to lower herself onto me, and all I can think about is how utterly amazing she feels.

"That's it, sweetheart. Take it slow," I instruct, watching as she gingerly drops down onto my cock.

She gasps when she's halfway rooted, her muscles stretching to accommodate me.

"Does it hurt?" I ask, suddenly worried it's too soon.

"A little, but it feels so good too." Her head falls back and her eyes close.

Gritting my teeth, I add, "Take your time." I don't care that my balls are starting to throb, that my body is begging me to thrust. I won't hurt this woman.

When she's finally seated on top of me, she opens her eyes and meets my gaze. "Oh God," she whimpers before lifting up a bit and sliding back down.

I force myself to remain still, lightly gripping her lower hips to help guide her. I take her all in. The swell of her breasts as she moves, the swirl of her hips as she finds a rhythm that feels good, the sight of my cock disappearing into her tight, wet pussy. All I can do is watch in complete rapture, knowing and understanding she's downright changing things for me.

For the better.

Life is so much better with her in it.

She flexes her nails into my chest, biting into my flesh. Her hips pick up the pace, and I know she's getting close. Her pussy muscles start to tighten around me, as she rocks her hips. "Gavin."

My name.

My fucking name on her lips as she starts to come is what does it. It triggers my own release and sends me reeling. My spine practically burns as it tightens and tingles, and this time, I'm unable to stop myself from flexing upward. She's squeezing me so firmly as we get off together, I can't really tell where I end and she begins.

As cheesy as it sounds, we're one.

Ava falls forward, her sweaty body pressing against my equally sweaty chest. "Wow," she mutters, her warm breath tickling my neck.

With my arms wrapped around her back, I hum in agreement. "You're a natural," I tell her, hoping to continue to boost her confidence where sexuality is concerned, because fuck me, Ava Rutledge is about as hot as a firecracker on the Fourth of July.

"I think I liked that," she confesses.

"I'm glad, because you're really fucking good at it."

She kisses my jaw, not seeming to be bothered in the slightest by the scratch of my scruff. "Not that I want to bring up my past at this moment, but I've never been on top before."

"The guys you've been with are idiots," I insist, kissing her cheek before claiming her lips. "Complete, utter wankers."

"Wankers?" she asks with a giggle. "Are you British?"

"Nope, but it seemed a little more PG than assholes, fuckers, or selfish douchebags."

She watches me for a minute. "They were all those things. You make me feel...alive. Valued. Different, but in a good way."

"You are different in the best way possible," I tell her before swiping my mouth across hers. "So fucking beautiful and sexual. I can't wait to see what other positions you like."

Again, she blushes. "Tell me more," she whispers.

I reach down and grab her ass, rocking my hips. The motion and friction cause my cock to kick with excitement once more. "We both need a shower, Miss Rutledge, and then, I'm gonna show ya."

Shower sex with Ava sounds like the perfect way to continue our day...

"I know it's probably too soon and violates our whole keeping this quiet thing, but I wish you'd come with me to dinner."

She pauses and turns around, her eyes wide.

Not wanting to give her a chance to tell me no right off the bat, I spell out what's been on my mind these last few minutes as she's gathered up her things to head home. It's a beautiful Sunday afternoon, and for the first time since I accepted the invitation to eat with my parents, I'm wishing I wouldn't have.

"My parents wouldn't say a word," I tell her. "If you ever want to join me at their house, they would be so thrilled and would keep it quiet if we asked them to. I'm not trying to rush you. I know this is a big step for you, so just know the invite is always there. I have dinner with them every week or two, especially if I have Annabelle. We join them at least once during the weeks I have her, but I also go over there when I don't have her. I know they'd love for you to accompany me." I take a deep breath, wishing I wouldn't have said anything at all. She looks shocked and maybe a bit perplexed. "All I'm saying is the invite is there. If and when you're ever ready, you're welcome."

She swallows hard and glances away for a moment. "Thank you for inviting me. I'm not sure I'm there yet, but I appreciate the offer."

I nod, hating that I feel even the slightest bit of sadness by her decline. "I didn't mean to make you feel uncomfortable."

"You didn't," she quickly reassures me, walking my way, her overnight bag forgotten. "I really appreciate it, honestly. And I hope we get to the place where I can join you." She runs her hands up my chest and around my neck, pulling me against her as she brushes her lips across mine. "I've never done the whole dinner with family before. It seems like a big step, but if I were ready to take the leap, it would be with you."

Her words are a balm to my heart. "You're the first woman I've ever wanted to bring home."

Her eyebrows pull together in question. "That can't be true. You were married."

I sigh and lean my forehead against hers. "I know, and yes, I did want to bring Julia home, but not as quickly. In fact, I dated her for about six months before I introduced her to my parents, and when that happened, it was because we were engaged." I give her a sheepish grin.

"Really?"

"Yeah. We met, started to date, and I asked her to marry me about six months later. The wedding happened pretty quickly, and she was pregnant with Annabelle not long after."

"Wow, kind of a whirlwind romance, huh?"

I nod. "Kinda, yeah. Looking back, I know it was all wrong. Don't get me wrong, I'll never regret the decisions I made back then because they led me to Annabelle, but Julia and I were all about the hot and heavy. It wasn't meant to last."

She blushes. "You're really good at hot and heavy."

I give her a wolfish grin. "It's my specialty. If we had more time, I'd give you another demonstration."

She laughs the sweetest sound. "I think my vagina needs a break from your hot and heavy for a bit." Then, as if realizing what she said, she blushes a deep shade of pink.

"Well, I'm always ready and at your service," I tell her, my cock focusing on her vagina and wanting another go. Sliding my mouth against hers, I confess, "You're not just sex, Ava. I feel it in my bones. Since the moment I first saw you, you've always been different. Having you here or being at your place is not just about sex. It's about you and me, and the fact I feel better in your presence than I ever have with anyone else. You make me feel...calm, for lack of a better word."

She gently lifts her leg and runs her thigh over my erection. "You don't feel very calm to me."

I bark out a laugh. "Yeah, well, get used to that. You evoke that kind of reaction regardless, whenever you're near. I'm like a walking hard-on in your presence."

She goes up on her tiptoes and brushes her lips across the underside of my jaw. "Let's table the parents' dinner conversation for a bit. Just know we'll definitely revisit it someday soon, because you feel different to me too."

My heart does this wild little gallop in my chest. It's a happy, content sensation I'm getting used to when it comes to her. "Sounds good."

Pressing her mouth to mine, we get lost in each other and make out like teenagers until it's past the time I was going to leave and am officially late.

"I should go."

"Yeah, but I wish you could stay," I tell her, taking her hand in my left and grabbing her bag with my right. We walk through my house and to the back door. I hold her bag while she puts on her boots and coat, and eventually, we make our way to my garage, where her car is parked. "Last night was incredible. All of it."

"It was," she agrees as soon as I place her bag in the back seat and hug her to my chest.

Brushing my lips across hers, I trail my finger over her cheek, memorizing the feel of her soft skin. "I've got all week without Annabelle, so if you want to have dinner or hang out, just let me know."

"I'd like that. I'm having dinner with my sister's family on Tuesday, but otherwise, I'm wide open."

"Sounds good." This time, I deepen the kiss. If I'm not going to get to touch or kiss her for more than a day, I'm going to need something to carry me through.

I pry my mouth away from hers, even though I'd rather not. "I'll text you later, if that's okay."

She gives me a gentle grin. "I'd like that. Have fun with your parents."

Ava climbs behind the wheel of her vehicle and waits for me to shut the door. Once she's started the car, I open the garage door and watch as she slowly backs out. It's after four and the sky is turning dark, so hopefully no one notices the woman leaving my garage. Not that I'd care, but I know Ava wants to remain private for a while. At least until my daughter is out of her class.

I totally understand and support her decision, but the moment Annabelle is officially moving on to sixth grade, all bets are off.

I want Ava. I want to be able to walk down the sidewalk, holding her hand. I want to sit across from her at the diner and share a meal. I want to kiss her in the park—okay, maybe not the park, but somewhere public, and I want everyone to see. Not to show her off, but to show the entire town how much I want her and how amazing she is.

I want them to know she's taken.

And she is, even if in just my mind.

We've not had the whole exclusive relationship conversation, but I know we are. Neither of us are serial daters or bounce from bed to bed. Sure, I've had a few girlfriends over the years, but none I've wanted to stand in the middle of the city square and declare my feelings for.

Ava makes me want to do that. To stand up and tell the world how I feel about her.

But let's not get into that right now. Because the truth is, I care about her. A lot. This isn't just a crush anymore. I'm developing real feelings, and with each moment we're together, those feelings grow. I can see myself falling for her, and despite the fact I should be a little worried to even think that right now after a few weeks, I'm not. Not worried in the least.

Because something tells me she's worth it.

Worth the risks and the potential heartache that comes with falling for someone.

Once she's gone, I close the garage door and return to my house to retrieve my keys and wallet. I could probably take the leftover cookies she baked, but I'm gonna be stingy and keep those for myself. Besides, my mom always makes desserts to go along with dinner, so I might as well just leave them here.

When I have my things, I lock up the house and return to the garage. My truck is parked in the first bay, but before I climb inside, I take a moment to study the empty space beside it. I liked having her vehicle here, in my garage. Hopefully soon, we won't have to hide when she's here, and if her car is parked in my garage, it's because it simply belongs there, not because we're trying to conceal it. Annabelle will be so excited to know I'm seeing her favorite teacher.

But that seems like forever away. Annabelle has about four months left of school. That's four months of sneaking around and hiding my relationship with Ava.

Just as I start to back out, my phone rings. My ex-wife's name comes up on the screen, and I'm certain it's my daughter calling, which makes me smile. "Hello, beautiful girl."

"Hi, Dad. Whatcha doing?"

"On my way to Grandma and Grandpa's for dinner."

"Awwww, I wish I could go, but we're getting ready to leave for dinner."

"Where ya going?" I ask, heading in the direction of my parents' house.

"The steakhouse. Mike and Mikey are going too."

"I'm sure that'll be fun," I reply.

"Yeah."

"Are you gonna have the chicken tenders?" I ask, knowing what response I'll get.

"Is there anything else to eat there?" she teases. She's ordered the chicken tenders and fries for as long as I can possibly remember.

"Maybe someday you'll actually try the steak. It's pretty good."

"Yeah, maybe someday, but today's not that day."

Smiling, I say, "I'm glad you called. I was thinking about you."

I leave out the part about why.

"Me too. I don't have school Friday for a teacher in-service day, and I get to go to work with Mom."

"That'll be fun," I reply as I continue to drive along.

"Yeah, but too bad you weren't still working on Miss Rutledge's house. I could go to work with you instead."

Smiling to myself, I answer, "I wasn't working inside her house except to install the new window. Everything else was outside. In the cold."

"Ehhh, okay, maybe that wouldn't have been as fun, but I still could have watched Tabitha."

"Maybe another time," I state, pulling onto my parents' road.

"Okay, Mom and Mike are ready to go so I better get off here."

"I'm glad you called. Have a great day at school tomorrow."

"I will," she assures me, and I know she will. She loves school. "Love you, Dad."

"Love you too, Belle. Talk to you soon."

"Bye."

I hang up, still smiling, as I pull into my parents' driveway. Talking to her always puts me in a good mood, even if it does cause me to miss her too. Her mom is pretty good about letting her use her phone, and for the most part, she gets to call when she wants. I love those surprise calls and look forward to them.

Shutting off my truck, I climb out and head for the front door. I love hanging out with Mom and Dad, but tonight, I'm looking forward to later. To calling Ava and chatting with her. Because at the end of this day, knowing I can talk to her until we're ready to fall asleep is the icing on the cake. I started today off with her, and even though we'll be in two different houses—two separate beds—I look forward to finding a way to end it with her too.

I'm totally gone for Ava Rutledge.
And that doesn't seem to bother me one bit.

CHAPTER
Twenty one

Ava

"Ava, special delivery."

I look up from my desk and smile at Rosa, the school office assistant, as she walks into my classroom with a gorgeous bouquet of flowers. My heart rate spikes as I take in the gorgeous array of blooms. "Oh wow," I comment as I stand up and take the vase from her hands.

"Who are they from?" she asks, leaning in and whispering.

Words fail me. I'm pretty certain I know who they're from, but that doesn't mean I want to blurt it out to Rosa and everyone else at the school. Thinking on the fly, I reply, "Probably my parents." I pray I sounded casual and convincing.

"Well, my parents never send me flowers like this," she replies as she hands them over. "I'll be honest, we were hoping they were from a man."

"Oh." I let out an awkward chuckle and turn to place the vase on my desk, praying she can't see the inevitable blush. "Sorry to burst your bubble."

"Oh well, no harm in asking," she replies, followed by the clicking of her heels on the floor. "Enjoy them, Ava."

"I will. Thank you for bringing them to my classroom for me," I say with a wave.

The moment she's gone, I reach for the sealed envelope. I rip it open and scan the words he handwrote on the small card.

Ava,

I've spent all day thinking about you. Dinner was amazing. Let's do it again. Very soon. Bring your overnight bag. Or don't. You don't need clothes anyway.

-G

My face flames hot as I read and reread his words. It's been six weeks since our non-date date to see the aurora borealis, which has been followed up by date dates. We've been spending time together in private, most of the time at either his house or mine and stealing the occasional time away to Hudson or St. Paul when he doesn't have his daughter.

It hasn't been easy.

So many times I've wanted to just say forget this and go have dinner with him at the diner or the steakhouse. It would be so much easier than sneaking around, hiding our vehicles in each other's garages so no one knows what's going on. Though, I'm certain my neighbors have figured it out. They've not said anything, but I caught the older gentleman on my left watching out his window when Gavin was pulling his truck into my garage last week.

Then, I recall what it was like to have my personal life dragged through the mud. One old—seemingly innocent—photo appeared on social media and turned my whole life upside down. It's just a prime example of why I don't have any social media pages, nor do I allow myself to be put in situations where a photograph could be taken and misconstrued by the masses. So, while I'd love to be a bit more public with my relationship with Gavin, I just don't want my life scrutinized and publicized again.

I glance down at the flowers. They're the most gorgeous arrangement of red roses and white lilies.

The bell rings, letting me know my quiet time is over. In a matter of seconds, my fifth-grade class will return from lunch and recess, and we'll be diving back into our studies. Fortunately, this afternoon consists of a quick math test, followed by watching a movie for science, which is always a welcomed change from the textbook reading we usually have.

The kids are excited.

As they start to file into the classroom, I slip the card into my top desk drawer. Standing up, I watch as the students who brought their sack lunches return their lunch boxes and bags to their cubbies where their coats and bookbags hang. Annabelle is chatting away with her friend, Madelyn, but offers me a wide smile as soon as she crosses the threshold. I can't help but return the gesture, especially since it reminds me so much of her father's. While Annabelle resembles her mom in a few features, she definitely has her dad's smile.

"Flowers!" Annabelle coos, making a beeline straight for my desk. "They're so pretty."

"Thank you," I reply, my heart beating a little faster all of a sudden.

"Are they from someone special? My dad always says flowers are sent to show someone you care."

A smile breaks out across my lips. "Oh yeah?"

"Yep. He doesn't send flowers though, because he doesn't have someone to send them to. I wish he did."

I feel my face blush as words fail me.

"Maybe someday my dad will send flowers to a girl. I want a baby brother."

My eyes widen at her statement, and there's no missing the excitement she clearly feels.

"You would make an excellent big sister," I finally say, not really sure what to add.

Annabelle nods. "Do you want kids?" she asks, leaving me flabbergasted. "You would make a really good mom. I bet you'd read to your kids every night and buy them lots of books."

I can't help but grin. "I'm sure I would."

The second bell rings, prompting Annabelle to say, "I better go put my lunch bag away," and taking off to the back of the classroom.

I take a few seconds to look at my flowers, warmth washing over me. Hearing Annabelle say her dad doesn't send them to anyone, yet knowing he took the time to explain to her what they can represent, lets me know I've got a good one. He took a risk by sending me the bouquet, knowing my coworkers would undoubtedly ask questions. Yet, he still wanted me to have them and know he was thinking of me.

"Everyone get ready for your math test. Nothing on your desk but your pencil," I state, getting ready to pass out the single sheet of paper. It's a pretty straightforward test, but it'll tell me who needs a little more help before we move on.

While the kids take their test, I quietly pull my phone from my desk and fire off a text.

> **Me:** I just received the most gorgeous bouquet of flowers. Thank you.

The little bubbles appear instantly.

> **Gavin:** Not as gorgeous as you, but they were too pretty to pass up. They made me think of you the moment I saw them. And you're welcome, beautiful. See you tonight?

> **Me:** I'll be there at five.

Gavin: If I'm not there, use the spare key.

Two weeks back, I arrived at his house before he got there. He didn't like that I was sitting, waiting in my vehicle, so he showed me where the spare key was hidden. I've never used it, mostly because I don't want to overstep, and I really don't mind waiting for him to arrive.

Me: Yes, sir.

Gavin: Hmmm. Sir. I like that. Maybe we can try that out later?

Again, my cheeks heat at his innuendo. This is definitely not something I've ever considered in the past, but the thought of trying something *different* with Gavin doesn't sound too scary.

Me: Possibly, but I can't talk about it now. My students are taking a math test, so I should get off here. Just wanted to say thank you.

Gavin: And again, you're welcome. Sorry if it causes you problems. I know people are probably asking questions, but my need to show you how much I've been thinking of you outweighed the rest.

Me: It was the best kind of surprise, and a first for me.

Gavin: Seriously?

Me: Yes. I've never had flowers sent to my place of employment from anyone other than my parents on my birthday.

Gavin: Mental note made. You deserve all the pretty flowers.

Before I can reply, he fires off another text.

Gavin: Have a great afternoon. See you in a few hours.

Me: See you soon.

I return my phone to my desk drawer and take a quick scan over the room. Everyone has their heads down, writing. My eyes land on Annabelle, who works diligently on her test. She's seated in the front row, at her request, and looks up, making eye contact. She gives me a smile, one that makes my heart sing. She's such a happy child. She can find joy in anything, especially books and crafts.

A girl after my own heart.

My mind flashes to her father. It's been six weeks since we started seeing each other. It started off very casual, but has transformed into something more. At least it has for me, and even though we've not discussed it, I'm certain it has for him too. I may not be ready to admit it out loud, but I've fallen in love with him. Our time together is always too short, and when one of us leaves, an overwhelming sense of sadness overcomes me.

And if the look in his eyes is any indication, I think he feels it too.

But we're not ready for more yet.

I have about three and a half months left of the school year, and then we can decide how we take the next step. I have a feeling we'll be taking that leap together.

His truck is already in his driveway when I pull in. I barely pause in front of the garage bay I've been using before the door starts to rise. I spot his sweatpants first, followed by his fitted long-sleeved T-shirt. His hair is a mess, and it's clear he just got out of the shower. He's also wearing a wolfish grin, one that conveys exactly how excited he is to have me here.

I park my vehicle as the garage door comes down, and as soon as I press the button to shut off the car, my door is open. After quickly releasing my seat belt, he extends his hand and helps me from the car, something he does each and every time I arrive.

The moment the door is closed behind me, I'm pressed against the car, his mouth claiming mine. There's an urgency, a fire in his kiss, as if I'm the very air he needs to breathe.

"Missed you today," he mutters, his hands roaming up my sides and beneath my sweater.

His erection is already standing tall, pressed firmly between us. My hips start to move entirely on their own, craving more of his touch, needing him where I ache. I push up his shirt, desperately seeking his hot flesh beneath my fingertips. Clothes start to fly immediately. His shirt is gone, followed quickly by my own. He pulls my bra down and sucks my nipple into his mouth, causing a moan of pleasure to fall from my lips.

I kick off my ankle boots, grateful to be wearing a slip-on pair. Gavin reaches for the button to my slacks and practically rips it off my pants, but I don't care. He can damage the zipper all he wants, as long as he helps alleviate this burn of desire settling between my thighs.

"Fuck," he groans, slipping his fingers beneath my pants and pressing them into me. "You're so fucking wet already."

A whimper falls from my mouth as I move. "Need you so bad," I confess, closing my eyes as the pleasure takes hold.

But as quickly as he's touching me, he's gone.

I open my eyes and find him pulling a condom from his sweatpants before thrusting them down his thighs. His erection is long, hard, and ready, and he makes fast work at covering it with the latex protection. I step out of my pants seconds before I'm lifted onto my car. The metal is cold from being outside, but my body is so hot, the temperature against my skin barely registers. The height of me sitting above the left front tire is perfect. My legs wrap around his waist as he pulls my panties aside and pushes inside me, filling me completely.

"Dammit," he mutters, trying to grasp at his control.

Reaching up, I shift the cups of my bra so both nipples are exposed. His eyes dilate farther, the hazel coloring now dark with his desire. "Don't stop," I tell him, desperate for more.

He pulls back and thrusts forward over and over, setting a fast, hard pace. I can feel my body starting to tighten like a coil, the release I'm desperately seeking just within reach. It's wild to me how I can go from work-mode to frantically needing him in such a quick amount of time. His touch, the desire he has for me does that.

Every time.

Gavin runs the pad of his finger over one of my hard nipples before pinching it between his thumb and index finger. I gasp, my internal muscles fluttering around him as he continues to drive inside me.

"I'm gonna come, baby. I need to get you there," he murmurs, slipping his hand between us and swiping it across my clit.

The friction is the gentle push I needed to send me flying over the edge. I come hard, crying out my release as the bliss crashes through me. He follows, thrusting hard and finding his own pleasure. His hips keep moving, which draws everything out until I'm left shuttering and exhausted.

"I'm sorry," he murmurs, taking my lips with his in a gentle kiss. "That wasn't what I was planning to do."

Throwing my arms around his neck, I pull him close, loving the way his chest feels pressed against mine. "No? If that's not what you planned to do, I think your original plan might need some work."

He pokes me in the side and chuckles. "No, I definitely meant to do *that*, but I was intending to get you inside my house first. Not take you against your car like a sex-crazed animal."

I kiss under his chin, right at the spot his facial scruff starts. I've learned over our time together; he really likes it when I kiss him there. "Hmm, I might prefer this sex-craved animal side of you."

"Yeah?" he asks, running his hands down my back. "You bring it out of me. I was planning to introduce you to my kitchen table the moment we got inside, but it appears I was unable to wait."

"Fine by me," I murmur softly, resting my face against his chest. I can hear the hard pounding of his heart and find so much comfort in the familiarity.

"Let's get you inside. It's not cold out here, but it's definitely not warm," he states, slowly pulling back and slipping from my body. He grabs the condom, gently and carefully pulling it off his cock before twisting it closed and tossing it into a nearby trash can.

"I'm comfortable," I insist. His garage is heated, since he does some woodworking in his free time, but mostly it's the fact I'm in his arms that causes me to be so content.

"Just think of how comfortable you'll be when I get you into my bed," he insists with a wicked smile.

"Hmm," I hum. "That does sound pretty darn comfortable."

"Let's get inside, beautiful. Do you have a bag?"

I shrug, hopping off the top of my car with his help. "I don't. I mean, you said I wouldn't need anything, since I'd be naked."

A Cheshire cat grin spreads across his devastatingly handsome face. "This is very true."

Slipping my pants back on, I add, "I know I have to leave early, since you'll have to go get Annabelle. I can shower at home."

The moment my pants are on, he pulls me into his arms. "Or you can just shower here and use my things. The thought of you smelling like my shampoo and soap brings out this caveman side of me."

Warmth begins to spread through my veins once more as desire pools between my legs. "I'm okay with that."

He presses a firm kiss to my lips, one that doesn't last nearly as long as I'd like, before reaching down and grabbing his shirt. He slips it over my head and carefully pulls it down, helping me slide my arms into the sleeves. He takes in my appearance in his shirt and grins. "I think seeing you in my shirt is the sexiest thing I've ever seen."

I bring the sleeve to my nose and inhale, loving the scent of his soap and detergent hanging on the material. "It's big and warm," I state, even though it's T-shirt material. "I might keep it."

"It's yours," he boasts, kissing my forehead. "Come on, beautiful. Let's get you inside," he says, reaching down and picking up my discarded sweater. He helps me step into my boots and shoves his feet into a pair of well-worn slip-on shoes.

I ignore the discomfort of my stretched-out panties and walk beside him to his house. He doesn't seem bothered by the fact he's not wearing a shirt, and thankfully, the walkway between his garage and house is concealed by trees and his fenced-in backyard. Otherwise, I'm sure the congregation at the Methodist Church next door would be scandalized by his shirtless chest.

Not that they're there on a Friday night. The lot was empty when I passed by.

The moment we're inside the house, he spins me around and presses me against the door. His erection is hard once more, as he rocks his hips against me. "I hope you're not planning on getting much sleep tonight. If I'm not going to be able to have you for the next week, I'm going to have to try to get my fill tonight."

I shrug, reaching between us and stroking his erection. "I can sleep tomorrow. Tonight, I'm all yours."

CHAPTER
Twenty Two

GAVIN

"I'll grab the stuff out of the dryer," Annabelle hollers the moment the appliance chimes in completion.

I finish putting the last of the dirty dishes from lunch inside the dishwasher and start a cycle. Once that's done, I return to my bedroom and grab the load of towels that'll go into the washer next. After flipping the clothes to the dryer and starting the towels, I join Annabelle in the kitchen, where she's folding the load already completed.

"What time are we going to Grandma and Grandpa's?" she asks, folding a pair of my lounge pants.

"About four. Aunt Ginger and the kids are coming too."

"Uncle Paul?" she asks.

"Nope, they've got a birthday party to go to, but Great-Grandma Zelda will be there."

"Really? Do you think she'll invite her friend, Betty? Last time she did that, Miss Rutledge came too," Annabelle states happily, her brown eyes filled with delight.

"I'm not sure," I reply. I can't just tell her no, that Ava isn't driving her grandma anywhere tonight, because then she'd want to know how I know. And that's a whole mess I don't want to get into.

"Well, I'm hoping she is. I like her."

I flash her a small grin, but don't reply. Mostly because I'm afraid my reply will go something like this. *I really like her too. In fact, I'm pretty sure I've fallen in love with her. I've been spending a lot of time with her without you or anyone else knowing, and she now consumes me. My thoughts, my dreams, my fantasies. She's all I think about, all I want.*

"Whose is this?"

I'm pulled out of my thoughts by my daughter's question, and stare dumbfoundedly at what she's holding up.

Fuck.

It's Ava's sweater.

How in the hell did that get mixed up with my laundry? I remember setting it aside, wanting to make sure it stayed in my closet until I could get it back to her. Yet, here it is, being waved in front of my face like a red flag.

My throat is dry, my tongue heavy. "I'm not sure," I reply, the lie like a punch to the gut.

Before I can reach for the sweater, Annabelle says, "This looks like the one Miss Rutledge was wearing at school yesterday."

Fuck. Me.

"Yeah? Well, I'm not sure where that came from," I state with an awkward chuckle. "Maybe it was mixed in with my work stuff from the truck. It could be Max's girlfriend's shirt." When she doesn't seem convinced, I quickly add, "Or maybe Grandma's. You know how she leaves stuff lying around every now and again."

I can feel her gaze on me, but I refuse to look up. I keep folding my clothes as if my life depends on it. When I continue to feel the weight of her stare, I look up, a big smile plastered on my lips. Reaching for the sweater that's still in her hands, I finally ask, "Are you sure it's not yours or your mom's? Maybe it got mixed up in the clothes you brought."

I know I'm reaching for straws here, but I can't help it. As much as I'd love to tell her whose sweater it really is—or confirm her suspicions—I can't. Not without talking to Ava first, and I'm certain she's not wanting my daughter to know. The risk is too high, the chance of her accidentally mentioning it to someone else—her mom, another student, *anyone*—is too great, and while I'd like to think I can trust my eleven-year-old with this secret, I'd never put her in any predicament. I'd never want her to feel like she has to lie to someone to keep my secret quiet.

"Dad, this is too big for me, and I'm pretty sure Mom would never wear something like this," she replies honestly. Internally, I wince. Annabelle isn't meaning to insult Ava, but I understand what she's saying. Ava wears sensible, comfortable, modest clothing, while Julia is more of the flaunt what your mama gave you type.

"Yeah, you're right. Must be Grandma's," I state, ripping the sweater out of her hand and tossing it aside.

Annabelle nods, returning her attention to what's left to fold. I'm so grateful she doesn't comment about the sizing. While she noted the fact the sweater's too big for her, she didn't pick up that it's too small for my mom. Mom isn't a big woman, but there's a difference between her large tops and Ava's small ones.

I gather up the folded clothes, as well as Ava's sweater, and take them to my bedroom. It only takes a few minutes to put everything away, and I make sure to add Ava's sweater to the top of my closet. This way, it's out of sight, out of mind, and hopefully, my daughter doesn't ask any more questions before I can return it to its rightful owner.

But I'll never forget the way she looked this morning when she left, wearing my long-sleeved shirt from last night. After our shower, and another round of unforgettable sex, I slipped my shirt over her head and insisted she wear it home. There were no complaints from her either, since she seemed to enjoy having it on. I just don't think she planned to leave her sweater behind, and I know I sure as hell didn't plan to leave it where my daughter could find it.

I take a quick look around my bedroom, seeing nothing that belongs to Ava, yet seeing her everywhere. In my bed, standing in front of my dresser, in the bathroom as she got ready to leave. Her image is imprinted on my life, and I realize instantly I don't want it any other way.

She's mine.

For as long as she'll have me.

She just doesn't really know it yet.

"Hi, Grandma," I greet, smiling as I enter the dining room.

"Hello, handsome. How are you?" she asks, patting the table beside where she sits. "Have a seat."

Annabelle is already playing with her cousins, so I take the opportunity to sit and spend a little time with my only remaining grandparent. "How have you been?"

"Right as rain," she insists. "How's my great-granddaughter?"

She's excellent. She'll come in and say hello shortly. She wanted to show Bethany some of the crafts she's been making."

Grandma waves her hand. "They're so energetic at that age and always going somewhere. Can't blame them for not having time for us old people."

I scoff at her statement. "We always have time for you," I insist, leaning over and kissing her aged cheek.

"I know you do, Gavin. You're a great young man," she says, offering me a grandmotherly smile. "You're my favorite, you know."

I chuckle at her statement. She's been telling me that since I was younger, insisting I keep it a secret. I'm the youngest, the last grandchild, and my grandma's always had a soft spot for me. Much like she did Paul, who is the oldest, and my sister, Ginger, who is the only girl. So, honestly, I'm certain there isn't real favorites, but I humor her just the same.

"You're just saying that because I come over and mow your grass."

She laughs. "Well, I do admit, that elevates you to a higher level, but that's not the only reason." She sighs and takes a sip of her coffee. "How have things been with you?"

"Busy," I reply, even though work isn't quite as hectic as it will be when the winter snow and cold finally thaw for the year. "Work's going good."

"I'm sure it is, but that's not what's putting that smile on your face."

The moment her statement registers, I pause. "What?"

"No man seems as happy as you appear thanks to work going well. That's the look of a man in love."

My throat goes Sahara dry, and it's suddenly hard to swallow. "I'm not...I'm not in love, Grandma."

Lies.

She just smiles widely. "Oh."

Clearly, she doesn't believe me.

I'm saved from having to dig deeper into this conversation by my mom entering the dining room. "I made a cherry chip pie," Mom announces to me as she leans over and gives me a hug.

"That sounds delicious. I'll take two slices," I state, kissing her cheek. "Your pies are the best."

"Kiss-ass," Mom mutters with a chuckle. "But thank you. We'll be ready to eat in about ten minutes."

"Grandma!" Annabelle comes running into the dining room, throwing her arms around my mom's waist.

"Hello, sweet girl. How is school going?" my mom asks Annabelle.

"It's great. Oh," she says, digging into her bag of stuff she brought to show Bethany. "I brought your shirt." She pulls the sweater out, handing it to my mom.

Mom looks at it with curiosity on her face. "This isn't mine," she tells Annabelle, and I swear, if the floor had the ability to open up and swallow me, I'd let it.

Hell, I'd jump in.

Annabelle just looks up at her grandma with confusion. "But...Dad said it must be yours. It was in the laundry."

That's when I feel all eyes on me. My mind goes completely blank. I have no clue what to do or say, because I know whatever comes out of my mouth will either be a lie—which I don't want to do—or will be the truth—something I'm not prepared to say.

Deflection it is...

"Interesting. Did you show Bethany that new game you wanted to play?" I ask, reaching out and grabbing the sweater again. I don't even want to know how she found and retrieved it from my closet shelf, but that discussion will have to be tabled for later.

Annabelle just stares at me. "We're going to play after dinner." Her eyebrows are drawing together as she asks, "So it's Max's girlfriend's? That's weird."

I shrug, shoving the sweater beneath the table onto my lap. "Max is weird."

"Dinner's almost ready," my mom says. "Why don't you run and see if your cousins are ready to eat?"

Annabelle takes off to the living room, and I feel two sets of laser-pointer eyes staring straight at me.

"I knew it," Grandma boasts, clapping her hands proudly.

"Knew what?" Mom asks.

"That Gavin is in love. He's practically glowing, don't you think?"

I open my mouth to argue, but nothing comes out. "Can we not do this here?" I ask softly, especially since my sister is in the kitchen and my nieces, nephew, and daughter, as well as dad and brother-in-law are all in the living room around the corner.

"Fine, fine, but don't think we haven't noticed the fact you're not denying it."

I sigh, resolved.

"Is this the woman you were buying wine and flowers for?" Mom asks, clearly not caring asked to table the conversation.

"What?" I ask, choking on air.

She shrugs. "Well, you were buying wine a few weeks back and told me you had a date. And then Emily's aunt Ruth saw you in the flower shop yesterday. Were you sending flowers to this mystery woman?"

"It's gonna come out eventually," Grandma announces, sipping her coffee without a care in the world.

I exhale deeply and rub my throbbing temple. "It will come out, yes, when we're both ready to share. Until then, keep your nosiness in your own lanes."

Mom throws up her hands. "Not trying to butt in, just curious as to why you're so secretive. And for the record, I think it's great. You haven't really dated much since you and Julia split, so I'm all for you finding someone, falling in love, and giving me more grandbabies."

"You're having a baby?!"

I glance over my mom's shoulder and find my sister standing there, wide-eyed and looking like she's ready to burst. "No, I'm not having a baby, Jesus," I groan, standing up and meeting all three of their gazes. "Yes, I'm seeing someone," I start quietly. "Annabelle doesn't know. I'll tell her—and all of you—when we're both ready. We're taking it slow. Very slow. End of story."

"Don't get upset, honey. We all want what's best for you."

"I know, and I appreciate that, really. When I have more to share, I will. Promise."

They all nod in understanding, and even though I'm certain they all want to press me for more details, they abide by my wishes and end the discussion.

Conversation flows around me as we eat dinner, but my mind is a million miles away. It's on Ava and the fact my family has figured out something's different with me.

Ava.

That's the difference.

She's a game-changer.

After dinner, I head to the kitchen to help my mom clean up. Annabelle is with my sister, showing her how to make flowers out of Kleenex, so I take the opportunity to steal a few minutes with Mom.

"Dad's back seems to be feeling better," I say, drying off a large bowl and putting it away in the cabinet.

"Much. He's been going to that chiropractor in Hudson the last few weeks. He's done wonders at helping alleviate the pain and discomfort he's been having. He says it's just going to take some time."

"I'm just glad he didn't break anything when he fell," I say, recalling that morning my mom called me. Dad was shoveling snow and slipped. He went down hard on his back and took an ambulance ride to make sure nothing was broken. It wasn't, thankfully, but he put an end to snow removal for a while.

"You and me both. It's been difficult enough to keep him comfortable and relaxed. You know your father. He wants to be up and doing something all the time, so for him to be forced to sit idle hasn't been easy for him."

"Or you," I add with a teasing tone.

"I love that man to death, but he's driving me bonkers."

Smiling, I take the casserole pan she's just washed and dry it off. "Let me know if I can help. Annabelle and I can come over and visit more often," I tell her, instantly feeling guilty for not offering to help more than I have been. I took on their snow removal so Dad wasn't tempted to do it himself, and have been helping anywhere else I can, but I have to just show up and do it. They never ask for assistance, despite Dad's back injury. Mom just steps up and does what she needs to do to get the work done. It was an argument for me to take over the shoveling, but when I wouldn't relent, she finally conceded to let me do it for a while.

"We're just fine, dear. Besides, you've been busy yourself lately," she replies with a knowing grin.

The look of excitement on her face makes me groan. I suppose I did walk right into that one. "Doesn't matter. I'd make time to do whatever you need."

She reaches over and places her wet, soapy hand on my arm. "I know that, and we appreciate it. We're managing just fine. Paul came over last weekend and took care of that limb that fell in the backyard. I didn't even have a chance to mention it to you before he showed up and cut it up."

My brother has a busy schedule, but he's always willing to drop what he's doing to help Mom and Dad. "I'm glad. I noticed he went ahead and took the firewood with him," I tease.

"Of course he did. Free firewood for the fireplace," Mom replies, giving me a look out of the corner of her eye. "Tell me about her."

I exhale but not out of irritation. I realize quickly I want to talk about Ava, even if I can't tell her exactly who I'm referring to. "She's...amazing. Simply the kindest, most beautiful person I've ever known, inside and out."

Mom smiles. "I'm so happy for you."

"Thanks. I'm pretty happy too. We're taking it very slow, like I said earlier. She has...rules. And until it's time, we're just keeping things on the down-low, but I'm hoping we'll take it to the level soon."

"Good. It does this mom heart good to see you smiling real, genuine smiles again. After the whole mess with Julia, I wasn't sure you'd ever risk your heart again. I'm glad you are, and I don't mind you taking it slow, for whatever reason. Just know I'm here, waiting to meet her when the time comes."

"You will," I assure her.

"Good. And don't worry about Annabelle. She'll love whoever you love, simply because you've taught her how to open her heart, give and receive love. She has every single one of your good qualities, Gavin. I know it hasn't been easy, but you've done an amazing job raising her. Julia too. I may not like that woman very much for the added stress and bullshit she's done to you, but I can appreciate how she's co-parented my granddaughter, even if I wanted to wring her neck a few times over the years."

I give my mom a big smile. "I love you," I say, throwing my arms around her shoulders and giving her a hard squeeze.

"I love you too. Now, let's get these dishes done so you can get out of here. Maybe there's time for you to go see your lady friend. You know, convince her to break all the rules. I'd like another grandbaby someday."

I chuckle and shake my head. "You're relentless."

She just grins up at me. "Where do you think you get it from?"

Don't I know it.

CHAPTER Twenty Three

Ava

"This looks amazing," Blair announces the moment she steps inside the community center where the double baby shower is being hosted today.

"Ava did the decorations. Aren't they amazing?" Ellie states with a huge smile on her face.

"Oh my goodness," Hallie coos, her eyes filling with tears as she and Logan enter.

"You two completely outdid yourselves," Blair adds.

"Well, we had help. The moms all pitched in too," Ellie says, looking around proudly.

She came up with an exquisite menu of sweet and savory treats, complete with a massive charcuterie board and homemade dessert bars, cookies, and cupcakes. The spread is impressive, but her presentation puts it over the top.

"Do you need help with anything?" Logan asks, looking a little nervous. While both he and Gabe are excited to become dads within the next month or two, I'm not sure the same could be said about attending today's baby shower.

"Gabe's in the kitchen," I tell him, to which he practically runs off to find the other man in attendance today.

"All right, so our two expecting mamas are going to sit in the rockers up front," Ellie states. "The future grandmas get the table right up front."

"And games?" Blair asks, giving a look toward Hallie.

"No games," I confirm.

"Thank you, Jesus! I hate playing games at showers. They're so awkward," Hallie says.

"Agreed. That's why we decided not to do them. We'll just snack on lots of delicious food and watch you ladies open gifts."

Blair gives me a grateful grin. "That sounds perfect, thank you."

The next two hours pass by in a blur of eating food and watching the two mommies-to-be open their gifts. I wrote the gift list for Hallie, while Ellie took care of Blair's stuff. They received some amazing necessities for their babies, and by the end of the shower, they were both on the verge of tears with gratitude and appreciation. Logan and Gabe hung in there too, helping open gifts by holding the contents up for the guests to see.

Of course, they really enjoyed the food too.

Now, there's only a handful of us left, cleaning up after the party. The guys, including TD, are loading up the gifts into trucks, while Ellie and I finish dividing up the leftover food into to-go containers. She had the forethought to bring several along, knowing there would most likely be extras.

The first few we packaged up went home with the moms, or the grandmas-to-be, as a thank you for helping us set up and clean afterward. Next, we're making sure Blair and Gabe and Logan and Hallie have goodies to take home. They'll have plenty to snack on while they're setting up the baby rooms with their new goodies. And if there's any left, which it appears there will be, Ellie and I will take those.

Since Gavin doesn't have Annabelle this week, I'm thinking about calling him to see if he wants to share some later. I snacked enough throughout the day I won't need to eat a big meal this evening, so leftover meat, cheese, fruit, and veggies might be just what the doctor ordered. Then, there'll be some of the sweet treats left for afterward. You know, dessert.

Gavin and cherry cheesecake bombs sound like an amazing way to end the evening.

Well, maybe topping it off with sex before heading home to my lonely bed.

"Earth to Ava."

I blink at Ellie, surprised I was spacing out enough not to hear her speaking to me. "What? I'm sorry, I was zoned out."

She gives me a slow, knowing grin. "I remember that feeling."

"What feeling?" I ask, keeping my hands busy by loading up the rest of the cheese cubes into the final two to-go containers.

"Being in love when it was still so new. It's a mixture of terrifying and exhilarating."

I stand here, wide-eyed, staring at my friend. "I'm not...I mean, I don't know..." I swallow over the massive lump formed in my throat and watch her. She has the softest grin on her beautiful face, and her eyes are filled with truth and wisdom. It wasn't too long ago she realized how much she truly loved her best friend. TD was always there for her and her teenage son, Brody, silently pining over her since we were in high school. When he finally decided to make his move, they realized his feelings weren't one-sided, and they've been together ever since. Of course, like any real relationship, it hasn't come without bumps in the road, but they came out stronger on the other side because of them.

"It's okay if you're not ready to admit it yet. Being in love is a huge step," she replies, closing the lids on the final two containers.

I open my mouth to argue, but nothing comes out. I can't deny it, because she's one-hundred-percent correct. I'm in love with

Gavin. Somewhere between our non-date date and stealing nights together, I fell madly in love with him.

But it's too soon, isn't it?

I know it's been a little more than seven weeks, but that doesn't seem long enough to get to know someone, finding out all the things that make them tick, and falling for them, good and bad. Yet, I feel like I know Gavin better than I know anyone else. He's kind, caring, supportive, and a tad bit on the bossy side. He's excellent at his job and worships his daughter. He's also a little crabby when his back hurts and he gets annoyed quickly in higher traffic cities like St. Paul. But he's still one of the best men I've ever met, and I'm so grateful he's willing to do this whole dating in private thing with me, because life has been a whole lot better with him in it.

Glancing over my shoulder to make sure we're still alone, I whisper, "I wasn't planning on falling for him."

Ellie flashes me a cheeky grin. "We never plan on it. Love just sort of swoops in and smacks ya upside the head. It comes out of nowhere, even when the person you fall for is right there all along."

I nod, understanding exactly what she's saying. Gavin has always been here. We've found ourselves at the same place at the same time throughout the years. I had parent-teacher conferences with him and his ex-wife last fall. We grew up in this town together, attending the same schools. Sure, we weren't ever in any classes together, but we did share the same halls. Isn't that where he said he saw me for the first time? In the hallway between classes?

My heart skips a beat just thinking about him.

"Go for it."

I turn my attention to her. "Go for what?"

Gavin.

I already know what she's going to say.

"Don't be afraid of it. Falling in love is totally scary, but it's so worth it," she says with a grin and a shrug. "I don't know where I'd be without TD. He's the second-best thing to happen to me." She doesn't have to explain the first is her son. "I can assume, since you're not talking about it and neither is anyone else in this town, you two aren't exactly public with whatever is going on, and that's okay. You'll get there. Just remember, this town has a way of finding out your secrets. And unfortunately, if they can't figure out the specifics, they'll just make them up."

I cringe at the thought. "Yeah, I definitely don't want that."

She leans in again. "I saw the way Gavin was looking at you on New Year's Eve. I truly hope he's everything you're looking for. He seems like such a sweet, kind guy. I don't remember him much in school, but I've waited on him and his daughter many times in the last few years, and he's a great dad."

I nod. "He is, and you're right about everything else too. He's just...amazing."

She grins widely. "I'm so happy for you," she blurts out, taking me in her arms and giving me a hug.

"Why are we happy for Ava?" Hallie asks as she and Blair approach, their bellies each leading the way.

Ellie doesn't say a word, not wanting to out me, but I know the two newcomers won't let it go without me giving them something. Especially Hallie. She's like a dog with a bone when she wants details, and by the look in her eyes, she's expecting them from me.

"I met someone," I announce, feeling a mixture of excitement and nervousness at finally telling someone about my relationship.

"Is it Gavin Pierson? I mean, you've always known him, but is he the one you're seeing?" Blair chimes in, eager for details too.

"Yes, Gavin! He's so pretty to look at," Hallie adds. "I bet he's spectacular without his shirt on. Those quiet, hardworking types usually are."

And...cue the blush again.

"She's blushing! That means yes," Hallie insists, her hands firmly on her swollen stomach.

My eyes widen and my cheeks heat up as I glance between the three woman who have become my closest friends. "How did you all know?"

"Are you kidding? You two were putting off major vibes at my place on New Year's Eve," Blair says.

"Totally. I mean, not the type of vibes Logan and I put out early on—"

"No one puts off those vibes. You guys were all 'I want to kill you, but I'll screw your brains out instead' vibes," Blair interrupts her best friend.

Hallie grins. "Those drunken pissed-off moments were the best," she mutters in response, a knowing grin on her face.

"Yeah, naked angry banging moments," Ellie murmurs, making us all giggle.

"Let's get back to the point here," Blair chimes in, redirecting the conversation. "Gavin seems great, and we can tell there's chemistry there."

Nodding, I confirm, "There is. A lot of it."

"I knew it! You two were practically smokin' at the party, and I remember how he was looking at you last summer at my birthday party. He was totally undressing you with his eyes that night, banging you in his mind."

"Oh my God." I laugh, lightly swatting at her upper arm. "You're incorrigible."

Hallie just shrugs. "I can't help it. Pregnancy makes my brain think only of sex."

"It's true," Blair adds. "Gabe and I had sex on his desk at work on Friday because he was wearing a blue button-down with the sleeves rolled up to reveal his forearms. I was so turned on, I literally stripped off my pants and climbed on his desk like a beached whale. These hormones are no joke."

"Truth. I could have sex three times a day and still want more," Hallie states, making my eyes bug out of my head.

"Seriously?"

Both she and Blair nod.

I glance at Ellie and see hurt laced in her eyes. I'm sure hearing our friends talk about their pregnancies is hard on her. She wants a baby so badly, it must be difficult to see others around you pregnant when you want it too, even if those others are your friends. She'd never begrudge them, but that doesn't mean she doesn't feel grief by the fact she's not pregnant too.

"What do you say we get the rest of this stuff picked up and get out of here," I suggest.

"I can't wait to tear into that cheese when we get home," Blair says.

"You eat cheese, while Gabe puts the baby crib and swing together," I propose.

"Excellent idea," she agrees with a laugh.

"I'm going home to take advantage of my boyfriend," Hallie states, turning and looking for Logan over by the door where he's chatting with her brother, Gabe, and TD.

"Maybe we'll give the baby making another shot tonight," Ellie says.

"Yes!" we all holler.

"Go home and make a baby," Hallie adds as we all gather up the rest of the stuff we brought and head for the door.

"We're supposed to just shut off the lights when we're done. They'll come by later and take out the trash and lock the door," Ellie informs us.

Slipping on my coat, I make sure I have my leftover food and purse and step outside with my friends.

"Thank you," Blair whispers, giving me a big hug. "Today was absolutely amazing. You helped spoil our baby girl, and we appreciate you so much."

"You're welcome," I reply.

The moment she steps back, Hallie is there, throwing her arms around me too. "Yes, thank you. Both of you. We have the bestest friends in the world," she informs us, making us chuckle.

I have to admit, it feels good to be so loved by these incredible women. Sure, we went to school together, but even with our small class, we didn't exactly hang out often. We were cordial and kind, always there if someone needed something. It wasn't until we were adults, we connected and became friends. Sure, Blair and Hallie had always remained in contact after Blair left town, and Ellie was here through the college years raising her son, but once we all returned to Pine Village and stayed, we developed the friendship we have today.

After I went off to college, I lost track of my old high school friends, and when I returned home, none of my college friends were near me. Over the years, the occasional texts and phone calls became less and less frequent, and before I knew it, I was moving through life with just my family and a few acquaintances. Having these three women and their men in my life has been eye-opening.

And so very welcome.

Add in Gavin, and I'm living a pretty rich life right now.

"You know, I bet that chocolate dip and those strawberries will come in handy later," Hallie says to me the moment we pull apart.

"What?" I ask, pretty sure I don't really want to know where she's going with this.

"You can dip the strawberries in chocolate, drizzle it over Gavin's abs—or better yet, his...you know," she says, dropping her voice down, "and lick it off. Food and sex go hand in hand."

My face flames hot, and yes, this was exactly where I expected her to go with her comment.

She grins cheekily. "Just think about it. He'll love it, promise."

And then she walks over to Logan, slips her arm around his waist, and they walk to his truck together to head home. "She's not wrong, you know," Blair chimes in before she starts to head toward Gabe. "I expect a report back tomorrow on the whole chocolate and strawberries thing."

Ellie and I both sigh as we watch the two mommies-to-be leave the community center. "I serve food all day long. The last thing I want to do is serve it up on my husband's abs."

TD chokes, clearly having heard what she said as he approaches. "Do I wanna know?"

"Hallie," Ellie and I both state at the same time.

"Ahh, should have known. You ready, babe?" he asks Ellie, slipping his arm around her and pulling her into his side.

"Ready. Thanks again, for everything, Ava. I think we knocked this shower out of the park."

I nod in agreement. "Sure did. Talk to you later," I holler, making my way to my vehicle and climbing inside. I set the leftover container in the passenger seat and fire up my little SUV, seeking warmth from the heater. It only takes a few minutes to reach a comfortable temperature, but before I pull out of my parking spot, I fire off a quick text.

Me: All done with the shower. I have leftover food if you're hungry.

Gavin: I'm always hungry...for you.

I grin down at the device in my hand as images of chocolate and strawberries and a very naked Gavin enter my mind. Before I can suggest he come over for a while, he shoots me another message.

Gavin: I'm still out at Logan's cabin finishing up the flooring. Wanna come out and keep me company?

Logan had called Gavin on Friday, hiring him to install a new pine floor before the baby arrives. Logan actually asked him if he could start it Sunday, since he has a couple of big jobs coming up. He wanted to squeeze it in before he has to help build a new addition on a house.

Me: Are you sure? I can just go home and hang out there.

Gavin: No way. I'd much prefer your company.

Me: All right then. I'll head out.

Gavin: See you soon, beautiful.

Smiling, I slip my phone into the cupholder and head toward the Bluff Preserves where Logan's cabin is housed. The sun is starting to set, but there's still plenty of light yet. The days are getting longer as we approach March, and as much as I enjoy the different seasons of weather we have in Wisconsin, I'm ready for spring.

I pull onto the road that leads to the cabin, passing a few vehicles. February is a great time at the Bluff. Yes, it's cold, but the lake is still frozen for ice fishing, and it's a prime time to snowmobile, if that's your thing. Most of the cabins are always rented, even in the winter, for long weekend getaways.

A string of snowmobiles pass me just as I'm turning into Logan's driveway, each one waving as they go. There's something magical about this place. Whether you're a summer or a winter person, there's always plenty to do at the park.

I stop my vehicle beside Gavin's work truck and climb out. Movement catches out of the corner of my eye, and when I glance up at the porch, I find him standing there. He's wearing well-worn jeans with knee pads and a flannel shirt with the sleeves rolled up. He looks positively edible and makes my mouth water.

Reaching up, he grabs the rafter above his head. The motion causes his shirt to tighten over his arms, and while I've never been big on appearances, the sight of Gavin with his corded muscles and killer smile makes my thighs clench.

"Get up here and kiss me."

My heart squeezes in my chest. My smile is automatic. My legs carry me quickly up the stairs and into his waiting arms. The kiss is electric. Everything fades away. The birds chirping, the snowmobiles running nearby, the world around us. It all just disappears until it's only him and me left.

Nothing else matters.

CHAPTER *Twenty four*

GAVIN

"Hi, Daddy," Annabelle says the moment I answer the phone.

"Hello, my beautiful daughter. How was school?" I ask, sitting in my recliner while I wait for Ava to get here. She had to stay after school for a bit today, which delayed her arrival for dinner. So, I'm showered up and ready to go when she gets here.

"It was good. Miss Rutledge tripped over a desk leg though and almost fell."

My heart skips a beat. "She did? Is she okay?"

"Yeah," Annabelle replies with a little giggle. "She was giggling afterward. She caught herself on the desk in front of the one she tripped over."

"Hmm," I reply, already making a plan to give her a massage later. "Anything else exciting happen at school?"

"Well, David dropped his lunch tray in his lap and had to wear wet pants until his mom could bring him another pair."

"That sucks," I reply.

"And we got to have extra recess time in the gym because the internet went out and Miss Rutledge couldn't print the math worksheet."

"I was always in favor of extra recess," I confess.

"How was work?" she asks.

"Good. Max and I finished up the floor in Logan's cabin. Tomorrow we get to start framing up an addition."

"Did you give his girlfriend back her sweater?"

My mind tries to figure out what in the hell she's talking about, and when it finally comes up with the memory. "Oh, yeah. All taken care of."

Ava was mortified when I told her about the whole sweater drama, how my daughter found it in the laundry and then took it over to my mom's to give it back to her. I never asked Annabelle how and why she took it out of my closet because I didn't want to give Annabelle another opportunity to put the whole thing under a microscope, but I wanted to. It was a reminder she's a bit nosier and more observant than she used to be.

We chat for a few more minutes before she has to go to help set the table for dinner. "Get your homework done after dinner," I say, even though I know I don't need to.

"I will. Mike will be in the living room playing video games, so I'll hang out in my room," she informs me.

I don't have anything against Mike, Julia's boyfriend, but he seems to be making himself right at home. "All right, well, have a good evening."

"I will, Dad. Love you."

"Love you more, Belle."

We hang up, and no sooner do I set my phone down on the armrest of the chair does it chime with a text.

Ava: Just now leaving. I offered to help gather some information for a grant the library is presenting at the board meeting on Wednesday night. Heading home now and then will be over.

Gavin: No rush. Take your time. I'll be here, waiting. Naked.

Ava: And that's supposed to cause me not to rush?

Gavin: Be safe. My nakedness will be here when you arrive.

Ava: On my way.

I jump up and stretch, taking a look around the living room. I'm anxious to have Ava back in my space. When she showed up at Logan's cabin yesterday, we never made it here. She watched me work for a bit, then we ate some of the leftover food she had with her. Finally, I sent her home when I was picking up my tools to head home because she was exhausted. I suggested she just go home and get a good night's sleep.

Heading to the kitchen, I check on the homemade pizzas I prepped and have ready to go in the oven, but I don't want to put them in quite yet. I'll give it another ten or fifteen minutes before I start to bake them, and if they're not done when she arrives, I'll use the free minutes as a time to steal a few kisses.

My phone rings from the living room, and I quickly retrieve it. My first thought is something's up with Ava, maybe her car or at her house. So when I see my employee, Max's, name on the screen, I relax just a bit.

"Hey, man, what's up?" I ask in way of greeting.

"Hey, sorry to bother you, but I wanted to make you aware of something."

"Shoot," I reply, reaching for the remote and turning on the TV. We won't necessarily watch it, but maybe we can find a movie to have on in the background while we eat.

"Uhhh, there's some pictures online."

The moment his words register, I stop. "What pictures?"

He hesitates before replying, "Pics of you and what looks like Ava Rutledge." Blood starts to swoosh in my ears, and I almost miss what he's saying. "At least that's who the post says it is."

"What post? Where?"

"Facebook. There's this group someone in Pine Village created, and lots of people share news, pictures, and event details there. Sometimes you get the occasional Karen in there bitching about something like the roads not being plowed enough to their liking or the chicken at the diner being drier than normal. Shit like that."

"Get to the point," I state with a little too much bite behind my words. It's not directed at Max, just at the fact I want to know what the hell he's talking about.

"Sorry, you can make anonymous posts, and someone posted some pictures. It says they were taken yesterday and it's you and Ava. You're standing on Logan's porch at the cabin and have your arms around her. You're clearly kissing in the first couple pics, and then you're holding hands and walking inside the cabin in the fourth photo."

I can see it, because I lived it. Yesterday, when she arrived at the cabin, the first thing I did when she stepped up on the porch was take her in my arms and kiss the hell out of her. I'd been craving those lips, her body pressed against mine, for too long. I didn't even stop to see if someone was nearby. Yes, I knew there were people nearby, snowmobiling and ice fishing, but I was so focused on Ava, I ignored everything and everyone who could have been around us.

"Who posted?"

"I don't know, man. It's anonymous."

"That's bullshit. Someone posts something like that, they should be required to use their damn name," I argue.

"I don't disagree, Gavin."

For the first time, I regret not having that damn social media app on my phone so I can see what's going on. "What does it say?"

"It says, 'Guess who was caught together on Sunday? Gavin Pierson and Ava Rutledge were busted sneaking into Logan Johnson's cabin. Clearly this teacher has problems and shouldn't be around kids. First, promoting underaged drinking, and now sleeping with a student's father? Our kids deserve better than this.'"

My heart is pounding so hard in my chest, I'm sure Max can hear it through the phone line. "Fuck."

"Is it true? Are you seeing Ava?"

I swallow hard. My first thought is to deny, since that's what I've been doing this whole time. Deny, deflect, and lie. Keep it under wraps.

But now, with these photos and the fact they're calling for Ava's job...again, I realize I can't keep quiet. Not because I don't want to, but simply because I won't let her face the firing squad of Pine Village alone.

Fuck that.

"Yeah, I am."

"Cool. She seems like a great woman. I remember you drooling over her last summer at the bar. Glad you finally made a move," he teases lightly, but with the weight of everything else parading through my head, I don't have the ability to joke back.

I rub my forehead. "I don't know anything about that app, man. So, everyone in there can see it? Are they replying, or whatever?"

He pauses a few moments before replying. "Yeah, there are comments. Quite a few, considering it was just posted about an hour ago. Looks like there are a lot of people who think the post is tasteless and gross, but...yeah. There are a handful of people who aren't saying very nice stuff about you two."

I couldn't give two shits about me. What I can't stand is anyone saying crap about Ava. She's an amazing human and an even better teacher, and I'm damn lucky to have her in my life. "This blows. I can't believe it's posted anonymously."

"It's bullshit, man. But you know how this town is. Eventually, it'll come out. Everyone talks."

I close my eyes and take a few deep breaths. "She's on her way over here. I'm gonna have to tell her."

"Yeah, I would, because by the number of comments on the photos, everyone in the city limits will know by morning."

"Can you screenshot it for me?"

"Yeah, sure. I'll send them right over."

"Thanks, Max."

"For what it's worth, I'm happy for you. I've noticed something different with you these last few weeks, and I hope she's that change. You're calmer and smile a lot more."

I don't reply, not really knowing what to say. She *is* the reason I've changed, and yes, all for the better. She makes me want to be a better man.

"I'll let you go. See you tomorrow?" he asks.

"Yeah. See you in the morning."

When I hang up, I stand here and just stare off into space. This is bad. Well, not *bad*, but definitely not ideal. Ava won't like this at all, and I have to be careful how I tell her. The last thing I want is for her to run scared out of my life, because, frankly, that's not an option.

A life without Ava isn't one I want to consider living.

I've fallen head over heels in love with her. We have to figure out how to get through this.

Together.

By the time she's pulling into my driveway, I still have no clue how to tell her what's going on. I scanned the images and post Max sent me, clearly posted by some nosy asshole who needs to mind their own business. This is one of the worst parts about living in a small town. People can't keep their noses out of everyone else's stuff.

I slip on my shoes and head out the back door to meet her. She's putting her car in the garage, and as I walk to the side door, I can't help but look around. Are my neighbors watching right now? Are they taking photos, preparing to post them and show the world we are, in fact, sneaking around?

"Hi," she greets with a big smile the moment she starts to climb out of her vehicle.

I admit, the happiness on her face almost makes all the other bullshit fade away. Almost. "Hey," I reply, taking her in my arms and kissing her lips.

She tastes like mint and honey, and all I want to do is get lost in her for hours on end. Unfortunately, that's not what can happen right now. We have some things to discuss tonight, because I'm certain Max is right and everyone in town will know by morning.

"Come on, let's get inside." I take her hand and lead her out the door, up the back steps, and into my house.

She takes off her sensible shoes and hangs her coat on one of the hooks at my back door. "What smells so good?" she asks as we walk to the kitchen.

I run my hand over the back of my neck, nervously. "Uhh, that's a candle wax warmer thingy with some sort of vanilla cookie melt in it. We're having pizza, and I meant to throw it in the oven when you were on your way, but I...got distracted."

She gives me a cheeky grin, clearly assuming I'm referring to something sexual, especially when her brown eyes take a slow, leisurely stroll down my body, landing on my groin. When she meets my gaze again, she must sense my hesitancy and uneasiness. "What's wrong?"

"Come in the living room with me," I suggest, reaching for her hand. "We have something to talk about."

She's clearly nervous but slips her hand inside mine and walks with me to the couch. "You're starting to freak me out a little," she finally says.

I take a deep breath and, while still holding her hand in mine, decide to rip off the Band-Aid. "Some photos were posted on social media today."

She looks confused. "Photos? Of who?"

"Us."

Clearly, by the look on her face, she wasn't expecting that. "Us? How? When?"

"They're pictures of you and me at Logan's cabin yesterday. Kissing on the porch and then walking into the cabin together."

Her wide eyes stare back at me, and I can read the fear, confusion, and sadness within. "Why would someone post pictures of us?"

"I don't know," I tell her honestly. "And we don't know who posted them because they're posted anonymously."

"How is that possible?" she asks, her voice getting smaller and smaller as the conversation continues.

"I don't know, but Max said you can post in groups without anyone knowing who the original poster is."

"Max? Max knows?"

I slowly nod my head. "Yeah, Max knows. He saw them and called me." Swallowing over the massive lump in my throat, I add, "A lot of people know. The photos have quite a few comments."

Her complexion grows increasingly pale as she watches me, trying to process what I'm telling her. "Can you..." She pauses and clears her throat. "Did he tell you what they're saying? In the comments?"

Fuck, this is hard, because I know I'm about to crush her.

"Yeah," I say gently, stroking my thumb over her knuckles as I continue to hold her hand. "A lot of the comments are very supportive of you. Of us."

She nods slowly. "But not all of the comments," she deduces, understanding where this is going.

"No, not all of them."

Her eyes fill with tears. "What are they saying?"

"It doesn't matter," I quickly state.

"But it does matter, Gavin. This is my job, my livelihood."

"I know it is, sweetheart, which is why I'm telling you right away."

"Then tell me what else they're saying," she insists, even though she knows it's going to hurt.

My mouth opens, but the words don't come yet. I know what I'm about to tell her will hurt, and fuck if I want to be the guy who crushes her.

"Tell me," she insists, lifting her chin.

"They accused you of being a real problem, first with the underaged drinking photo and now by sneaking around with one of your student's dads."

She closes her eyes, but I briefly saw the moment my words hit their mark. The devastation was clear, and I'm certain it's something I'll never forget. "I know this isn't ideal," I start, but she cuts me off.

"Not ideal? This is exactly what I didn't want to happen, Gavin. People are talking about me sleeping with a student's father. They'll assume—"

"That's right, they'll assume. They'll assume because they have no idea how much you really mean to me, and I assure you, my feelings for you have absolutely nothing to do with you being my daughter's teacher." I take her other hand and bring it to my lips, brushing them against her knuckles. "Listen, Ava, I know this sucks. It sucks huge hairy balls, but maybe this is a blessing."

Her eyes widen in shock. "A blessing? Everyone thinking you're sleeping with me to get your daughter a better grade is a blessing?"

"We don't know that's what they're thinking," I argue.

"Of course they do! I'm the teacher who had to face the school board because an underaged photo of myself drinking was posted online. I'm sure they'll find all sorts of reasons why our relationship isn't appropriate, which is why I wanted to keep it quiet. I couldn't risk the public scrutiny."

"I know that, and I respected your position. It's not our fault we were outed on some stupid website, where nosy assholes get to post whatever they want without caring who they hurt."

Her eyes fill with tears, and when the first one slides unchecked down her cheek, it feels as if someone reaches into my chest and rips out my heart. "What am I going to do now?" she whispers to herself.

"We're going to get through this, together."

Ava shakes her head, as if not wanting to hear my words. "I need to think," she blurts out, suddenly standing up and taking a step back.

Holding on to her hand, I say, "Listen, I know this is a big deal for you. I get it, really. But we can't let them win by tearing us apart, Ava. Whoever did this is trying to drive a wedge between us and hurt your reputation. If we show them they can't break us, we win."

A few more tears slide down her cheeks. "I appreciate your confidence, but I don't quite share it. If the school board catches wind of this, I could lose my job."

"There's no clause saying you can't date a student's father."

"No, but I'm already being watched like a hawk, Gavin. Can't you see that? This gives the board and the superintendent an opportunity to fire me for negative press."

"They can't fire you for dating," I argue, starting to get upset now too.

"No, they can't, but they can fire me because of my reputation."

"You're an amazing teacher, Ava. They'd be stupid to let you go just for dating me."

"Welcome to living and working in a small town," she counters sadly. She takes a deep breath before adding, "I'm going to go home. I need to do some thinking, and I'll probably need to talk to the superintendent tomorrow."

Standing up, I take her in my arms and breathe her in. "I don't want you to go."

She curls her hands into my chest, holding my sweatshirt tightly. "I don't want to go, but I need to."

Sighing, I pull back, meeting her sad gaze. "I need you to know I'm fighting for you, for us. When you go through something hard, you go through it with me by your side. We may not have been ready to go public, but now that it's happened for us, I refuse to let you face the firing squad on your own. I'll be right beside you, Ava, because that's what you do when you love

A whimper breaks from her lips as she throws her arms around my shoulders and holds on tight. I squeeze a little harder than I should, desperately needing to feel her body against my own.

When she pulls back, she sniffles and gives me a dejected look. "Thank you. Give me a little time to process this and deal with whatever fallout I'll have at work."

"I'm not kidding, Ava. I'm not going anywhere. I'll be right by your side through all of this."

Her small smile, while sad, tells me how grateful she is. She may not understand what it truly means to have someone in her corner like this, but she's about to find out. I'm not going anywhere, and I'll fight every single one of the bastards who try to hurt her.

Watch me.

She steps forward and goes up on her tiptoes, her hands pressed to my chest. I swipe my mouth against hers, savoring the feel of her and refusing to rush this kiss. I need her to know—to *feel*—exactly how much I love her.

When she pulls away, the normal heat I'd see reflecting in those brown eyes is void. Instead, those orbs are full of fear and concern, two things I hate to see. I guide her to the mudroom and watch as she slips her shoes back on. Grabbing her coat, I hold it open for her and watch as she shivers at the slightest contact of my hand against her arm.

At least I know I still affect her the way she does me.

"This isn't over," I insist. When she nods, I add, "Not by a long shot, Ava. We're going to get through this together."

"Okay," she whispers.

"The only reason I'm letting you go is because kidnapping is illegal in Wisconsin."

The corner of her mouth ticks. "I'm pretty sure it's illegal in all states."

"I'm not going to force you to stay, even though I want to. I want you to stay and come up with a game plan with me. I want to go to school with you tomorrow and face every single one of the people who dare to say a cross word to you or look at you in a way they shouldn't. This fight, if there is one, isn't just about you. I'm involved too, but even if I wasn't, I'd still be right here, waiting for you. So, go home and take the time you need to process what's happening, but know I'm here. I'm always right here."

She relaxes and nods. "Thank you, Gavin. For everything." She goes up on her tiptoes and presses a chaste kiss to my lips once more. I want to take control, to deepen the kiss and show her exactly what she means to me, but I don't.

I let her walk out the door.

Helping her into her vehicle, I open the garage door she had just pulled into a short time ago and watch her back out of my driveway. I stand there even after she drives away, wishing she'd come back so we can deal with the fallout of those photos together.

With a loud exhale, I lock everything up and head back inside. My heart aches for her, at the hurt reflected in her eyes as I told her what was found online. It hurts for another reason too. One I wasn't expecting.

I had told her I loved her.

But she didn't tell me back.

The pain in my chest just continues to grow. Something tells me, it won't get better until she's by my side once more. By my side and in my arms.

Time to put a plan together.

Time to show her exactly how I feel.

Time to let the whole world know she's mine.

CHAPTER Twenty five

Ava

I manage to hold it together until I get home. The moment I pull into my garage and park my vehicle, the waterworks start and don't stop.

This is exactly why I didn't want anyone to know I was seeing Gavin. This is why I fought the attraction to him in the beginning. I knew this could blow up in my face, as it has.

I know if that old photo of me hadn't been posted, then me seeing Gavin wouldn't be a problem. I wouldn't have the rule about not getting involved with the dad of one of my students and we wouldn't have had to hide. Yet, here I am, reliving one of the worst times in my life, professionally, because more photos have appeared of me on social media.

I know I need to talk to the superintendent. I need to tell him about the photos before he hears about them from some of the people against the idea of me dating a student's father. But I also need to see the post. I didn't think to ask Gavin to see it, which clearly he did. I'm assuming someone sent it to him, most likely Max, since he's the one who found it and called.

God, I can't believe I'm the subject of drama.

Again.

This is exactly what I've been trying to avoid. This is what I was afraid of happening.

But then I picture Gavin's handsome, smiling face, and all I want to do is run straight back over there and let him hold me in his arms. I know he wanted me to stay with him, to figure this out together, but I needed space. I needed time to breathe. I need to figure out how I'm going to talk to my bosses and do damage control on my reputation.

Boy, that thing has sure taken a beating these last few years.

My phone keeps chiming with unread texts and ringing, but I ignore them for now. I'm certain it's my friends, having heard about or seen the latest post about me. Grabbing my phone, I fire off a text Gavin.

Me: Are you able to send me copies of what's posted online?

He replies right away.

Gavin: Yes, I can send you the screenshots Max sent me. Hold on.

His message is proceeded by four snapshots of an online post from Anonymous.

Gavin: How are you? What do you need?

Before I click on the images, I fire back a response.

Me: I'm okay, and I don't really know yet. I'm going to call the superintendent and see what he thinks.

Gavin: I'm here, Ava. Please don't shut me out. We're in this together.

I smile at his reply, warmth washing over me. He truly is one of the good ones, and I'm dang lucky to have him in my corner.

Me: I know, and I appreciate that so much. Give me just a little time.

Gavin: Take all the time you need, but not too much. I miss you when you're not here.

Me: I miss you too.

Gavin: Don't even think about pushing me away, all right? I won't go. You jump, I jump. Or whatever it was Leonardo DiCaprio said in *Titanic*.

I chuckle at his comment, smiling down at the screen. Even when it feels like everything is crashing down around me, he knows how to bring a smile to my face.

Gavin: You smiled, I know it. I felt it. Every time you smile, it's like being bathed by the sun. It's the best feeling.

Even though I blush, his comment hits its intended target, and my heart skips a beat.

Me: I did smile. Thank you for that. I needed it.

Gavin: I've got lots more ammunition in my arsenal, beautiful. Come over when you're ready, and I'll make you smile all night long...amongst other things.

Me: I promise, when I'm ready, I'll be there.

Gavin: My door is always open, beautiful, but don't take too long. My bed is cold when you're not there.

I don't reply, mostly because I'm not sure what to say. He's not wrong. I hate sleeping alone, even though I do it more nights than I have with him. Those nights we've been together are just...special. That's the only way to describe them. And there haven't been too many on account that he has his daughter every other week, but we steal a lot of time together on those off weeks, especially Friday and Saturday nights.

With a deep sigh, I click on the images he sent. The first thing I do is read the headline for the photos.

Guess who was caught together on Sunday? Gavin Pierson and Ava Rutledge were busted sneaking into Logan Johnson's cabin. Clearly this teacher has problems and shouldn't be around kids. First, promoting underaged drinking, and now sleeping with a student's father? Our kids deserve better than this.

A massive lump forms in my throat, making it hard to breathe, but I force myself to keep going. Clicking on the images, I scroll so I can get a better look at the screenshots. The first three pictures are of us kissing. If I stand back and objectively look at them, all I see is a man and woman sharing an intimate moment. It's not scandalous. There're no ulterior motives. Just two people in love.

In love.

Guilt slams me in the chest. When I close my eyes, I hear his words.

I'll be right beside you, Ava, because that's what you do when you love someone.

He told me he loved me, and I didn't acknowledge it. I didn't say it back, even though I feel the same way. I was overwhelmed by everything happening around me, and I didn't take the time to listen to his words. To reciprocate them. To tell him how madly in love with him I am, and how much I want to make this work between us.

But there will be time for that. First chance I get, I'll figure out the perfect way to say the words to him.

The fourth picture is of us smiling at each other, holding hands as we enter Logan's cabin. I remember hanging out in there for about an hour, watching him work, before I ran out to my vehicle and got the container of leftover food. We ate and chatted until the yawns started and I struggled to keep my eyes open. It had been a long day. Instead of going back to either my or his house, I ended up alone and promptly fell asleep as soon as my head hit the pillow.

That night, despite being about twenty-four hours ago, suddenly feels like a lifetime ago.

At the bottom of the fourth photo, I'm able to see some of the comments. The first two are complimentary, stating that it's no one's business who I date and finding the anonymous post tacky. But the third one definitely isn't in my favor.

"This doesn't surprise me. She's a terrible teacher. My son almost didn't pass fifth grade because of her. She needs to be fired." Reading those words aloud is like a knife to the chest. It burns and aches in the worst way.

I recognize the name attached to the comment, and honestly, it's not surprising. I had her son in class two years ago, and he was a huge struggle from day one. He didn't want to be there, created drama amongst his classmates, and refused to do the work. I tried everything to engage him and help him learn. His mother enabled him, telling me it was my job to get him to do the work, and she gave no encouragement, no help from home. So when he nearly didn't pass the grade, of course, it was my fault.

Sighing, I click out of the picture and pull up my contacts. I need to call the superintendent, even though I don't want to. It's after six, and I hate bothering him at home. But I feel this can't wait. Things like this will only continue to grow and fester until they erupt with toxicity.

Tapping on Mr. Jones's name, I listen while the call connects and rings. "Hello?"

"Hi, Mr. Jones, this is Ava Rutledge. I apologize for calling you at home in the evening like this," I say.

"It's no problem. What can I do for you?" he asks.

"Well, I, uh, I'm not sure how to say this, but I'm having an issue you need to be aware of."

"Go on."

I explain the situation with the photos and give him a rundown on the comments I was able to see. He doesn't say anything at first, but eventually breaks the silence. "Well, I hate that your name is being dragged through the mud on social media. I'll give Dana a call and discuss the matter with her."

Dana is Principal Dunn, who's in her second year at the position. "I was planning to call her after I spoke to you."

"You're welcome to, but I'll still do it. As you know, matters pertaining to employment and discipline also are brought to the board's attention."

My throat goes dry. "I know."

"I'm not saying there's any disciplinary matters here, Ava. Frankly, you're entitled to a personal life. I've known you for several years, and you're a fair, competent educator and employee."

"Thank you, sir."

"But this is also a small town, and yes, the people here have a way of making your business their own. If it weren't for the issue you had a handful of years back, this wouldn't even be discussed."

"I know, and I get it."

"You're welcome to take tomorrow and Wednesday off. We have a board meeting Wednesday, and with that, an executive session to discuss any employee matters. If I know the board, they'll want to discuss the accusations against you."

It's hard to swallow over the lump of emotion lodged in my throat. "Could I...Is there a chance I'll be fired, sir?"

"I wouldn't think so."

His reply doesn't exactly soothe the worry and ache in my chest. "I'm not sure about taking the days off. I don't want it to appear I'm hiding."

"I understand that, and only you can make the decision. But you have the time saved up, and if you need to take a couple days to calm down, I'd understand. Dana will approve it, I'll make sure. If you don't take them off, be prepared for questions and probably some comments. Good and bad. You know this town as well as I do, and when drama arises, everyone has an opinion to state, and they will state it."

I nod in understanding, even though he can't see it. "Thank you, sir. I may go ahead and take a few days off."

"I'll let Dana know, and she can arrange for a substitute. Keep her posted if you want to take more than just the next day or two."

"I will, sir. Thank you for taking my call."

"It's no problem." He pauses before adding, "You're an amazing educator, Ava. I know you've had your fair share of issues over the years, but our district is very lucky to have you. If asked, I pledge my support to you. You're allowed a personal life, and I'm certain there will be no findings of misdoings where your student is concerned."

"There won't be. Annabelle Pierson is a bright student. The grades she's received have been earned, not given because I was seeing her father. You could ask Mr. Parmelee," I state, referring to the fourth-grade teacher.

"I'm sure it won't come to that, but I'll take it under advisement."

After a few seconds, I ask, "Should I plan to attend the board meeting on Wednesday?"

"You're more than welcome to, as you are with any public meeting. There's a portion on the agenda for public comments, and if you'd want to speak to the board, that would be the time."

Ugh, the thought of getting up in front of the board and the community members who attend is enough to cause me to break out in hives. Give me a classroom full of kids, and I'm fine, but there's something about speaking in public like that, especially to defend myself, that makes me want to crawl into a hole and hide.

"Call me if you need anything. Otherwise, plan to take the next two days off, and if you want the rest of the week, just let Dana know."

"Thank you, again. I appreciate your support."

"You're welcome. Talk soon."

We hang up, and even though I appreciate his candor and kind support, it doesn't help settle the tsunami of emotions in my chest. My heart hurts. Being a teacher brings a certain level of scrutiny. Not all parents will support you. I get that. But this is different. This is public scrutiny, and I'm not in favor of it. In fact, I despise it completely.

I give Dana a call after waiting about thirty minutes. As suspected, she has already spoken with the superintendent, but she's also fielding other calls and comments. A small group of parents have already stepped forward, outraged by my actions and calling for my dismissal once more. She didn't state who is leading the charge, not that it matters.

The damage is done.

My dream of working in my hometown until retirement may very well be in jeopardy.

The board might look at me as a problem child, for lack of a better phrase, and decide my contract isn't worth keeping. There may be a nationwide teacher shortage, but sometimes you have to cut yourself loose from things that bring you grief.

What will I do then?

I can't imagine any other school district jumping at the chance to hire a teacher who's constantly being talked about and may or may not have lost her previous job because of public backlash and scrutiny.

The thought of having to find another job makes my stomach roll. I love my students, my school, and this town, despite the fact they're throwing me under the bus right now.

But I love Gavin more.

How quickly my perspective changes when I think about him. He's simply amazing, and if I have to choose between working at Pine Village Elementary School or finding another job so I can continue to date him, I already know which one I would choose.

Guess it's time to freshen up my résumé, huh?

I shake my head at the thought. I'm not afraid of it, but I really hope it doesn't come to that.

My time with Gavin has been special, and looking back, I wouldn't change it for anything. Even now, knowing I could lose everything I've been working toward my entire career.

As I get ready for bed, my phone chimes with a text alert. Even though I have dozens of messages I need to reply to from colleagues and friends, I click on the one name that brings me comfort during this mess.

Gavin: Heading to bed and thinking of you. I wish you were here, so I could hold you while you sleep.

Gavin: Please don't stress and worry, beautiful. I'm sure that's easier said than done. I can practically hear the wheels in your head spinning from here. You will get through this. We'll do it together.

He keeps saying that word.
Together.

Gavin: I'm glad you're taking the next couple of days off. No reason to put yourself directly in the spotlight while you're trying to work. Your dad is right, you don't take nearly enough time for you.

Try to relax. Read a new book. Create something beautiful in your craft room. Just be you.

After I talked to the principal, I called my dad. He was outraged on my behalf, but seemed genuinely happy when I told him who the man was. He's known Gavin for a while and has the utmost respect for him professionally. Personally, he's now his biggest cheerleader, and during the conversation, he kept offering his approval.

Once I filled my dad in on what's happening, I messaged Gavin with an update. He knows I'm taking the next two days off and will be attending the board meeting Wednesday night. I still don't know if I'll speak, but I want to be there, to hear what others will say to the board. Maybe then I'll decide to speak on my behalf.

Gavin: I have something to say to you, and I'm going to say it the first chance I get. But not in a text. I want to look in your mesmerizing brown eyes when I do.

Gavin: Sweet dreams, sweetheart. I'll talk to you soon.

Smiling, I reply, wishing we were lying in bed, snuggled together beneath the blankets.

Me: Good night, Gavin.

I insert the heart emoji, hoping it conveys how I feel without saying the words. I can assume to know what he's wanting to tell me, and it most likely is the same thing I want to tell him. Face-to-face. So I can throw my arms around him and show him how I feel in a kiss.

Sleep doesn't come easy, but it eventually does. Dreams of me, Gavin, and Annabelle carry me through the night until I'm awakened by more phone calls and texts.

These next couple of days won't be easy, but I'll get through them.

I always do.

CHAPTER
Twenty six

GAVIN

"Hi, Belle," I greet the moment I see my ex-wife's name on my phone.

"Hi, Daddy."

I'm instantly on alert. My happy daughter sounds anything but. "What's the matter?"

Annabelle sighs. "Well, Miss Rutledge wasn't at school today. We had a substitute, Mrs. Bridges, and she told us Miss Rutledge was sick."

My heart skips a beat at the mere mention of Ava's name. "Well, I'm sure she'll be feeling better and back to class soon." I don't tell her I already know she'll be out tomorrow, and the reason isn't exactly because she's sick.

"I hope so, but then I came home, and Mommy said she was going to be fired."

I sit straight up in my seat. "She said what?"

Annabelle sniffles, clearly upset by this news. "She said Miss Rutledge is going to get fired and not teach at my school anymore."

I sigh and rub my forehead. "I don't think Miss Rutledge is going to be fired, honey. That's not something you should worry about."

"But...she's such a great teacher. I love being in her class."

"I know. I'm sure a lot of students feel the same way," I reply.

"The substitute is okay, but she doesn't make me smile the way Miss Rutledge does."

Same.

Clearing my throat, I tell her, "Try not to worry. I'm sure Miss Rutledge will be back in class very soon."

"I hope so. We're supposed to watch another science video on Friday, and even though they're kinda boring, she makes them fun."

A grin spreads across my face. "Aren't you supposed to be at karate?" I ask, noting it's Tuesday night.

"Yeah, I'm waiting on Mom to tell me it's time to go. After class Mike and Mikey are having dinner with us."

"That'll be nice," I reply absently, my mind on Ava, as it has been since everything blew up yesterday.

"You know, I've been thinking," she starts.

"About?"

"I think you should date."

I cough, choking on the breath I was taking. "What?"

"Here me out, Dad. You deserve to have nice dinners too, and even though I don't really want to know, my friends' moms say you're hot."

"Uhh, thanks?"

"I think you should ask out Miss Rutledge."

There's no stopping my smile now. "Yeah? Why do you say that?"

"Because she's super pretty and nice and loves to read. We can talk about books, and she'd make stuff with me because she loves to craft like I do."

"That is true," I find myself saying. "Miss Rutledge would be a catch."

"She really would. And when she came over to Grandma and Grandpa's on Christmas Eve, you said she was pretty."

"I did say that."

"So, think about it. I bet she'd say yes, unless she's dating someone. She did get flowers not that long ago. She didn't tell me who they were from, but she smiled a lot when she looked at them."

The thought of Ava appreciating the flowers I sent fills my mind, as does the fact I feel like Annabelle has completely opened the door for me. She's encouraging me to date her teacher, which means she'll probably be ecstatic when Ava and I decide to take our relationship public. Since those photos appeared online, that'll likely happen sooner rather than later, but I'm fine with that.

As long as she's content with everyone knowing.

Not that she really has a choice, but she could still insist on keeping our relationship under wraps for a while. There are still three months left of school, and she could choose to chill until then. I'd respect it, as long as she doesn't push me away completely. But I'm hoping it doesn't come to that.

I'm hoping to convince her to take a chance on us.

Publicly.

Together.

"I gotta go, Dad. Mom is hollering it's time to go."

"Have fun at karate," I tell her before we sign off. "Love you."

"Love you too, Daddy. Talk to you soon."

I hang up the phone and the euphoria I felt running through my veins at how encouraging my daughter was for me to ask Ava out vanishes.

Why in the fuck did Julia tell Annabelle that Miss Rutledge was getting fired?

Needing to know the answer to that question, I fire off a text, knowing she won't be able to talk on the phone in front of Annabelle until they arrive at karate.

Me: Call me when you can talk.

It takes a solid thirty minutes before my phone rings. With each minute that passed, I grew more irritated with my ex-wife, angrier that she said something to our daughter, especially because she knows how much Annabelle loves her teacher. Not to mention the man in the middle of this whole mess is me.

"Hello?" I ask, unable to mask my annoyance.

"I've got about five minutes. What's up?"

My annoyance level elevates immediately, mostly because I know she's not doing anything but sitting there, waiting for our daughter to finish her karate class. "Why did you tell Annabelle her teacher is getting fired?"

Julia laughs. She actually laughs at my question. "Because she is?"

"You don't know that," I argue, "So why you would tell our daughter, who absolutely loves her teacher, that is beyond me."

"Are someone's panties in a bunch? You're just mad because those photos outed you. Your sneaking around is over."

"You know nothing about any of that, so I'd watch what you say."

"Or what? Listen, Gavin, I'm terribly sorry your booty call came to an end, but did you have to sleep with our daughter's teacher? How cliché and tacky."

"Don't ever call Ava a booty call again," I spit out, my tolerance of her bullshit reaching the end of my rope. "She's a hell of a lot more than that."

"Well, maybe you should have protected her precious reputation instead of mauling her on Logan Johnson's cabin porch. Did you not even consider you're surrounded by a public park where anyone can see and take pictures?"

The hairs on the back of my neck stand up.

"Listen, I don't care who you screw, but you involved our daughter when you decided to drop your pants with her teacher.

Now, she's going to lose her job because she's sleeping with one of her students' fathers. Looks like perfect Miss Rutledge isn't really perfect at all. Maybe it's time she got knocked down a notch or two."

I'm left completely speechless. I've never heard Julia speak ill of Ava, and I wasn't prepared for it now. Before there was ever anything between myself and Ava, Julia had nothing but good to say about our daughter's fifth-grade teacher, so what changed? Why all this hostility now?

"I have to go, Gavin. Mike is here, and we're going to grab coffee across the street while the kids finish class." She doesn't say anything else before disconnecting the line, hanging up on me.

I stare at my phone, trying to comprehend what in the hell just happened. Julia's always blamed everyone but herself for everything, but I don't understand her venom toward Ava. Sadly, I probably won't ever know the reason. Julia does what Julia wants to do, and doesn't care who she hurts in the process.

I spend the rest of my Tuesday night thinking about Ava. Tomorrow is the board meeting, and she needs support. I hope all those people who were championing her on that post all show up, because if it's only the ones who think she's doing something wrong, then it might not go as it should with the board.

And the school district isn't the only one who would suffer a disservice by letting her go.

I would too, because who knows where she'd end up. The thought of her having to leave town to take a job elsewhere is unacceptable.

Time to put my plan into motion.

Operation Show Ava How Much She Means to Me is about to commence.

271

The parking lot is packed. So full, I have to circle the block and park on a side street.

I hate that I'm running late, but despite facing one of the most important moments of my life, I got delayed at the end of work, having to talk over a few issues with the homeowner. By the time I left, I barely had enough time to rush home, shower, and get back on the road.

Now, I'm here, ready to stand beside the woman I love.

With a deep breath, I grab the door that leads to the room where the school board conducts their meetings. The moment I step inside, it's almost chaotic. There are people everywhere, as if the whole town is in attendance for tonight's meeting.

I scan the room, finding Ava sitting in the back row. She looks completely overwhelmed as she sits beside some of the other teachers from the school. Standing directly behind them are her friends—Hallie, Logan, Blair, Gabe, Ellie, and TD, as are Marcus and Cameron, who own the steakhouse. But that's not all. Her dad, grandma, and sister are here, silently showing support for their loved one too.

"Does anyone else have anything to add during public comments?" a man at the front of the room asks.

Stepping forward, I raise my hand. "Yeah, I have something to say."

CHAPTER Twenty seven

Ava

The sound of his voice has my heart pounding in my chest and my eyes seeking him out. Gavin is walking toward the podium at the front of the room, looking as gorgeous as I've ever seen him in jeans and a fitted black shirt with his company logo across the chest. There's confidence in his movements, a familiarity in the thump of his boots on the floor, and just before he reaches the front, he turns and gives me a grin.

One that goes straight to my lady bits and pieces.

He clears his throat. "I'm Gavin Pierson, and I'd like to say something about Ava Rutledge."

I swear my heart is going to beat right out of my chest, and I'm pretty certain I'm not breathing as I wait to hear what he has to say.

"If you weren't aware, I'm the man in the photographs that were posted about Miss Rutledge, and the caption is wrong. It's absurd for multiple reasons. To insist what was documented without our knowledge as being anything more than sneaking around is ridiculous. Even if that were the case, it would be not one person's business in this room. Any relationship she has on a personal level has nothing to do with how amazing she is at her job. I could pull dozens of former students and parents of hers up here to the front of the room to preach her praises, but I'm going to assume a few of them spoke tonight before I arrived. Her students, her school, it all comes first to her, which is why she's so effective at teaching. We're fortunate to have many great educators in this district, and Ava Rutledge is one of them."

He takes a deep breath and glances around the front of the room. The seven members of the board are at the very front, as well as the superintendent. Principals for both the elementary and the junior/senior high school are seated to the side, and all are listening and watching.

"I know what has been said about her, about us. I've read the comments, some by prominent members of the community sitting right here in this very room. I can't imagine having my name dragged through the mud, not once, but twice by the people sitting in this room."

I can't help but notice a few people shift uncomfortably.

"I can speak to you all day about her character, about her ability to teach and how much she loves this school. But I also know if you choose to make the decision to let her go, based on juvenile bullshit posted on the internet by a coward who won't even show their name, then that's your call. It's the wrong one, but that's on you. I know she'll be fine. There isn't a district in this state that wouldn't jump at an opportunity to have a teacher like Ava Rutledge on their staff, and if you let her go, it will be someone else's gain, I know it."

He glances over his shoulder and meets my wide-eyed gaze. "They called our photos inappropriate. How is a man welcoming the woman he loves home inappropriate? No, we weren't at either of our homes, but what does that matter? If we were dating or married before my daughter began her class, would we be here, having this discussion? The answer is no."

His eyes return to the front of the room. "This is a wonderful small town. You get things here you can't find in a bigger city. The level of support and appreciation is second to none. So why are we picking and choosing who gets that support? Don't let the bad shit in a small town outweigh the positive. Ava Rutledge *is* the positive. She's the best person I know, and if I'm lucky, someday, I'll get to call her mine forever. Thank you."

My jaw must be hanging down to my chest, but I can't seem to close it. All I can do is watch as he walks past the crowd of people and back out the way he came.

Panic sets in.

He's leaving?

After he just told the entire town he was in love with me, he's walking out the door?

I jump up. "Excuse me, excuse me," I mumble to the people I pass, trying not to step on their feet as I scurry toward the exit.

Pushing through the door, I burst outside into the cold of night. "Gavin!" I holler, my eyes scanning.

"There's no reason to yell."

I whip to my right to find Gavin leaning against the wall, waiting. "I thought you left."

A grin cracks across his lips. "Not without you."

"But...why did you come out here?"

He sighs and shakes his head. "Because I didn't want to listen to anyone say one bad thing about you."

Giving him a smile, I step forward and press my hands to his warm chest. "Hardly anyone said anything negative. If they were there to advocate my dismissal, they didn't say a word. They didn't have a chance, really, because my coworkers and former parents started speaking, everyone else seemed to get real quiet, real fast."

"Good," he says, slipping his arm around my waist and pulling me toward him. "I'd have to have words with anyone who spoke ill of the woman I love."

Unable to contain my smile, I go up on my tiptoes and press my lips to his. "I love you too."

He opens his mouth, claiming mine in a bruising kiss that makes my toes curl. "For the record, I'm done pussyfooting around this. I want everything with you, Ava."

My heart pirouettes in my chest. "I want that too."

He kisses me again, his tongue sliding inside my mouth as his hands slip beneath my sweater. Cold fingers brush against my lower back, sending a shiver through my body, but the heat of the kiss more than makes up for the frigid temperatures around us.

"Should we go back inside?" he asks, resting his forehead against mine.

"No, I think we should go home. Whatever happens next is out of our hands. What will be, will be, right?" I ask, repeating his words from Monday.

"That's right," he replies, taking my hands in his. "Let's go home. And maybe get naked," he suggests, a wolfish grin on his gorgeous face.

Before we're able to take off, the door opens, and the attendees start to file out.

"There you are!" Grandma hollers, making a beeline for Gavin and me. "We thought you took off for some nookie."

My face flames red as my dad looks on, uncomfortable. "No one thought that but you," my sister argues, shaking her head.

"The meeting's over?" I ask.

"No, but there's nothing more we can do. They'll do their executive session like always, but the superintendent spoke and pledged his support of you before they went back for the closed-door meeting. He said it would be an outrage to the school if the board voted to remove you, and he'd hate to see what sort of fallout would happen," my dad informs me, a look of pride on his face.

"I watched the board members the entire time, and most of them seemed to really listen to those who spoke up for you. The only one I thought seemed shady was that Mark Bollinger. He kept subtly shaking his head in disagreement."

"Mark? His wife is Julia's best friend. I saw them Sunday—" Gavin stops speaking, his eyes wide with realization. "Shit, I saw him and his wife on Sunday. They were snowmobiling around the Bluff. Son of a bitch, I know who took the photos."

I watch him as he turns concerned, sad eyes my way.

"Kelli, Julia's friend. She had to have taken the photos, I'm just not sure which one posted them."

"It doesn't matter," I tell him, wrapping my hand around his.

"The hell it doesn't. If my ex-wife had anything to do with those photos being published, I'll—"

"Don't make it worse for anyone. Someone tried to drive a wedge between us, tried to ruin reputations. Let's not let them win," I insist. "Besides, I don't want to cause more problems between you and Julia, especially where Annabelle is concerned. The best revenge is to not let their scheming bullshit take us down."

He flashes me a quick grin and pulls me into his arms. "Did you just say bullshit?"

I feel my cheeks flush a bit. "This seemed like the right occasion."

"Of course it did. What someone did was bullshit," Grandma states bluntly.

"Mom, it's getting cold out here. Why don't I take you home?" my dad suggests, having picked my grandma up to bring her to the meeting to show me support.

"I'm fine, but I bet these two want to get going and get back to the nookie."

My cheeks flame red, my entire body burning with embarrassment. "Grandma!" I groan at the same time my dad screeches, "Mom."

She just chuckles and gives Gavin a kiss on the cheek. "Take care of my granddaughter."

"I will, Miss Betty," he replies. He glances over and extends a hand toward my dad. "I hope it's okay I date your daughter, sir. I seem to have fallen in love with her over the last couple of months."

My dad just smiles. "I think that's wonderful."

"Come on, let's get out of here. Sis, I'm sure it'll all work out for you," Analise says, pulling me into a tight hug.

I can't help but glance over at Gavin. "It already has."

After making sure my family gets off without any issues, I take Gavin's hand and let him walk me toward my car. "Well, which place is it going to be? Mine or yours?"

The corner of my mouth curls up as I glance his way under my eyelashes. "Yours is closer."

Gavin barks out a laugh as he opens my driver's door. "I like the way you think, Miss Rutledge." Once I'm seated, he leans in and presses his mouth to mine. "See you in a few minutes."

I nod, reaching for the door and pulling it closed. Starting the engine, I roll my window down and holler, "Gavin?"

He's not far, only walking a few feet back before he goes to his own truck. "Yeah?"

A wicked smile full of intent spreads across my lips. "Race you."

Even in the darkness, I can see his eyes dilate with desire. "You're on, Miss Rutledge."

Then, he takes off running toward the side street where his truck is parked, which of course, is closer to the way we need to travel to reach his house. But even if he beats me there, am I really losing?

Nope, definitely not.

Something tells me there'll be no loser tonight.

As I drive toward his house, following behind him, I realize I'm okay. Even without knowing what the board will decide, I'll be fine. I may or may not still be working in the school district come tomorrow, but I'll figure it out, and I'll get through it. Despite the blow to my reputation, I'll be okay. Because I have the love of a man I hope to spend a lot more time with, publicly.

But for now, I'm going to focus on the alone part.
You know, the nookie.
I'm relentless like that.

EPILOGUE
epilogue

Ava

Three months later

The bell rings, signaling not only the end of the shortened school day, but the end of the school year. I've been looking forward to it yet dreading it for the last month.

"Make sure you have all of your things," I holler over the excitement of leaving school for the summer. "Enjoy your summer," I add as they all start filing out of the classroom on their way to freedom.

I step out into the hallway and make sure everyone is where they need to be. The atmosphere is one of excitement and anticipation. Not that I blame them. I'm pretty excited myself. Not only to get a couple of months to enjoy my own summer.

And this year will be a little different, because I'll have a visitor every day.

Speaking of visitors, I head back into my classroom to find Annabelle. "Do you have everything gathered up?" I ask, finding the now sixth grader waiting for me by my desk.

"Yep! But not yet."

"No?" I ask with a chuckle, going to start gathering my own things. I won't take too much with me, just my coffee mug and a few personal belongings. Everything else will be locked in the room until I start cleaning and organizing in August for the new school year.

"Nope. But I'll be ready soon," she informs me with a big grin on her face.

Well, I suppose I'll wait a few more minutes until she's ready to go. "Are you excited for junior high?"

"Yes and no. I'm eager to get a locker and switch classes, but I'm going to miss you."

I flash her a quick grin. "You see me all the time," I remind, considering I'm dating her dad.

"Yeah, but not during the school day. We won't be in the same school anymore," she replies, the sadness evident.

"I know, but you're going to love junior high, I promise. Plus, we get weekends together."

A wide grin spreads across her face. "That's true. By the way, I was thinking, maybe we can do a *Ghostbusters* marathon on Saturday."

"I think that's a great idea," I reply, pulling out my keys and preparing to lock my room. "Are you ready now?" I ask when there's nothing left but to shut off the lights.

"We're ready."

Startled, I glance toward the familiar voice and find Gavin standing in the doorway, holding a bouquet of red roses and lilies. My heart starts to pound as a smile takes over my entire face. "What are you doing here?" I ask, heading his way.

"Brought flowers to my favorite ladies on their last day of school." I notice he's holding two bouquets, one a smaller version of the larger. "These are for you," he states, handing over the large vase and placing a chaste kiss on my lips. "Hi."

"Hi," I reply, taking the flowers. "These are beautiful and a wonderful surprise."

"You're welcome," he says. "Give me one minute."

Then, he turns his attention to his daughter and starts to hand her the small bouquet. "To my most favorite girl in the world," he informs her as he hands them over.

Annabelle giggles.

"Do you remember what flowers represent?" he asks, crouching down and gazing up at her.

She nods. "They mean you care."

"That's right."

Annabelle leans forward and whispers, "But I thought you were just bringing them for Miss Rutledge."

He winks and gives her a smile. "Well, I care about two ladies, and they both deserved flowers on their last day of school."

Annabelle giggles. "Can I ask her now?"

What is she talking about?

"You sure can."

And when they both turn to face me, I can tell by the matching determined looks in their eyes, things are about to change.

My life will never be the same.

Gavin

"Go ahead," I encourage my daughter, knowing she's both anxious and a little nervous.

Annabelle steps forward and smiles up at Ava. "My dad and I have been talking. I'm really excited to get to stay with you during the summer, and I know I'll be a huge help with keeping Tabitha out of trouble."

Ava smiles. "I love having you there, and she loves playing with you."

From what I've been told, Tabitha wasn't a super friendly cat, only wanting to be petted when she wanted it, but since Annabelle started going over to Ava's with me, Tabitha has taken a liking to my daughter, always wanting to snuggle and play with this weird fish on a stick toy Annabelle insisted she get her.

"Well, Dad and I think it would be kinda cool if we were all together, under the same roof."

I watch as shock registers on Ava's face before she glances my way out of the corner of her eye. "You do?"

"Yep," Annabelle replies. "And if you wanted to stay in your house, then maybe we can come stay with you all the time. But Dad and I also talked about getting a whole new house, one big enough for our craft room and a bedroom for me. And maybe a spare bedroom we can use for a little brother or sister someday. Dad and I didn't talk about that, but I wanted to throw it out there because that would be really cool."

Ava's eyes fill with tears as she grins at my daughter. "I think that sounds amazing," she replies with a sniffle.

"Which part?"

"All of it," Ava states with a decisive nod.

"Really? You'll let us move in with you or you'll move in with us?" my daughter asks eagerly.

"I'd love to move in with you. Your home has a little more space than mine does, but I think a new house would be perfect."

Annabelle jumps up and down with elation. "This is the best day ever!" She spins around and levels me with an emphatic look. "Can we start looking now? I mean tonight? When you get home from work?"

Chuckling, I step forward and ruffle her hair, even though she hates it. "We'll figure it out, Belle. We don't have to get it all planned tonight."

"No, but we could get a big start. Like finding a house with four bedrooms and making sure Tabitha is excited about having me for a roommate."

Ava and I both laugh, and even though my daughter did all the heavy lifting, I figure it's time for me to add my two cents. As Ava sets the flowers down, I step toward her and pull her against my chest. Her arms wrap around my waist, her fingers threaded together at my back.

"Is this really okay? I don't want you to feel pressured into doing something you're not ready for," I tell her.

She cups my cheek with her hand, and I instinctively turn into her touch and kiss her fingertips. "I'm very sure. I'm not attached to my house, other than it was my first one. But we'll need more space for two crafters and the little brother or sister Annabelle wants."

It's my turn to blush. Even though that wasn't part of the original plan and conversation Annabelle and I had, I'm not sorry she said it. "Negotiations are definitely on the table."

"Good." She goes up on her tiptoes and kisses me. "Yes, I'd love to move in with you and Annabelle."

"Fifteen-year-old me is on cloud nine right now, you know that, right?"

She giggles and shakes her head. "You're incorrigible."

"I'm relentless, baby, especially when I see something I want. And in case you didn't know, I want you."

"You have me."

My life is pretty damn close to perfect. I have a daughter who is my entire world, and the woman of my dreams. The one I used to pine over all those years ago in high school. I'm not joking. Freshman Gavin would flip his shit if he could see me now.

"Good," I reply, taking her hand and kissing her knuckles. Leaning in so little ears can't hear, I add, "What do you say we go home and work on that little brother or sister."

The look she gives me has my cock hard in record time. "Deal."

MARCUS

Finally.

Time to go home.

As the Memorial Day weekend kicks off, so does the busy summer tourist season, and with that, my workload increases. Sure, owning the only residential snowplow in town during the long winter is exhausting, but that's nothing compared to summer. From working six days a week at the auto repair shop to running the tow truck, I'm about to embark on a five-month, four to five hours of sleep a night trek of madness.

Something about summer brings out the stupid in a lot of people.

It's pushing nine o'clock at night, and the streets of Pine Village are still active. As tourists move into the campgrounds and cabins at the Bluff Preserves National Park for weekend getaways and boating excursions, I'm reminded I still need to find another mechanic to hire at the shop. I love what I do, but as I approach my late thirties, I realize I can't do it all. With the influx of work, it can be hard to keep up.

Case in point: working until almost nine tonight to repair two boat trailer tires for someone in town for the weekend.

I pull onto Lowe Road, headed for home, when I come upon a disabled vehicle on the side of the road with their hazards flashing. The vehicle is right after the big curve, which is a terrible place to stop, considering you can't see who's coming around the bend. Sighing, I flip on my own flashers and stop behind the SUV. It's a big one, and by the way it's leaning, I'm certain it has a flat.

Reaching into the back seat of my old truck, I grab a neon vest and hop out. As I shove my arms into the vest, all thoughts of taking a nice hot shower being put on hold, I hear the high-pitched sound of a woman.

A woman in distress.

Catching movement ahead, I walk to the front of the SUV and find the most beautiful creature I've ever seen pacing back and forth, yelling into her phone. There's just enough sunlight left to catch her features, from her long, dark blond hair to her striking dark eyes.

"5G my ass! Why won't you work? Someone is getting fired over this."

"You've hit a dead spot. You gotta go about three or four hundred yards back up the road to get service, but even then, it's spotty at best." It's one of the reasons I love living out here.

The woman shrieks and spins around, holding her phone out like a weapon. "Don't come near me," she demands, her eyes wide and her manicured hand covering her heart.

I hold up my hands in surrender and take a step back. "All right, I'll just get back in my truck and leave then. Good luck getting ahold of someone to come help without walking about a mile in those ridiculous heels you're wearing. Oh, and when you do finally get your call to come through, they're gonna call me, since I'm the mechanic and tow truck driver here. Watch out for the black bears too. They're hungry this time of year. See you soon, Princess."

Just as I spin to return to my truck, I hear, "Wait." It's followed by a deep feminine sigh that does something strange to my insides. "I need your help."

Don't miss a single reveal, release, or sale! Sign up for my newsletter.

http://www.laceyblackbooks.com/newsletter

BOOKS ALSO BY
lacey black

Rivers Edge series

Trust Me, Rivers Edge book 1 (Maddox and Avery) – FREE at all retailers

Fight Me, Rivers Edge book 2 (Jake and Erin)

Expect Me, Rivers Edge book 3 (Travis and Josselyn)

Promise Me: A Novella, Rivers Edge book 3.5 (Jase and Holly)

Protect Me, Rivers Edge book 4 (Nate and Lia)

Boss Me, Rivers Edge book 5 (Will and Carmen)

Trust Us: A Rivers Edge Christmas Novella (Maddox and Avery)

> ~ *This novella was originally part of the Christmas Miracles Anthology*

With Me, A Rivers Edge Christmas Novella (Brooklyn and Becker)

Bound Together series

Submerged, Bound Together book 1 (Blake and Carly)

Profited, Bound Together book 2 (Reid and Dani)

Entwined, Bound Together book 3 (Luke and Sidney)

Summer Sisters series

My Kinda Kisses, Summer Sisters book 1 (Jaime and Ryan)

My Kinda Night, Summer Sisters book 2 (Payton and Dean)

My Kinda Song, Summer Sisters book 3 (Abby and Levi)

My Kinda Mess, Summer Sisters book 4 (Lexi and Linkin)

My Kinda Player, Summer Sisters book 5 (AJ and Sawyer)

My Kinda Player, Summer Sisters book 6 (Meghan and Nick)
My Kinda Wedding, A Summer Sisters Novella book 7 (Meghan and Nick)

Rockland Falls series
Love and Pancakes, Rockland Falls book 1
Love and Lingerie, Rockland Falls book 2
Love and Landscape, Rockland Falls book 3
Love and Neckties, Rockland Falls book 4

Standalone
Music Notes, a sexy contemporary romance standalone
A Place To Call Home, a Memorial Day novella
Exes and Ho Ho Ho's, a sexy contemporary romance standalone novella
Pants on Fire
Double Dog Dare You
Grip
Bachelor Swap, A Bachelor Tower Series Novel
Perfect Kiss, Mason Creek Series book 9
Waiting For Love, The Love Vixen Series book 11
Quarterback Keeper, a surprise baby novella
Kissing A Stranger, book 4 in the multi-author The Kissing Games series

Burgers and Brew Crüe Series
Kickstart My Heart, book 1
Don't Go Away Mad, book 2
Same Ol' Situation, book 3
Wild Side, book 4
What's It Gonna Take, book 5
Home Sweet Home, book 6
Too Young to Fall in Love, book 7
Without You, book 8

Time For Change, book 9
You're All I Need, book 10

Pine Village Series
Pretty Remarkable, a free prequel short story
Pretty Incredible, book 1
Pretty Dependable, book 2
Pretty Drunk, book 3
Pretty Relentless, book 4
Pretty Wild, book 5
Pretty Desperate, book 6

Snowflake Falls Series
Merry Little Mix-Up, book 1
Merry Little Sugar Rush, book 2

Co-Written with *NYT Bestselling* Author, Kaylee Ryan
It's Not Over, Fair Lakes book 1
Just Getting Started, Fair Lakes book 2
Can't Get Enough, Fair Lakes book 3
Fair Lakes Box Set
Boy Trouble
Home To You, a second chance novella
Beneath the Fallen Stars, Never Too Far book 1
Beneath the Desert Sun, Never Too Far book 2
Tell Me A Story
Royal – Writing as Rebel Shaw
Crying Shame – Writing as Rebel Shaw
Watch and Learn – Writing as Rebel Shaw

ABOUT lacey black

USA Today Bestselling Author Lacey Black is a Midwestern girl with a passion for reading, writing, and shopping. She carries her e-reader with her everywhere she goes so she never misses an opportunity to read a few pages. Always looking for a happily ever after, Lacey is passionate about contemporary romance novels and enjoys it further when you mix in a little suspense. She resides in a small town in Illinois with her husband, two children, adorable black lab puppy, crazy cat, and three rowdy chickens.

Website: www.laceyblackbooks.com
Email: laceyblackwrites@gmail.com
Facebook: https://www.facebook.com/authorlaceyblack
Instagram: https://www.instagram.com/laceyblackwrites/
Bookbub: https://www.bookbub.com/authors/lacey-black
Amazon: https://www.amazon.com/Lacey-Black/e/B00MW2UGZI
Twitter: https://twitter.com/AuthLaceyBlack
Goodreads:
https://www.goodreads.com/author/show/8414783.Lacey_Black

www.ingramcontent.com/pod-product-compliance
Lightning Source LLC
Chambersburg PA
CBHW070637260626
47161CB00007B/2731